W9-CCT-664

Tonight, or at least, this moment, she was going to do exactly what she wanted to do. Hang the consequences.

She was about to take matters into her own hands for a change. And right now, she wanted to find out what it was like to kiss a scoundrel.

"Who's there?" Rothbury nearly growled, straining against his binds, the muscles in his gloriously tanned arms bunching and tightening.

She didn't answer him. Instead, she took a deep breath, and padded purposely toward the earl, kicking another slumping tasseled pillow aside.

Tied up and blindfolded as he was, she would have her way and be out the door before he could ever guess who she was.

And once he'd returned to the ballroom, she would have herself a secret smile. He'd never know, he'd never guess his shy friend would dare to taste forbidden fruit. Besides, what damage could one little kiss do?

Romances by **Olivia Parker**

TO WED A WICKED EARL
AT THE BRIDE HUNT BALL

ATTENTION: ORGANIZATIONS AND CORPORATIONS
Most Avon Books paperbacks are available at special quantity
discounts for bulk purchases for sales promotions, premiums,
or fund raising. For information, please call or write:

Special Markets Department, HarperCollins Publishers,
10 East 53rd Street, New York, New York 10022-5299.
Telephone: (212) 207-7528.   Fax: (212) 207-7222.

To Wed A
WICKED EARL

Olivia Parker

AVON
An Imprint of HarperCollinsPublishers

This is a work of fiction. Names, characters, places, and incidents are drawn from the author's imagination or are used fictitiously and are not to be construed as real. Any resemblance to actual events, locales, organizations, or persons, living or dead, is entirely coincidental.

AVON BOOKS
An Imprint of HarperCollins*Publishers*
10 East 53rd Street
New York, New York 10022-5299

Copyright © 2009 by Tracy Ann Parker
ISBN 978-0-06-171278-4
www.avonromance.com

All rights reserved. No part of this book may be used or reproduced in any manner whatsoever without written permission, except in the case of brief quotations embodied in critical articles and reviews. For information, address Avon Books, an Imprint of HarperCollins Publishers.

First Avon Books paperback printing: September 2009

Avon Trademark Reg. U.S. Pat. Off. and in Other Countries, Marca Registrada, Hecho en U.S.A.
HarperCollins® is a registered trademark of HarperCollins Publishers.

Printed in the U.S.A.

10 9 8 7 6 5 4 3 2

If you purchased this book without a cover, you should be aware that this book is stolen property. It was reported as "unsold and destroyed" to the publisher, and neither the author nor the publisher has received any payment for this "stripped book."

In loving memory of
My father,
Frank J. Ventura Sr.
July 24, 1940–April 13, 2005
A very smart man, indeed.
And for my mom.
Thank you.

Acknowledgments

My love and gratitude to my entire family, including Diane next door, and to my friends of the NEORWA, and anyone else who listened with even half an ear to all my fears, doubts, and marathon babbling sessions.

To Wed a
Wicked Earl

Chapter 1

*A Gentleman never hesitates to
rescue a Lady.*

The Bride Hunt Ball, Castle Wolverest
August 1813

"**M**y word, child. You look lovely this evening."

Miss Charlotte Greene leveled a blank stare at Viscount Witherby. She should smile, to be polite of course, but her lips wouldn't budge. So instead she simply murmured, "You are much too kind, my lord."

"Kindness has little to do with it." His broad, nearly connected white eyebrows waggled as his greedy gaze swept over her bodice. "I say, you are a *temptress*," he hissed in a raspy whisper, most likely so her mother wouldn't overhear.

Giving a distracted nod in acknowledgment of the absurd compliment, Charlotte pressed her lips together, suppressing a smile. The balding, elderly viscount might mistakenly consider it encouragement.

"Will you do me the honor of a dance in this next set?" he asked her bosom.

Absolutely not! she wanted to shout. Her proper upbringing, of course, kept the thought from tumbling past her lips, but just barely. Taking a measured breath, she scrambled to find a suitable response.

At her hesitation, his bushy brows raised in haughty disbelief. Truly, if he had half as much hair on his head as he did on his eyebrows, he'd have quite the coiffure.

"Ah, I mean to rest for the time being, my lord," she managed, watching the viscount's spine stiffen as she spoke. "However, I do thank you."

As her mother stepped closer beside her, Charlotte heard her frustrated sigh.

Apparently, Charlotte should have been eager for his attentions, or any attention for that matter, considering her well-known wallflower status. However, Charlotte just couldn't summon the required gratitude.

"You'll have to excuse my daughter," her mother interjected. "She's just being shy."

Charlotte inwardly cringed at her mother's muttered excuse. *Shy*? Why did that word always rankle her? Her mother's well-meaning conciliations never failed to make her feel like a girl of seven. Still, the fact remained that being accursedly timid around men had little to do with it. The real reason she refused to dance this evening was simply that no one had asked her.

Well . . . no one who wasn't foxed, looking for a victim to grope, or old enough to be her grandfather. Or all three as was the case with Viscount Witherby.

Even so, Charlotte hadn't the time to wallow in self-pity. It was nearly midnight, and if her calculations were correct, a long-awaited dream of hers was about to come to fruition.

She just might find herself engaged to none other than Lord Tristan Devine.

As luck would have it—though there were those who thought it was more of a miracle—Charlotte had been selected to participate in the Duke of Wolverest's bride hunt for his younger brother, a man she had been enamored of for so long—ever since that fateful day when he had rescued her mother and herself from their mangled carriage.

Since then, she had been completely, irrevocably besotted.

She bit her lip, thinking of the other bride hopefuls and wondering again of her chances. Besides herself, there was her friend Madelyn Haywood (who Charlotte suspected would soon marry Lord Tristan's brother, the duke, instead), the Fairbourne twins, and Harriet Beauchamp. Out of all of them, Miss Beauchamp was her only real competitor, as the twins had their eyes on Madelyn's duke.

A waltz would be played next, and then the remaining women would line up at the north end of the room to await his decision.

Charlotte's heart hammered inside her chest. It was almost time.

Thankfully, Witherby decided to leave Charlotte to her musings. He offered his arm to her mother, who clutched at it as she often did when her rheumatism ailed her.

"Good luck to you, my dearest," Hyacinth Greene said quietly for Charlotte's ears only. "If he has any sense in that handsome head of his, he'll make the right decision."

Charlotte gave her mother a small smile as the pair tottered off to a settee set against the wall, her mother throwing Charlotte an encouraging grin from over her shoulder.

A shaky sigh escaped her. Surely, Lord Tristan would pick her.

Just the night before, he had pulled her aside after dinner and told her that she was a cut above the others. He told her she was the only genuine one of the lot and that if he truly had to spend the rest of his life with any of them, it would be her.

Certainly, he must have been sincere? But if she was so certain, why did she feel overcome with doubt?

Perhaps because his words, however pleasing for her to hear, sounded a bit *rehearsed*.

She blinked out of her musings when she noticed a man walking purposefully toward her. She squinted, willing her eyes to focus. Tall, raven-haired, and just a bit of a swagger. Lord Tristan.

She needed to pinch herself. Was she really here, in his ancestral home, waiting for his proposal? It was all so terribly romantic . . . even if it was a scandalous way to find a bride.

"Good evening, Miss Greene," he said with a smile, holding out his hand.

She took it without caring where he was going to take her. He led her to the middle of the ballroom, her feet having no need for the glossy parquet floor, for she was surely floating.

His timing was impeccable. The first notes of

the waltz began with their first movements. And as they danced, swirling and dipping, no words were spoken, though she couldn't stop a giggle or two from escaping. Charlotte simply relished the joy of being in his capable arms.

A rush of heat spread down her back, making her shiver. She looked over her shoulder to see Lord Tristan's friend, the notoriously wicked Earl of Rothbury, gliding past with his dance partner. She caught the handsome rogue's glance for a second, but in that second all her giddy enthusiasm froze.

Not only was she unaccustomed to having men as attractive as Lord Rothbury give her anything more than a fleeting look, the earl's glance held an intensity, a *forewarning.* Gone in an instant, it unnerved her.

She forced herself to brush it off, telling herself she either imagined it, or caught his stark look by mistake. Perhaps it was in response to something his dance partner had said.

Too soon, the waltz ended, and Lord Tristan walked her back to her mother. Breathlessly, she curtsied and managed a wobbly smile, all thoughts of Lord Rothbury and "his look" gone.

Bowing, Lord Tristan paused before straightening fully and then . . . and then he winked.

Winked! With a half-roguish grin, he then sauntered away, disappearing into the crowd.

Charlotte's entire body felt as if it would burst
with delight. Glancing down at her mother, she
wanted to gauge her reaction to Lord Tristan's
behavior, but Hyacinth Greene sat nestled in the
overstuffed cushions of the settee, busily searching for something in her reticule.

Turning back, Charlotte glanced at the line of
women assembling at the top of the room. It was
time to join her competitors. There were only a
few minutes until his lordship announced his
chosen bride, minutes that up to this point Charlotte thought would be torturous. But that all
changed after *the wink*. Now Charlotte was absolutely certain—she was the chosen bride!

"Hmm . . . now which tart shall it be?"

Adam Bastien Aubry Faramond, Earl of Rothbury, studied the line of women standing on the
far side of the ballroom. "Come now," he murmured with a grin. "I had thought they were all
proper, respectable ladies."

"I'm speaking of the pastries, as you well
know," Lord Pickering replied while eyeing the
sweets greedily. With stubby fingers, he selected
a honey-slathered scone and proceeded to cram

it in his mouth. "So, whom do you think Tristan will pick to be his bride?"

Caught by surprise, Rothbury expertly dodged a crumb set free from Pickering's mouth.

"I've stacked my blunt on the Haywood chit," Pickering continued, flying bits of scone and all, "though Oxley claims he'll pick one of the twins to be his bride. Ha! But we all know one thing's for sure, he'll not pick that awful timid gel. Miss . . . ah . . . Miss . . . Devil take it! Don't suppose *you* remember her name?"

"Miss Greene," Rothbury answered flatly, taking a self-preserving step back. Narrowing his gaze, he studied the five handpicked young women, coming again to a full stop on the only wallflower among them, the painfully shy Miss Charlotte Greene.

As he watched, she plucked at the band of lace ribbon at her waist, looking as if all the hundreds of pairs of eyes fixed upon her and her competitors had set jabbing pins to her nerves. As if she could truly *see* them anyway, with her spectacles tucked inside her bodice. She liked to pretend she didn't need them, but he was one of the very few who knew of her little secret.

An odd sting of something akin to pity bit at him. Oh, even a jaded man like him could muster at least some smidgen of compassion for the poor creatures, including Miss Greene. After all, they had been subjected to participate in this wicked game that had scandalized all of London. Except him.

Rothbury despised himself for admitting it, but the duke's plan to marry off his errant younger brother, Tristan, was sinfully devious. According to the strategy, Tristan would pick one lady from the group to be his bride at the end of a fortnight. And that group had been selected by the duke himself, allowing Tristan a choice, albeit a supervised one. And now that deciding moment had finally come upon them.

The air thrummed with loosely contained anticipation. Men rushed to place last-minute wagers on who the young lord would pick, and mothers and guardians of the chosen women prayed it would be their charge singled out for the esteemed betrothal to a member of the ducal family.

Behind Rothbury, the familiar twittering of feminine whispers broke through his musings. He threw them a glance over his shoulder and each one flushed pink and broke into giggles.

"If they weren't so terrified you'd ravish them, you could have your pick from the lot, I'd wager." Pickering chortled.

"There is only one I want."

As if on cue, Lady Rosalind Devine skirted past him without sparing him a glance.

"You mean the one you want right now, or the one you want only because she is denied to you?"

"Perhaps," Rothbury muttered with a shrug. "Though I see little difference between the two."

As was his habit, he let Pickering believe they were speaking of Lady Rosalind.

Over the course of his life, and especially for the past six years, Rothbury had honed his skills at hiding his true feelings, which of course came in handy at the card tables. It was amazing what people could be led to believe if given (or not given) all of the facts. He considered himself a private person and detested society gossip and speculation. So he turned a jaundiced eye to their wagging tongues, often working hard to steer them onto the wrong path should they begin to dig close to the truth.

He had no desire to enlighten them. Let them believe what they will.

Pausing while reaching for another sweet, Pickering shot him a disbelieving look, then burst out with a bark of laughter. "Well, there is that. You do love the thrill of the chase. More so than the winning, I'd wager. All things considered, then, can't say I blame the duke for forbidding his sister to accept your suit. I'd do the same myself should I have a sister."

He cleared his throat when Rothbury's narrowed eyes homed in on him. "It's the truth," he sputtered in defense. "The Rothburys are a fiendish lot. Have been for decades, as you well know. Lord knows once you tire of her, you'll send her on her way. She's exquisite, for sure, but clearly not interested in you. *If* she wanted anything at all to do with you, she'd ignore her brother's restrictions and find some way to be near you. As it stands, she hasn't even looked at you once this—"

"Pickering?"

"Yes?"

"Just eat your sweets."

Across the room, a footman handed Tristan a bouquet of roses. Excitement leaped through the crowd, for Tristan was to present the bloodred hothouse blooms to the one woman he'd chosen.

"Do tell, old boy!" Pickering urged, their attention brought back to the event unfolding across the room. "You are good friends with the bloke. Who do you think he'll choose?"

"He'll pick the Beauchamp girl," Rothbury said simply, though his gaze fastened once again on a trembling Miss Greene.

Poor little lamb. Her heart and gullible aspirations were about to be crushed. Timid creature never had a chance.

"Deuce take it," Pickering exclaimed, tossing his hands in the air. "You knew days ago who Tristan would pick, didn't you?"

He gave a distracted nod, though Tristan had never disclosed his choice to him; Rothbury had figured it out by simple observation.

"Bah! Serves me right, I guess. With your luck at Newmarket, I should have realized you knew how to pick a winning filly." He plucked a sugared biscuit from the table and turned to leave, muttering under his breath.

As Pickering tottered off, nursing his spoiled bet with sweets, a hush spread across the crowded ballroom. Stealthily, Rothbury moved through the wedged guests in order to keep his gaze fastened on the top of the room. He watched Tristan saunter down the line of women, hesitating before Charlotte.

Guilt teetered on the edge of his mind as Rothbury watched her pale skin blot with nervous red splotches. But try as he might, he could not turn away.

Why did he feel compelled to await her reaction? Was it true? *Was* heartlessness hopelessly entangled in the threads of his soul? What was he hoping to see in her eyes? Hurt? Pain? Rejection?

Relief. A small voice whispered from the depths of his thoughts.

He should turn and leave, the event of the Season finally at its end. None of this mattered to him.

At that moment the crowd seemed to lean forward in expectancy, blocking Rothbury's view.

"Damn," he muttered in initial frustration. No matter, he told himself, redirecting his thoughts. He knew the end result. Miss Beauchamp would win and the other ladies would turn into instant watering pots. He shuddered at the thought. Tears always left him cold.

It was time he left. He lifted a glass of wine from the tray of a passing footman and swiftly tossed the contents back. Finished, he made for the door, but packed near shoulder-to-shoulder as they were, traversing the ballroom was a lengthy process.

A short minute later there came polite gasps of delight from some guests and insulted shudders of masked outrage from others. It seemed the most anticipated event of the Season was finally over. Tristan had chosen his betrothed. The orchestra broke into a lively waltz where the newly—and very publicly engaged—couple would open the dance.

The anticipated denouement now over, the guests quickly swept back into motion. Rothbury strode across the parquet floor and was glad to see the crowd thinned as others now joined the dance.

Just before he would have made it to the hall leading to the guest wing, he dared a glance over his shoulder at the line of jilted women. Instead of finding a bunch of women caterwauling like a nursery full of babes, they had all disappeared into the waltz with dance partners now happily obliged to ease their transition back into the marriage mart.

All but one.

Miss Greene stood alone, wringing her gloved hands together, her face inflamed with a scorching blush.

Surely, someone would claim her for the dance. They had all been handpicked by a duke. They were all highly suitable, eligible young women, and . . . Why the hell should he care if Miss Greene stood alone while the others danced?

No. Her partner was coming. Certainly some gentleman—a group in which Rothbury was not included—would dance with her, alleviating the pain of rejection.

He took two steps, his ankles feeling as if weighted with chains.

"Ah, hell," he muttered. His restraint gone, he turned back around . . . and almost slammed into her.

Or rather, *she* was seconds away from bumping into *him*. Hurriedly backing her way out of the room, Miss Greene came at him with surprising speed.

His breath hitched as her backside brushed against his thighs. "Oh!" She spun around, nearly whacking her forehead on his jaw when she looked up. "Lord Rothbury! I didn't know you were there."

"As you do not have eyes on the back of your head, I wager you would not." By design, he gave her a slow, wolfish grin, expecting her to react like most virtuous females did: break into a giggle and flounce away.

She only blinked up at him.

But then again, he didn't really know how bad her vision was. There was a chance his face was just a blur to her. Besides, she seemed to be busy muttering something under her breath. It sounded like a chant of *I-will-not-cry-I-will-not-cry-I-will-not-cry*.

And that's when it happened. Twin, fat tears,

dislodged from the tips of her lashes, no doubt from all her furious blinking, raced over her cheeks and splashed onto his dark green waistcoat.

He stared down at those small damp splotches. And while he did, his stomach clenched. *What the hell was wrong with him?*

His gaze darted to her face. She was taking deep, gasping breaths, her teary eyes growing wider, he guessed to keep any more tears from falling.

The crestfallen look on her face left him feeling as if she had sucked the air straight out of him. How absurd. It wasn't as if *he* was the one who broke her heart. Furthermore, he hadn't a conscience even if he *had* been the one. He was debauched. His lifestyle was decadent, overflowing with good wine, questionable pursuits, and plenty of feisty, beautiful women. Women he walked away from with ease when they became possessive or his attention waned. After all, he was a man of varied carnal delights. And damn proud of it too.

But this . . . this felt different. Despite Miss Greene's being known for her timidity, Rothbury had always observed that she was one to be quick with a smile—even when she was left standing in the corner watching while all her friends danced.

Right now, however, he reckoned she couldn't summon a smile if he offered to pay her for one. But then even he knew that of all the potential brides present this evening, Miss Greene was the only woman who sincerely liked Tristan. Hell, even Tristan *himself* knew that.

At his continued silence, she looked down, her cheeks growing redder by the second. Good God, she wasn't going to swoon, was she?

"May I ask where you were dashing off to, Miss Greene?"

Delicately, she cleared her throat. "I needed to get a bit of fresh air."

"Leave, you mean?"

She answered with a nearly imperceptible nod.

"Whatever for? Because Tristan didn't choose you?"

When she didn't answer, he tilted her chin up. A tear had settled at the corner of her mouth. In his mind's eye, he used his thumb to gently wipe the moisture. Such a telling action would certainly give him away, not to mention supply the hundred or so guests swarming around them into a feeding frenzy of gossip and speculation, so he held back. But as he continued to gaze down into her fathomless blue eyes, he felt himself losing purchase, slipping deeper.

Her bottom lip started to tremble and she made a tiny, heart-breaking squeak of a sound.

"Shhhhh," he said in a whisper of air, sounding, even to his own ears, like a wolf comforting a lamb right before he devoured her. He rushed to think of what to say before she sobbed uncontrollably. "Did your dance partner wrench his ankle?"

"Pardon?"

"Your partner? I could not help but notice that you are not engaged in the last waltz of the evening."

"I haven't a partner," she said softly. "I was not asked."

"Oh. Right, then. Would you do me the honor?" He took a step back, holding up his bent arm.

Someone should mark this day down in history. He was doing something nice and the truth of the matter was, he very likely wouldn't be gaining a bloody thing from sacrificing his time.

She sighed loudly, taking his arm with a shrug.

"Not quite the enthusiasm I was hoping for," he drawled, holding back a chuckle as he walked her toward the swirling couples.

"Oh. I'm terribly sorry," she said on another sigh as he swept her easily into the twirling steps of the dance. "I'm just not having a good day."

"No need to apologize." She felt so delicate in his arms, like he was dancing with air. In reaction to the sensation, he tightened his grip at her waist, else the next turn shoot her straight into the wall.

"It's just that . . ." she continued, clearly oblivious to his worry. "It's just that I liked him for so long. Since I was . . . well, for a rather long time." She cleared her throat. "Did you know that once, when our carriage overturned in the market, he pulled my mother and I from the wreckage? He even tended to our driver and calmed our horse."

"Heroic."

"Quite. I thought for sure that this was fate—being chosen to attend this ball." She sighed. "And then today he . . . he *winked*."

"Winked?"

"Yes. *Winked*."

"Well, then, there you have it. For everyone knows what a *wink* means."

She blinked. "What does it mean?"

"I have no bloody clue. You seemed so certain it meant something, I thought I should agree."

With masked delight he watched a glimmer of humor sparkle in her gaze, but it was soon gone, replaced by glum acceptance. "I guess it really doesn't matter now, does it? But still, I tried so hard to be what he wanted."

"And how do you presume to know what he wanted? Did you make a list?" He gave a low chuckle.

"Yes. Yes, I did. I knew all of his favorite things. His likes, his dislikes—"

Ridiculous. He had nothing to say to that, other than her actions bespoke a schoolgirl's infatuation. But then that sort of adoration often faded quickly, and Miss Greene had been quite tenacious in her esteem for Tristan over the years.

"And I . . ." She swallowed hard, quite like she was still concentrating on not crying.

He swirled her faster.

" . . . and I thought he liked me. He alluded many times . . ."

"I can only guess he was toying with you," he said sharply.

He couldn't help it. Friend or not, Tristan's actions of the past fortnight reeked of immaturity, a certain lack of diplomacy, if you will. Besides Rothbury knew the ways of wicked men, he *was* one, only until now he had never remained long enough to bear witness to the pain and the anguish of the rejected woman.

She looked up at him for the first time since they joined the dance, her eyes a deep, sorrowful blue. "I'm not stupid. Surely I would have noticed his falseness."

"No, you wouldn't. You were too busy bumping into furniture and walking into walls. Wear your spectacles, Miss Greene."

She lifted her chin. "I can see perfectly well, thank you."

"No, you cannot."

"Yes, I can."

"All right, then." He made a purposeful arc that brought them dancing past the terrace doors, where a long row of chairs were set up against the wall, some occupied, some empty. "Tell me, Miss Greene, does your mother still repose on one of these seats?"

She pulled her pale pink bottom lip into her mouth as she stared around his shoulder. Soon, a small, satisfied smile curved her lips. "Why yes, my lord. Indeed, she does."

"Counting from the corner, which seat do you believe she's in?"

"The third chair," she answered without hesitating.

He raised a brow. "Really? Are you sure?"

"Yes. Yes, of course." But uncertainty shone in her eyes.

"Now that I know you are most positive, Miss Greene, I must tell you that what you claim is your mother is in actuality two walking sticks and a stack of ladies' shawls, should someone decide to take a stroll outside."

"Oh dear," she said, her voice small. But to his surprise a small, low chuckle tumbled from her lips.

Rothbury tamped down a surge of unexpected pride at making her laugh. "Contrary to what you believe, rendering yourself nearly blind to attract suitors could never work to your benefit."

"I wasn't trying to attract all suitors, just him. And before you should think me a fool, I had overheard him say that he didn't fancy women who wore spectacles. So naturally I . . ." She stopped, her eyes narrowing on him in suspicion. "Why the sudden change?"

He wasn't quite sure he heard her correctly. "I beg your pardon," he said, bending his head close. Her soft lemony scent teased at his senses.

"*You* came to my rescue, my lord."

Her stress on the word "You" was not missed by him. She might have well said "despicable beast" instead.

"I wanted to dance," he replied, with a small shrug. "You flatter yourself by thinking more of it."

"No. I bumped into you as you were leaving."

"*No*," he countered, his jaw tightening. "I was looking for a partner."

"In the empty doorway?"

"Miss Greene," he said, feeling quite like he had been caught in a lie. "Do you always interrogate your dance partners?"

"What provoked it?"

Bloody hell. She was the embodiment of aggravation. Couldn't a man ask a lady to dance without being asked twenty damn questions?

"Do you know what I think, my lord?"

"I do not doubt that you are going to tell me."

"I think you desire a chance to redeem yourself. Transform yourself into a gentleman, perhaps."

"Is that so?" He did not bother withholding the note of sarcasm in his tone.

"Am I correct?"

"Absolutely not." His gaze trailed across her lace-edged bodice before returning to her eyes, just in case she failed to take him seriously.

Charlotte, however, knew better than to believe that a man like Lord Rothbury was truly appraising her figure. She might be a bit gullible and trusting, but she was well aware that his shocking assessment of her girlish charms—or lack thereof—had less to do with genuine interest and more to do with the fact that he was trying to scare her off the scent, so to speak. And she was not so easily deterred.

His reaction to her assumptions stirred her curiosity. Perhaps she was correct.

"I think you are on your best behavior this night," she said, "because a certain someone is in the room. A certain Lady Rosalind Devine."

"And I think you are wholly misguided—"

"I disagree."

"—and incredibly nosy."

"Well, I wish you all the luck, my lord," she said as gently as possible. "You'll need it."

Charlotte could feel the tightness of his shoulders underneath her fingertips at her words. However, she just couldn't seem to stop herself. She was just trying to be helpful.

"Honestly," she went on, "how could you possibly expect a different outcome? Hasn't the earldom of Rothbury been synonymous with sin and scandal for hundreds of years?" Indeed. Renowned for trickery and vice, the Rothburys were not to be trusted. "Perhaps therein lies your problem, my lord. I know it's terribly disappointing to hear, but it is entirely plausible that you will never be able to rise above the weed-filled path of debauchery the men in your family have so heavily sowed."

A muscle in his cheek twitched. At once she regretted her words.

They neared an alcove made by swaths of towering cream silk draped along alabaster columns. Before she could say another word, he disengaged himself from the pose of the waltz and grabbed her by the waist.

In a whirl of movement he lifted her and then deposited her inside the silken cocoon, which deftly hid them from view.

Her heart thundered in her ears. "I have said too much," she rushed out, making for what she hoped was the narrow opening in the fabric.

Nodding menacingly, he took a step toward her, blocking her escape. His warm, whiskey-hued eyes hardening to crystals of amber. "The middle of a ballroom isn't the most ideal place to use our tongues as weapons, is it?"

She rubbed her arms as a shiver shot through her. He was a prideful man. Her dearest friend, Madelyn Haywood, always said he reminded her of a tawny lion. Charlotte must have wounded his pride with her stark words, that's all. Of course it wasn't the smartest thing for her to have done, she supposed. Nor the most gracious. He had asked her to dance after all. And now she insults him?

Up until this point all she managed to do was

embarrass herself. Now, however, her big mouth just might have gotten her into a particular class of trouble she had no idea how to handle. Somehow, Charlotte mused, a simply apology would do nothing to placate him.

This man was a renowned rogue. In fact, should it strike his fancy, he could make her life a miserable one. Starting with a ravishment in the middle of a ballroom, just for sport.

He had a reputation for using women. Leading them to believe he sought their hearts only to walk away in search of his next willing victim. And she had heard they were always willing, only to be lured into believing it was love in his eyes instead of lust.

She looked up, willing her features to remain impassive. He was so devastatingly handsome, it was difficult to do. A silky ash-blond lock loosened from the leather queue he always used to tie back his hair and slid against his temple.

An absurd thought popped into her head. Maybe he cast some sort of spell on women to get them to do what he wished.

Suddenly she felt like a mouse caught under a lion's claw. And everyone knew what cats did with their quarry—they dragged it off to the corner to play. Before devouring it.

She swallowed hard. "What are you about, sir?"

"It's really very simple," he drawled. "No need to look as if you fear I'll gobble you up in the next second."

"I'm f-fine," she said, mortified that she stuttered. "Women like me are not your natural prey, so I can assume that I'm perfectly safe here . . . alone with you . . ." she made a vague gesture to the silks surrounding them ". . . hiding behind this curtain. Alone. Very alone."

While she stumbled her way through her reasoning, Rothbury crossed his arms over his chest and studied her with a cool gaze. "One should never assume, Miss Greene, " he countered darkly.

"Yes, well, I must be on my way."

"Quite. Before you go, however, you must tell me why you believe Lady Rosalind is . . . above my reach, shall we say? I cannot wait to hear your reasoning."

In that instant, her shoulders relaxed. Of course he hadn't plucked Charlotte from the ballroom to have his wicked way with her. How could she have thought otherwise?

He must have whisked her away simply because she happened to be acquainted with Lady Rosalind, not to mention the fact that Charlotte was quite possibly the only virtuous young lady who could talk to Rothbury without immediately diving into a swoon.

She sighed. Apparently, he didn't like to be told the truth either. She supposed the polite thing to do was placate him. "It's just that . . . I believe the only way you would ever have a chance at winning her would be with help."

"*Your* help?"

"Perhaps."

A hint of masked stubbornness hardened his chin. "Preposterous." His mesmerizing gaze remained steady on her. "I do not need help. Most especially yours."

"Good." *Insufferable man.* "For I was not offering it."

Outside their linen-draped cocoon, the waltz was coming to an end.

"I must go," she announced. But despite the need for haste, she hesitated, wondering what it would be like to be a sought-after woman. To be admired, envied, and desired. To be pursued by men—by *this* man. Would her manner be comparable to that of Lady Rosalind? Would she be able to resist his attentions?

She gave her head a little shake, vowing to finally put an end to her penchant for woolgathering. Giving Rothbury a tight, polite smile, she excused herself from his company and made to skirt around him.

In a burst of movement, he took her up into his arms, smoothly sliding out from their hiding spot. Seamlessly, they rejoined the other dancing couples. To onlookers she supposed it looked as if they had become clumsily caught up in the duke's lavish decorations.

Charlotte felt scorching heat radiate from where his steady hand pressed on her back, the smooth grasp of his other hand over hers. He had moved so quickly, her breath felt trapped in her throat.

The music concluded with a flourish. Gently, he released her from his hold, her skirts swinging back into place.

"I didn't mean to pry," she explained, feeling like she ought to say something. "And I didn't mean to insult you."

"It is of no consequence, I assure you."

Her lips parted on a shaky exhale. "I don't suppose you'll walk me back to my mother."

"Er, no. But I think you understand why. I find I'm not in the mood to be pummeled into submission just for dancing with you."

"Oh dear. That's right. She did do that once, didn't she?"

Prior to that incident, Rothbury had thought reticules had no purpose other than to compliment a lady's frock. He had no idea they could be used as a weapon. Miss Greene's mother believed otherwise. "I shall never forget it."

She cringed. "I'm sorry. She's very protective and you are . . ." Her cheeks bloomed with a blush as she realized what she was about to say right to his face.

He smiled tightly at her hesitation. "A very bad sort?"

"Quite," she said looking relieved.

"Well, then," he said, lifted one side of his mouth in a grin. "We must assume *the bad sort* puts you at ease, then."

"Oh, I don't know about that. Whenever I see you, I can't help but think of all the wicked things you've done, and then my skin feels as if it's ablaze." She gasped and turned scarlet. "That didn't come out right at all."

He smiled grimly. "I don't suppose there *is* a right way. "

If there had been a boulder nearby, Miss Greene looked as if she would have loved to do nothing better than to dive behind it.

"It's all right, Miss Greene. I've been called worse. Much worse." And he deserved just about every moniker thrown at him, he supposed. However, Miss Greene was a proper young lady and proper young ladies did not spew insults, no matter how deserving the person happened to be. "Besides," he added, "it is not as if you are insulting the archbishop or the king for that matter. I know what I am."

After a brief hesitation, she dipped her head. "Thank you for the dance."

He inclined his head.

With that he turned to walk away, but after about five steps, he glanced over his shoulder. With an odd sense of satisfaction, he watched as she plucked her spectacles out from the inside of her bodice and placed them on her nose where they belonged. He bit back a smile, bemused, as always, by just how this one managed to get under his skin.

Indeed, the earldom of Rothbury was synonymous with debauchery, gambling, too much wine, and too many women for generations. The men in his family certainly never took it upon themselves to rescue bespectacled wallflowers from the indignity of being the only young woman without a dance partner.

Rothbury turned to leave the room, ignoring the curious looks of a few guests who obviously wondered why in hell he would bother paying any attention at all to the reigning wallflower of London. He, the reigning scoundrel. No doubt they all thought she was to be his new conquest.

He did not blame them. Because in truth, that's what he did, that's what he was. Seduce and dominate. Charm and manipulate. A user of women.

How they would scoff, Rothbury mused bitterly, if they knew that he was secretly in love with the silly little chit, spectacles and all.

Chapter 2

*A Gentleman courts his Lady Love in
the proper manner.*

London
April 1814

" 'G oodnight, goodnight! Parting is such sweet—' "

A fat pot of pink begonias sailed through the crisp evening air and crashed upon the lawn in a scrambled mess of broken porcelain, water, and abused blooms.

Apparently, standing below the second-floor window of one's beloved whilst quoting Shakespeare didn't hold the exact air of shiver-inducing sentiment one would expect. Especially if the man doing all the quoting was most definitely drunk

. . . and terribly unwanted, if the objects being tossed out the window were any indication.

Looking out her second-floor window into the garden of the house next door, Charlotte leaned her elbows on the sill, her chin resting in her hand.

Renting a house next to the stunningly beautiful heiress Lady Rosalind was certainly turning out to be entertaining. All day long, men strutted like roosters past her front door, back and forth, hoping for either a chance meeting or a little glance at the sought-after woman. Charlotte shook her head. The woman never had peace. Should the poor dear ever venture out to a ball, the following day men would call upon her in droves. They brought flowers, baskets of sweets, sang ballads, and one even brought her a horse. Some of the men were admitted inside, but most were politely turned away. Perhaps the one below was one of the rejected, drunk and determined to win her somehow.

Clearly oblivious to her presence—not to mention the near miss with the potted plant—the man below alternately mumbled and whistled as if calling for his collie. Charlotte's lips quirked and she shook her head sadly. Men could be such fools around beautiful women.

The first streaks of light were beginning to glow on the horizon; the first chirpings of the sparrows sounded far in the distance, for the romantic drunken sot below most assuredly frightened all of their birds away with his shouting.

Why hadn't anyone sent for the magistrate yet, she wondered? Perhaps because most of her neighbors had just gone to bed after exhausting themselves after an unending string of parties. In truth, Charlotte and her mother had only just retired after returning from a ball themselves. And Charlotte often had trouble winding down enough to fall sleep after nights such as these and would often lie abed for hours.

"Ah, hell," the man grumbled loudly, looking about. "Now where the devil did you go?"

Though it was nearly dawn, it was still dark and quiet. There didn't seem to be anyone else about, at least in the shadowed gardens behind this particular row of mansions. Who did he think he was speaking to?

As he swaggered his way toward a dense grouping of trees, Charlotte straightened her spectacles, surveying the myriad of other items strewn across the lawn.

There was a wedge of soap, three decorative pillows, an ornate inkwell, several candle stubs, a lady's brush, and what appeared to be a small wooden duck. Evidently the man had been here for some time.

The sound of flapping paper caught Charlotte's attention. She glanced over just in time to witness a writing tablet drop down from the window. For a fleeting moment she wondered if the man wasn't drunk after all, but simply suffered the effects of being walloped in the head by any or all of the items.

Looking down, she realized she had lost sight of him. Had he left? Peering through the darkness, her eyes barely made out the tall shadow amidst the trees. He had a hand braced against the trunk of a birch tree, giving the impression he was keeping it from falling over, though it was most definitely the other way around.

Although a thick, naked branch hid most of his face, she could discern that he wore no coat or waistcoat, just a loose white shirt, scandalously unbuttoned to the center of his chest.

For a second she entertained the notion that he was a common man, perhaps even an errant footman, but there was something unmistakably regal about him that set him apart, despite his inebriated state.

Even in the dim light emanating from the few

illuminated windows of the mansions, Charlotte could see that this man's body was athletic and pleasing to the feminine eye. This was no young, besotted whelp declaring his undying love. This was a man.

A clearly stubborn one, but a man just the same. Long and lean muscled, a trim waist and narrow hips, and strong legs encased in black breeches that he must have inched his way into. *Inexpressibles*. Charlotte almost sighed.

Why couldn't she be oblivious to such things? She ought to shut the window and go to back to bed.

The man under the tree started mumbling, bringing her attention back to the present. This one definitely belonged in the scoundrel category, a group of men she had recently sworn to avoid at all costs. Not that they had been beating down her door, but still.

She watched him pluck an empty brandy decanter from the grass. Frowning, he closed one eye to peer inside the narrow glass neck. Finding it empty, he shrugged, then tossed the bottle over his shoulder.

At that moment the wind picked up, bringing with it a chilly reminder that winter still nipped at the heels of spring here in London. Charlotte shivered, pulling the edges of her woolly white shawl closer together.

'"What's in a name?'" The man tucked in the shadows suddenly proclaimed, his deep voice booming loudly in the dark, making Charlotte nearly jump out of the thick, woolly stockings she wore to bed. '"That which we call a rose by any other name would smell as sweet.'"

After punctuating the quote with an ill-timed hiccup, he took two long, lazy strides out from under the shelter of the tree . . . and then promptly had to duck for cover under the branches.

Add one large boot to the inventory of objects scattered across the ground.

Charlotte gasped. Not because of the boot, although that was indeed unexpected. No, her breath caught for she had finally recognized the inebriated man.

It was none other than Lord Rothbury: renowned profligate, devious debaucher, and gambler of cards, horses, and numerous women. Not to mention her reluctant rescuer from the night of the Bride Hunt Ball of last autumn.

The epitome of tawny masculine beauty—beguiling, if such a word could be used for a man—the earl's charred reputation caused suitable, marriageable ladies to give him a wide berth, but that didn't stop them from staring . . . and sighing.

An excellent dancer, Lord Rothbury had asked Charlotte to dance seven and a half times within the last four years. The half was for the time her mother marched on the dance floor and forcibly pried Charlotte from his hold, slapping his forearm repeatedly with her reticule.

However embarrassing that had been, it didn't stop Charlotte from watching him over her shoulder as she was ushered out of the room by her mother. And he had watched her departure as well. She always wondered why he had.

Still, daydreaming about Lord Rothbury was a horrible, sinful weakness on her part, on any young lady's part, really. The Rothbury earldom had been linked to sin and scandal for hundreds of years. It was a good thing for Charlotte and her reputation that she just happened to be invisible to him. It was his habit to bestow attention only on the most ravishing of females.

Except, of course, for that night.

His kind gesture had shocked her to her toes. However, she had recently learned to not let such acts go straight to her head. He was simply being kind, she supposed. Nothing more. Undoubtedly, to him it was only a dance. Wicked or romantic,

Lord Rothbury had no designs on her. If he had wanted Charlotte, she would have known about it an age ago.

But he really was quite gorgeous, she thought with another sigh. Tall and virile, the earl maintained a cultured grace in dress and comportment that belied his wicked mind. Whatever it was that he did—walking, dancing, conversing, or riding— he did it while looking utterly captivating.

Except, apparently, for this evening.

But love, Charlotte mused, must do that to a man. Weaken his will, test his resolve, tilt his judgment, make him do idiotic things—like stand under a window at four o'clock in the morning and get pummeled with personal objects.

Of course he'd be here on this particular morning. Even though he was good friends with Rosalind's younger brother, Lord Tristan, he was barred from visiting when the duke wasn't there. And the duke and his new duchess were traveling in Wales on their wedding trip presently.

Which of course left Lady Rosalind dreadfully devoid of her older brother's unflinching protection.

A small sigh eased past her lips. Would Rothbury ever learn? The beautiful Lady Rosalind could have any man she wanted. Why in the world would she choose to associate herself with scoundrels? And just what had come over Rothbury this evening? She hadn't thought he was the sort to behave so hopelessly besotted. She couldn't quite believe it.

She shook her head in disdain, certain she would never fully understand the ways of society's elite. Before pushing off from the sill and returning to her bed, she stole one more glance at him.

He was now emerging from under the tree once again, the branches no longer offering him shelter as they undulated in the rising wind.

Expertly overstepping the litter, he sauntered over to a nest of dense shrubbery. Minus the leather queue he always used to tie back his hair, his tousled, dark gold locks feathered against the back of his neck in a deceptively boyish manner.

"What say you?" Rothbury drawled the question, sounding less like a drunk and more like the skilled seducer he was reputed to be—most probably because he was now speaking French.

Charlotte continued to listen in, grateful for the fact that she actually had paid attention to her French lessons.

"Are you going to hide back there all evening,"

he asked, "or are you going to come out and help me?"

A huge, dark shadow emerged from behind the thick cluster of tall bushes nestled close to the mansion wall under Rosalind's window. The beast's glossy coat shimmered in the low light. Other than that, the beautiful horse was nearly invisible in the dark.

"There you are." Reaching up, Rothbury ruffled the tousled ebony locks between the horse's ears, much as one would the hair of a doted-upon child.

What sort of man talked to his horse as if it were a person? In French, no less?

"Just as I thought," he said softly to the animal. "You little coward. Afraid of a woman."

The horse snorted, shaking its elegant head.

"What do you know anyway?" Rothbury grumbled. "How could she know my heart is not engaged? Thinks she's a bloody mind reader? I'll win her yet."

"Goodness, I doubt that," Charlotte snickered, then gasped. Dear heaven, had her voice travelled to him?

Rothbury's tawny head jerked up in her direction.

Apparently, it had. Too late, she clamped a hand over her mouth just the same.

"Who is there?" he queried, now in English. "Reveal yourself."

Every muscle froze. She held her breath, hoping the earl would soon dismiss what he had thought he'd heard. She slid her foot back, thinking to simply slip into the depths of her bedchamber.

Movement coming from the window next door caught her attention. Her mouth fell open in shock. Unbeknownst to the earl, someone, most likely Rosalind, was now holding a rather large tome out of the window.

Directly above his head.

The intent was obvious.

Charlotte lurched forward, panic making her speech stilted. "Your lordship!" she shouted from her window, pointing. "A book!"

Seemingly unsurprised by her declaration, no doubt from the effects of heavy drinking, the usually elegant and dignified-looking earl merely arched a brow. "A book? I beg your pardon, but *I* am not a pilferer of books, miss. "

"NO! Duck, you lovesick buffoon!"

"Duck? If you want one of those, *chèrie*, I think I

saw one over there." He gestured toward the lawn with a negligent hand.

He looked up. But it was too late. Before he could blink the book landed on the earl's head with a thunk. His horse cantered off to hide behind the bushes once again.

Groaning, he crumpled heavily into a heap, his hand sliding off his broad chest, falling listlessly onto the grass.

"Oh-dear-oh-dear-oh-dear," she chanted anxiously, moving from side to side, wondering what she should do.

Grasping the sill, she peered outside. Nothing stirred. Not another living being was about. Even the birds in the distance had quieted.

Should she just leave him there and go back to bed? Yes, definitely yes, she should . . . but she wouldn't. How could she not go to the rescue of a man who had rescued her? Good Lord, he could be dead!

Racing across her room, she shoved her feet inside a pair of boots without tying the laces. They flapped at the sides as she padded speedily down the steps and into the front hall. Moving through the house as quietly as she could, she headed toward the back. Reaching the back door, she slipped outside and rushed over, slowing her pace only momentarily so she could step over a low hedge. She nearly tripped on her laces, which would have sent her flying atop his lordship, but she caught her balance just in time.

Panting from exertion, Charlotte put her hands on her hips, studying the earl's prone form. She was relieved to see his chest rising and falling, slowly and steadily. Her gaze trailed down his hard, lean-muscled body, noting the charmingly disheveled clothing. She knew she shouldn't be thinking such things at this particular moment, but he seemed so . . . so long. Truly, he must sleep in a huge bed, or else his feet would hang off the end.

Lifting her chin, she threw a brief glance at her window across the way, silently telling herself she was an idiot for coming down here to assist him.

Good Lord, soon it would be daylight. But she couldn't just leave him here. Perhaps she could rouse him up quickly and be on her way before anyone should spy her in her night rail in the garden with a scoundrel.

"Perhaps I should leave," she murmured, a worried frown marring her brow. "Even unconscious you're dangerous to my reputation."

Chapter 3

A Gentleman's mind is always fit, his
reflexes sharp.

"**M**y lord? Are you all right?"
Rothbury inhaled the fresh, almost
lemon-tinged air wafting before him, the scent
seeping deep into his lungs coaxing forth an unexpected pang of responsiveness.

Eyes of sapphire blurred and spun before his
gaze. " 'Tempt not a desperate man.' "

"I believe that's enough Shakespeare for one
evening, my lord."

For a moment the air seemed to sparkle about
her head, causing him added confusion. "Are you
an angel?" he heard himself mutter.

"Are you all right?" her soft voice asked, sounding like she withheld a laugh.

He closed his eyes as a shard of pain stabbed at the back of his skull, tempting him to succumb to the blissful realm of weightless oblivion. "Bloody hell."

"I think you hit your head on a rock when you fell. And please don't curse, my lord," the angel replied from above him.

"Am I dead?"

A beat of silence, then came the soft hush of rustling fabric. It sounded as if she surrounded him. Her scent certainly did, delicate citrus and warmth.

Mmm. He smiled. "You smell like sunshine."

What a ridiculous thing to say. Maybe he *was* dead . . . and in heaven. No, that couldn't be. Too many people had told him he was solely responsible for the fiery trail into hell.

"No, you're not dead," the angel said, her tone flat. "But I think I know someone who *wishes* you were."

"Cheeky, angel," he muttered. Eyes still shut, he rose up to lean back on his elbows. A sudden wave of lightheadedness gave him a spinning sensation. "Hell and damna—"

A dainty palm clamped over his mouth, surprising him and smothering his curse. "I told you," she admonished lightly, "no more cursing."

Her palm felt warm against his lips.

"You have no one to blame but yourself for what happened," she scolded, sounding very much like a tight-lipped nursemaid. "The lady does not want you."

Lady? What lady? This lady?

Her hand of course, muffled his next comment. If he were in a different frame of mind and not in such terrible pain, he would have enjoyed taking a bite, if only to hear her scandalized gasp. Presently, however, he decided the best course of action was to simply lie there. Besides, she smelled simply gorgeous.

"Do you promise not to employ vulgar language, sir?"

"Mmph." Which she had better damn well know translated as "yes" or he definitely *would* bite her. He put a hand over his heart in case she didn't understand.

"All right, then," she said, suppressed laughter tucked within her tone. "What is it you would like to say?"

His mouth was uncovered, but he suspected her hand lingered near just in case. "What in the h . . ." He paused, catching himself. "What happened?"

The hair at his temples was smoothed away with dainty sweeps. "I can only guess, really."

"Well, why don't you give it a try," he replied, happy to note that his inherited trait of impatience was still intact.

She sighed, light and feminine. The urge to look at her emerged, but he worried he'd be ill if he dared open his eyes.

"Can you recall what happened?" she asked tentatively.

"Not precisely."

"I believe a rather angry female dropped a rather heavy tome from her window."

Rothbury's memory came flooding in then. A torrent really. When one thought emerged, it was swept away by a new one.

He remembered sitting in his town house. Alone. He remembered drinking half a bottle of whiskey in celebration of the fact that his best friend had chosen someone other than Miss Greene. Then, he remembered that even with Tristan out of the picture, he dared never to reach for Miss Greene. Then he remembered the second half of the bottle of whiskey. After that, he couldn't remember anything of much consequence at all.

Well, that wasn't entirely true. He was a man who could hold his liquor . . . occasionally. That is, if he ate a heavy lunch. And an enormous dinner. He gave his head a shake to clear it. No, he did, in fact, remember staggering from the house, heading for the stables, thinking he'd ride out here and throw his whole heart into courting the duke's sister. And why the hell not? He needed to marry. And she was beautiful. And she was kind. And she was . . . well, he really didn't know much about her after all. But that was how they all were, really. Beautiful strangers. All but one.

The other one, the one who crept into his heart with her subtlety, the one whose unprejudiced smile dared him to think there was good in him— now, she could truly hurt him. So he stayed away. Feigned indifference. He was a coward.

While she batted her lashes at Tristan for six years, never sparing Rothbury a single glance, he chased other women so that hopefully, one day, one of them could chase away his regard for her. Make him forget her, forget that she was in love with his best friend. He had hoped her affection for Tristan was only a schoolgirl's fancy, but even if it wasn't, it was love of a sort, *she* was offering it, and he wanted it all for his own.

"Given your reputation and how society regards you," the angel pointed out just then, "I suspect a man such as you provokes such altercations quite often."

He started to negate her assumption but changed

his mind. It was about time he opened his eyes to see just to whom he was speaking.

After several quick blinks, he managed to do just that, gazing up into a small, heart-shaped face. A pretty face. Not one of a curvy seductress or a cool-hearted courtesan, but a feminine, delicately featured face. He knew this face. He adored this face.

"Miss Charlotte Greene," he stated finally, taking a risk and raising his head to get a better look.

Sitting at his side, the white skirt of her thick night rail tucked around her legs, she smiled down at him with concerned eyes of deep blue. Gorgeous sapphire eyes often hidden behind the rims of small, round spectacles.

Truthfully, she happened to be the complete opposite of what he was usually attracted to. She was a bit too thin, too short, and too quiet for his tastes, which had always leaned toward the voluptuous, the tall, and the spirited. Normally, she wasn't one to stand out. And he rather suspected she preferred it that way.

However, while most young bucks readily discounted her merits and furtively joked about her quirky behavior behind her back, Rothbury had always sensed a subtle undercurrent of passion in her dark blue gaze. Unlike the "diamonds" of the *ton* and demimonde, who slinked across assembly rooms completely aware of their beauty and the power that accompanied it, Miss Greene moved like a woman who hadn't yet realized how utterly fetching she truly was. She clung to the walls, sometimes barely raising her eyes from the floor, rarely spoke but to her closest friends, and shied away from situations that demanded she converse with the opposite sex.

Strange it was for him to notice those facets in such an unassuming woman. Strange it was he should have noticed her at all. But he always did. The second she walked into a room.

A sudden irritability pricked him.

He found himself somewhat mortified that *she* should see him in such a ghastly state. He gave his head a shake in an attempt to clear it. Had he just been spouting Shakespeare at Rosalind's window? He stifled a groan and silently vowed to never touch gin again. Or wait, it was whiskey, wasn't it? Christ, he couldn't remember any longer.

"Miss Greene, if you promise never to utter a word of my rather idiotic behavior this evening to another living soul, I shall owe you one large favor."

She gave him a small smile. "Agreed. Are you feeling any better?"

He nodded slightly, his thoughts still marred by spirit indulgence and a throbbing skull.

"Good," she said with a sigh. "At first I had worried she had killed you and I might get blamed."

"Your selflessness astounds me."

His comment only prompted a wry grin. "Quite foxed and still acerbic. I daresay, it's rather impressive." She scooted closer and whispered conspiringly, "Concerning the lady," she pointed to the window, "I believe she entertains no interest in your attentions whatsoever."

"I know," he whispered back, watching her closely with hooded eyes.

She looked at him thoughtfully. "And you are *still* determined to pursue her? Everyone knows the duke will not let you anywhere near his baby sister."

He knew that, of course. Certainly, Lady Rosalind wasn't the only woman he attempted to court who denied him, or was denied to him. But their rejections never penetrated. He shrugged them off with ease.

"Because I am a scoundrel, is it?"

"Yes," she said, flatly. "I suppose rakish reputations do have the habit of getting in the way."

"I agree." *Especially when one least wants to own up to it.*

He tried to give her a dark, seductive look, something to either get her to cease her prying into his private affairs, or better: send her running back to her lax chaperone. But under his current physical limitations, he couldn't even muster a raised brow.

"Where did you come from anyway?" he asked, suddenly wishing he hadn't indulged so heavily. "One minute you weren't there and the next you were."

"I was awake."

"At this hour?" Not that he had any real grasp of time at this moment himself. But it was still dark at least, though he suspected dawn would break soon.

Visions of a slumbering Miss Greene drifted through his thoughts. He imagined that her wheat-colored hair would be unbound, streaming across the pillow like a golden banner. He rather thought she'd toss around in her sleep a lot, which would cause her nightdress to become rucked up to her hips, revealing her thighs, smooth as cream, and her silky—

"Would you like me to summon a doctor?" she asked. "You are starting to look flushed."

He swallowed, shaking the absolutely lovely thoughts out of his head. "No. I'll be fine." And he would be. He always managed to be. Actually, he had become quite the expert at pretending he was just fine. Nothing that a little whiskey couldn't manage.

At Miss Greene's acknowledging nod, Rothbury's gaze swept over her hair, pulled back into a long rope of a braid, which rested against her breast. A few curls framed her ears and there was one long, loose strand that had somehow escaped the twist of the braid.

He smiled, his gaze raking the rest of her, from the white ribbon woven through the high neck of her night rail all the way down to where he imagined her feet were hidden under the folds. When he finally returned to her face, she gave him a small smile, vulnerability stealing across her lovely features.

"Now that I know you're fine, I must go. Someone could discover us."

"Come here," he heard himself whisper. It was the oddest, most singular feeling he had ever had. For reasons unbeknownst to him, he found himself quite needing to embrace her. Good Lord, maybe he did need a doctor.

And to his further surprise, she didn't bolt

off in the opposite direction. She actually crept closer, stopping next to his hip. And she wasn't some smooth, avaricious coquette either. She was a proper, respectable young lady. Exactly the sort who steered far away from the likes of him.

Within touching distance now, he reached out and tugged at a pale curl near her ear, which bounced like a spring when he let go.

She should slap his hand, he mused. He deserved it for being so forward. But she didn't. However, her eyes gradually narrowed on him as if she were studying him closely.

"Now," he said, closing his eyes with a slow blink. "I think you should return to your bedchamber."

"Do you know what I think, my lord?" she suddenly asked.

"Tell me," he said with a small grin.

"I think we need each other."

His smile fell. In fact, all Rothbury could do was blink. He hadn't any idea where this conversation was going and he didn't intend to find out. Besides, he reminded himself, he needed to leave before Rosalind threw anything else out the window. He'd feel terrible if anything meant for him should hit Charlotte.

"Might I trouble you to help me up?" He hated to ask her, but figured if he didn't he might fall.

Ah, hell. Who was he kidding? It was simply an excuse to feel her touch upon him again.

"Of course." She stood, extending her hand to him.

He took it, coming to his feet cautiously, careful not to topple over.

Once vertical, he steadied himself by grabbing firm hold of the nearest tree branch above his head. The angry pulse in his head came to an alarming crescendo before settling back down to a dull ache. He closed his eyes for a moment, and when he opened them Miss Greene stood before him, wringing her hands together.

"Are you sure you're all right?"

"As well as I'll ever be, I suppose."

"It's cold. Would you like to use my shawl?"

He shook his head, hiding his smile at her sweet offer with a grimace.

She stepped forward to swipe leaves and dirt from his shoulders and from his hair. Standing on tiptoe, she lightly examined the spot where he was hit. He inclined his head so she could see.

"There isn't any blood," she said. "Just a small bump. Put some ice on it when you get home and it should go down."

He nodded, feeling for a moment like he was someone else. Someone who deserved attention from a proper young lady, and not her censure. "Now, you were saying that we need each other, yes?" Curiosity bit at him.

"Quite. You see, how ever will I find a suitable husband after Lord Tristan's rejection? And how will you win Lady Rosalind, or any suitable bride for that matter, if everyone thinks you a despicable scoundrel?"

"Hmm. Yes, it has been a bit of a problem." A problem that grew larger with every passing year. Sometimes he wondered if he was destined to wander ballroom after ballroom, chasing the wrong woman, all the while cursing himself that he *had* found the right sort of woman but she was in love with someone else and kept getting pulled out of his path.

Still, he couldn't fathom why Miss Greene thought he needed her. Or maybe now that Tristan was out of the picture . . .

"Miss Greene, are you proposing I marry you?"

Her lovely eyes grew round and then she laughed. "Oh, good heavens, no," she scoffed, waving a hand in the air. "Don't be ridiculous."

Covering her mouth with her hand, she continued to chuckle. Not uproariously, mind you, but hard enough to make him think she'd remember this one for days and still chuckle at the thought.

And just what was so ridiculous? Surely he expected her to negate his suggestion, but why in the name of depravity did she find the prospect of marrying him particularly *hilarious*?

"I could never marry you . . . or anyone like you, for that matter. I might be a bit impulsive at times, but I've certainly learned my lesson about trusting a scoundrel with my heart. And you are, as everyone knows, a scoundrel of the highest order."

"Then what, exactly are you proposing I need you for?" he asked, aware that he could not hide the irritation from his voice.

She sighed, reigning in her grin. "All I was proposing, my lord, is friendship. We could offer each other suggest—"

"*Friendship?*" he echoed blankly, unable to believe his ears. Perhaps he was still unconscious. He couldn't possibly have heard her correctly.

She grinned in such a fashion as to make him feel like she was infinitely wiser than he. "You've heard of the word?"

He narrowed his eyes, giving a dark look that, hopefully, told her he didn't find her amusing at all. "Of course, I have many friends."

"Female friends, acquaintances, I mean."

"Indeed," he drawled, "I have many of those."

She twirled her eyes. "Yes, but do you have any *real* lady friends? Those whom you do not have intimate relations or a torrid history with? Or, to be more precise, female individuals who would never find themselves provoked into causing you bodily harm?"

There was no need to think on it. The truth was in his silence.

"You see," she said cheerfully, then shrugged. "You need me."

He felt his lips working, but for a few bizarre moments, he couldn't speak. Was this little slip of a girl truly offering her companionship to him? Why? Associating herself with him was a daring venture.

He dragged a hand over his jaw. Christ, she was an innocent.

"Ah," he began, giving her a doleful smile. "You have forgotten a most important factor, Miss Greene."

"And that is . . ."

"Men and women cannot be friends. It is impossible."

Her brow furrowed. "And why not?"

He bit back a smile. Lord, she was an easy one to fool. If he had a mind to fool her, that is. She was so gullible; he had no idea how she made it through life so far without being compromised, fleeced, or coerced into buying a three-legged horse at least a half a dozen times.

He cleared his throat to keep a cynical grin from creeping in. "Because, my sweet, sweet naive creature, lust would, undoubtedly, get in the way. You've heard of lust, correct?"

Pressing her lips together, she nodded. "Of course."

"Damn. I should have liked to explain it to you in excruciating detail. Showing you examples, of course."

"Lust is a sin."

"Yes, indeed it is. My favorite one." He gave her a wicked grin. She only blinked at him.

"You were saying," she urged, clearly unmoved.

He sighed. "Well, one day or another, one of us would start having . . . thoughts about the other." Truly, he had quite taken the lead on that facet already.

Her eyes narrowed on him in that half-annoying, half-adorable assessing manner once again. "Think you're utterly irresistible, hmm?"

His mouth opened, presumably to utter some quip, but then his mind realized the bizarre spectacle this woman had just witnessed. He laughed instead. "Well, naturally, I'm not irresistible right now. But usually . . ."

"Your modesty astounds me," she returned coolly.

"Believe what you will. But the truth of the matter is that eventually we would become completely obsessed about finding out what it would be like to finally—"

"Are you trying to say that you've tried this before and failed?"

"No," he said. "What I'm saying is that people do not simply *decide* to become friends. We are not in our leading-strings, Miss Greene. And furthermore men and women cannot *be* merely friends. It just doesn't happen." He held up a hand when it looked as if she'd interrupt. "And even if it does, eventually, attraction, wonder, and temptation would supersede the relationship." And on his end, it had already started. Being "friends" with her would just make it worse, he imagined.

"Now you are the one forgetting a most important factor, my lord."

"And that is . . ."

"I do not inspire lust. All I provoke are whispered promises from a man who, with his next breath, asks another woman to marry him. Furthermore," she added a bit forcibly when he made to interrupt, "I should think I can manage restraining myself when it comes to you. Therefore, all things considered . . . "

"And why bother anyway? What do you suppose can be gained by such an alliance, I wonder?"

"That's all up to you, my lord." She extended her hand.

He stared at her dainty fingertips for a second, perversely wondering what he could do that would stir this particular woman's ire and inspire her to toss objects at his head like Lady Rosalind. Looking at Miss Greene's friendly, pretty face, he couldn't even imagine it. She couldn't be real. This whole encounter could be a part of a bizarre dream provoked by too much whiskey and the knock to his skull.

Reaching out he touched her hand, for a second cradling her fingers within his before pressing his palm to hers for a handshake.

She flicked a nervous glance at their joined hands when he failed to pull his away.

Lifting her hand to his mouth, he pressed a soft kiss to her knuckles.

Strangely, seduction was not at the forefront of his mind. Right now, he was preoccupied with trying to figure her out. Did she have some sort of motive? Was she befriending him just because he happened to be good friends with Tristan?

"I should go," she muttered, a flash of something akin to distress apparent in her gaze. She turned to leave, then stopped, spinning back around. "Perhaps I shall see you at the Hawthorne's annual costume ball in July?"

He was invited every year, but never attended. Aubry Park was near the Hawthorne estate in Northumberland, but Rothbury had always found other things to do. There was nothing for him there. "It's three months from now. Already know you are attending, Miss Greene?"

She nodded with a wry smile. "We go every year. My cousin Lizzie insists upon it. Besides, my mother loves everything metaphysical, and there are those supposed 'haunted' pathways and caves nearby. She's forever dragging me on one of her excursions."

He nodded, not knowing what else to say. He didn't think he'd ever had a friendly, no hidden-motives conversation with a woman before. Odd but true. He was forever coaxing, manipulating, and seducing. Or letting those things to be done to him.

"Good night," he said.

"Good night." She smiled, turning to leave. "Do you know," she added from over her shoulder, "I'm not supposed to be speaking with men like you?"

"It's going to be a little hard being friends with someone you're not allowed to converse with," he murmured, but she had already gone. He watched her retreating form, his sinful mind fixating on her small, pleasantly rounded bottom, which had a wiggle that was definitely unintentional, but quite engaging.

Apparently deeming it safe to come out again, his stallion, Petruchio, came out from hiding. The beast nudged Rothbury in the back, breaking his concentration.

"I beg your pardon," he muttered to the horse. "I do not have the attention span of a butterfly when it comes to women."

Grabbing the pommel, he swooped into the saddle, the quick action making him momentarily dizzy. He bit it back, then urged his mount into a trot.

The window above and the woman to whom it belonged long forgotten, he focused instead on Miss Greene during the short ride back, and her utterly naïve, utterly perplexing offer.

Part of him hoped she'd forget all about this nonsense. Surely, she'd realize the folly of her association with him. And part of him thought maybe it *would* be better being friends with her, rather than nothing at all.

But still another part of him felt like grinning.

A derisive huff blew past his lips. He pushed that thought to the back of his mind. Miss Greene was an innocent. A peculiar one, but an innocent all the same. Women like her did not get involved with men like him.

When he finally returned to his town house, a mere block away, he relaxed in his study, sipping a horrid concoction conjured up by the housekeeper, who promised the vile liquid would clear his head.

His favorite wolfhound lay snoring at his feet, and a tumbling tray of correspondence awaited his attention near his elbow—one a letter from his grandmother, the dowager countess, he realized with a groan.

The dear woman was slowly going senile, and the contents of her letters were always a surprise. Sometimes she remembered who he was, sometimes she did not, and sometimes she confessed to having had tea with Napoleon and a giant talking rabbit named Mrs. Nesbitt every afternoon.

All in all, she had to be watched carefully. Not only did she have some harmless quirks, but she kept threatening to sell off parts of the earldom if he didn't marry soon.

Lucky for him, they were all entailed properties, except for Aubry Park and its horse-breeding facilities. But insofar as he knew, she hadn't threatened to sell it in order to get him to conform to her wishes.

Leaning back into the chair, he closed his eyes. He never enjoyed the quiet, the emptiness. It reminded him of other times, long-ago events he would like to forget.

Thankfully, amid his dark memories, a tumble of pale blond ringlets and a shy smile rose unbidden in his mind as it always did when he was alone.

Opening one eye, he spied one letter that stood out from the rest. He plucked it from the others and turned it over in his hand, revealing the Marquis of Hawthorne's seal.

Their annual costume ball. The Hawthornes, with a son who would be looking for a bride soon, rarely came to Town for the Season. Families with unmarried females wouldn't dare balk and miss out on the opportunity to attend their ball, even though it meant they'd have to pack up and leave London in the middle of the Season for a week.

It was about time he attended, he told himself. The Hawthornes had always been loyal friends of his family over the years, particularly of his mother and grandmother, he mused, giving the dog at his feet a pat on the head.

Besides, it wasn't as if he'd decided to come just to see a certain young lady who possessed gorgeous sapphire eyes, asked way too many questions, and now suffered under the grand illusion of being his friend.

Chapter 4

*A Gentleman values his friends, even
when one drops in unexpectedly.*

Three months later

Lord Rothbury slept in the nude.

Which was why, one could suppose, a jolt of annoyance ran through him when he found himself awakened by the unmistakable sound of someone climbing up the rose trellis just outside his bedchamber window.

Damn. And he had been in the midst of such a peculiar and lusty dream too. "Peculiar" because he had never in his life thought he harbored a secret attraction to shepherdesses and "lusty" because he couldn't seem to keep his hands off of her. Though he couldn't see her face, she was quite luscious, with rosy-tipped breasts peeking over the edge of her bodice. He had lowered his head. . .

A creaking sound followed by the snap of thin wood yanked him straight out of his sleep-drenched musings.

Rising up to lean back on his elbows, Rothbury managed to blink open one eye just in time to watch a frilly parasol pop up and over the windowsill. It landed on his floor with a rattle.

What the bloody hell?

Since when did the thieves, cutthroats, and ne'er-do-wells of London do away with pistols and clubs in place of decorative umbrellas?

He shook his head in an effort to clear it. Despite the unique weapon choice, he still needed a swift plan of action in order to quickly overpower the miscreant intent on breaking in. But he hadn't much time and he couldn't be all that threatening to an intruder if he were to spring from his bed brandishing nothing more than a night's growth of beard stubble.

Although, he thought with a sleepy grin, he'd wager a stable full of his coveted Arabian mares that he'd have the element of surprise on his side.

Just then, a series of soft, decidedly feminine

grunts came from the vicinity of the open window. His grin crumbled.

"Ah, hell," he muttered, letting his shoulders slump back to the mattress. "Yet another blasted woman?" Truly, a man could only take so much.

In the past, Rothbury's admirers tended to keep a safe distance from him, watching him from behind their silk fans, winking at him from across the ballroom . . . or discreetly grabbing his thigh from underneath the dinner table.

He had grown quite skilled at selecting only those beauties who suited his tastes and then persuading them into the one position he happened to value above all else—which, naturally, happened to be underneath him in bed. And of course with his looks and money, it wasn't that hard of an objective to accomplish.

But that all changed this season.

Now, they came at him in droves. And all because a circulating scandal sheet had reported that he intended to cast aside his wicked ways for the benefit of a wife.

A simple statement, yes, but the columnist of that paper might as well have tied a slab of beef to his arse and let loose all the marriage-hounds.

However, being a wicked sort himself, he was doomed to attract the wicked sort—a woman who would harbor no reservations about breaking in to his house.

A scuffling sound followed by a thump against the side of the town house drew his attention. Whoever it was attempting to scramble up the side of his house was apparently having a difficult time of it.

"So, who will it be this time?" he muttered, tossing his bangs from his eyes. An intrepid lover determined to find her way back into his bed one way or another?

He cringed. More likely one of those empty-headed chits hoping to trap him into a compromising situation in order to wheedle a marriage proposal out of him, lest he be shot by her father.

Either way he would be bound to endure the aggravation of tossing her out. After all, he would never take advantage of her desperate state. Well, at least not anymore, he reminded himself. He was supposed to be behaving.

Blue-tinted moonlight cast tall shadows across the floor and a soft southerly breeze sent the long, sheer drapes billowing into motion. He would have considered it a rather pleasant evening, one meant for sleeping, if it wasn't for the small pants of exertion growing closer by the second as the woman finally made it to the top.

With an odd mix of impatience and dread, he watched as a gloved hand grasped tightly at the sill. In another minute, he'd learn the identity of this newest little intruder.

The brim of a bonnet adorned with a frilly lace ribbon rose into view. A young woman, then, but her form blocked out the light from the moon, casting her features in shadow. With a squeak and a grunt, she struggled to hoist herself up by bracing her forearms on the casement.

A long ripping sound followed as she swung her leg up and over the sill. Most likely a flounce on the hem of her gown had snagged on a thorn, he surmised. She mumbled a curse and a second later quite literally fell into his room.

"Oomph!"

He would have waited for her to stand to make his presence known, but she seemed quite content to lie there upon his floor, staring up at the ceiling.

Naturally, his gaze homed in on her bosom, which quickly rose and fell, no doubt from the strain of her recent climb.

Rothbury sat up and then swung his legs to the side of the bed. The thin sheet slid to his waist, but he chose to ignore it. Glancing down at himself, he considered his state of undress. After all, there was now a lady present. He shrugged, deciding to forgo yanking on a pair of breeches for modesty's sake. After all, he didn't have any to spare. Modesty. Not breeches.

Before long, the chit, apparently done with her little respite, scrambled to stand, then tripped on her ripped hem, which trailed under her feet as she strode to the window. She leaned on the sill, then peered out, signaling to someone below with a small wave.

Rothbury shifted his weight, eyeing the window and wondering if her father and a vicar were waiting in the bushes.

Turning back around, she tilted her head as if searching the dark for someone. She was trembling, he could hear it in her breath, almost feel it shuddering against his skin.

She took two soft, deliberate steps in his direction.

"Looking for me?"

"OH!" She jumped back, nearly falling out of the window.

He lurched forward at his waist, his sheet nearly slipping to his knees.

"I'm all right," she said, throwing up a hand in assurance, her other hand grasping the window frame. "You just startled me is all."

"I gave *you* a start?"

"Indeed." She pushed away from the window, dusted a scattering of leaves and petals off her skirts, then removed a glove to examine the tip of her smallest finger. With a shrug, she soon dismissed whatever it was she saw there and tilted her head, evidently searching the dark for his location. "Where are you?"

"Oh, over here," he said casually, like it was an everyday occurrence to welcome intruders inside his home. "On my bed."

"What?" she shouted the question. "On your *bed*?"

"Quite."

"How in the world is that possible?"

"Well, as this is my bedchamber and most bedchambers do, strangely enough, have beds in them, I fail to see how this should come as such a shock."

"Surely, you're jesting," she said with a little laugh, quite like she hoped he was merely teasing, but doubt lingered near. "That's enough time for jokes, don't you agree?"

He folded his arms over his chest. "I must ask you," he said cautiously, "just where did you expect to be?"

"In your study, of course."

"Of course," he echoed warily, wondering if there had been a report of someone escaping Bedlam recently and he had missed it.

"Now," she said in the prim and proper tone of a tight-lipped nursemaid, "are you ready to begin?" She tilted her head, apparently searching the dark for his location once again. "I should like to get started straight away. Where shall I sit?"

"There aren't any chairs in here."

"Whyever not?"

"For the simple fact," he stressed, "that you are standing in my *bedchamber*. Unless, of course, you were hoping to hop up on my bed . . . or have a cuddle upon my lap. In that case, any other night I would love to accommodate you. Although . . ." he scratched the dark-gold bristles on his chin in roguish thought ". . . it might be fun should you fancy to sway my mind."

Her nearly imperceptible gasp whispered in the room. "I–I am in your bedchamber, aren't I?" she asked softly. Her voice sounded achingly familiar.

His next words were spoken slowly. "For the third time, yes." Surely, his interloper couldn't be . . .

She bent to snatch up her parasol. Apparently, she thought to use it as a weapon. However, when she straightened, a glimmer of light reflected near her face, making him realize she wore spectacles.

His eyes narrowed. He knew of only one young woman of his acquaintance who was of a similar delicate figure and wore spectacles. But Charlotte was astoundingly timid. Certainly, she was not one to lay siege to a bachelor's town house and infiltrate his bedchamber. It couldn't be her. His mind must be muddled from sleep.

Reaching inside her bodice, she yanked out a sheet of wrinkled paper and held it up to the moonlight. "Dear me, this map is all wrong." She tapped her foot in aggravation.

"Since you brought up the point," he replied, "do you know whose bedchamber you are in?"

"Well, of course I do." She looked in his direction, waving her arm in an animated fashion. "Do you think I just go around tossing myself inside windows of unsuspecting men?"

"I can't say that I would know the answer to that question." What the hell was going on? Was he still dreaming? He cleared his throat. "I do know one thing, however."

"And that is?"

"I never expected to find you sneaking inside my town house in the middle of the night."

She shrugged. "What other time is better for sneaking into someone's town house than at night?"

She had a point there.

"Besides," she said as if he possessed the intelligence of a wheel of cheese, "I couldn't very well knock upon your front door and awaken the entire neighborhood."

"No, no. We couldn't have that."

"Rothbury, are you well?" she asked. "Why do you sound so out of sorts? I regret entering your bedchamber—an honest mistake—but after all, you knew I was coming."

"I did?"

"Well, of course you did. Your town house was the only location where we could meet in secret in such a short notice. It's not as if you frequent the same society events as I do. Our circles of friends do not overlap, as you well know."

"I can assure you, my clearly mad darling, that I had no idea you were due to arrive here."

Her mouth parted slightly at his words. "Do you mean to say you don't know . . ." As her words trailed away, her spine straightened with what could have only been a burst of indignation. "Of all the nerve! You *have* been ignoring me, haven't you?"

"Could be," he admitted with a shrug. "I ignore a great deal of women all the time. I assure you it is entirely necessary. There certainly isn't enough time in the world to pay attention to them all."

She began to pace the length of windows, muttering under her breath. Rothbury couldn't make out a single thing she said except for a few key words: "arrogant," "stubborn," and "buffoon."

"Wait," she said, coming to a full stop directly in front of him, but still far enough away that she couldn't possibly see him fully. "You did *get* my letters, didn't you?"

Letters . . . letters. His mind raced. He received letters from women all the time. Per his orders, his solicitor threw the lot of them away.

She sighed in apparent exasperation. "The letters I've been sending you, telling you that we must meet in secret—tonight. It's a matter of urgency."

"Again," he said, his patience fading, "I receive such letters all the time."

"Think, Rothbury."

All he could think about was the fact that he was abed and naked and they were quite utterly alone in his room. She obviously hadn't a care for her virtue, so that left only two reasons for sneaking into his bedchamber in the middle of the night.

Either she wanted to set up an arrangement with him as her lover or trap him into marriage. Maybe both. But she hadn't done more than be cross with him, which completely bewildered him and put him on his guard.

He sighed, threading his fingers through his already tousled hair. "Just tell me what you want and be on your way, miss."

"Miss? Since when do you call me 'miss'?"

He could do nothing but give his head a slow, befuddled shake.

"It's me," she said, in a tone tinged with a familiar vulnerability that never failed to strike a chord within him. "Charlotte."

All right. This wasn't a dream. It was a bloody nightmare.

His mouth felt slack. He might as well have been dreaming. The utter astonishment of just who stood before him hit him square in the chest.

She stepped into a beam of moonlight, which alighted upon the curve of her cheek, the elegant lines of her neck, and a fat pale ringlet that had become tangled in the ribbon of her bonnet.

Charlotte. Shy, quiet, and usually quite predictable—except for tonight, evidently.

He didn't know what provoked her desperate climb into his room, but he intended to find out.

After all they were friends, or she kept claiming they were anyway. And quite adamantly too.

He humored her, of course, letting her believe what she wished, whatever pleased her.

According to her, their friendship had started the night of the Bride Hunt Ball. Charlotte had claimed he had saved her from certain mortification after not a single gentleman in attendance asked her to dance. She had called him her "reluctant hero." Which wasn't true.

But he allowed her to keep her little story, even found himself laughing while she retold the event animatedly for the hundredth time.

Charlotte was a lovely woman. Clearly an impulsive one, but a lovely one just the same. She had seen him at his worst. Well, maybe not *the* worst, but the fact remained—she had offered him kindness. For a man like him, it was rather remarkable. Who knows, with the knock to his skull coupled with his drunken state that night outside Rosalind's window, he could have very well caught his death if Charlotte wasn't there to rouse him back to consciousness.

And he desired her, but secretly vowed to never cross the proverbial line. Granted, there were three extremely helpful notions that helped keep him walking that particular tightrope.

One: she thought the prospect of marrying him was utterly ridiculous.

Two: he suspected she was still enamored of his friend Tristan.

And three: she had "adopted" him as her newest project, her friend.

Lord, he hated that word. "Friend."

Too bad for Charlotte that her little friendship mission had to be conducted entirely in secret. Her mother, like most mothers, considered him a despicable rogue and banned them from speaking to or being near each other. So they met at the park and various other places, timing their social outings so that they'd "bump" into each other.

It was an odd relationship, when he thought on it. And they were an odd pair, he mused, catching a glimpse of his tawny hair, loose and resting against his collarbone. Quite like the lion and the mouse.

Oh, how bloody absurd. Clearly, he'd finally gone stark raving mad.

"Charlotte," he muttered again, rubbing his temples. "I can't believe you're in my house, in my bedchamber."

"Well, who did you think I was?" She shook her head in derision, settling her map upon his shaving table—but not her parasol, he noted. "Really, who else did you expect this eve?"

"Any great number of women."

She didn't like that comment, if the way she crossed her arms tightly over her chest was any indication. It was a defensive gesture. And one of the things he was astonishingly good at was reading body language. Especially *her* body language.

He flicked a glance at the window. "You're quite the determined lass. Agile too." He paused to yawn and stretch out his arms above his head. "The last woman who tried to climb into my town house ended up getting the laces of her dress tangled on a hardy rose vine. Poor creature. She wasn't discovered until dawn, hanging nearly upside down." He hadn't been home at the time, but the gardener claimed she'd paid him handsomely for his secrecy after he'd cut her down.

"Thank you for your very arrogant story."

"Anything to please you." He ran a hand through the hair atop his head.

"You," she said pointedly, "are a shameless flirt."

A lock of hair now hanging in his eyes, he leveled a stare at her. "Believe me when I say that your accusation has offended me. How dare you besmirch my character."

"*You* are supposed to be behaving."

"And I was," he said, in mock offense. "Cleary, *you* are not."

"Be serious."

"I am. For someone determined to avoid scoundrels, you're doing a deplorable job."

"Don't be silly. It's just you." Her foot tapped an impatient staccato upon his floor. "Seriously now, we must get down to the matter at hand . . . though I suspect you don't even know why I'm here."

"I'll guess. Could it be that you've had a sudden epiphany? Yes, that must be it. Let's see . . . After months of searching for the perfect gentleman, you now crave a steady dose of wicked men and you've decided to start with me." He patted his lap, knowing she couldn't see the gesture in the dark. "I don't think I should like you finding another, so I shall work hard to hold your attention."

Inhaling deeply, she was evidently trying her best to bite back a retort. "Has she accepted any of your calls?" she asked, speaking of Rosalind, the woman he was "trying" to court, only her brother deemed him and his reputation unfit to lick her half boots. Charlotte thought he had been leaving his calling cards with her footman for the past week. Unbeknownst to her, he hadn't left a single one.

"No," he said, watching Charlotte closely.

What would she do, what would she say, he wondered, if she knew the only reason he still pretended to want Rosalind was to be close to Charlotte? She considered him her little project, and it unearthed a buried self-confidence, something he doubted she would have ever thought she possessed. Something that attracted him to her like a beacon. As if he needed more encouragement.

She thought she was helping him, when in fact, she was wasting her time. Oh, he knew that pretending he was still infatuated with Rosalind just to be close to Charlotte was a tad underhanded, but he couldn't help himself. Besides, being underhanded was his specialty.

"Don't worry," she muttered. "I have another idea."

"I'm not worried," he said with a shrug.

But she should be.

He had warned her that day at Wolverest that women and men could not be merely friends, that one day one of them would undoubtedly desire the other. Of course, he left out that he was already at that point and beyond.

However, he knew nothing would ever come of their relationship, other than being friends. Noth-

ing more. Surely, his feelings would fade away
. . . eventually. And he would try to behave until
then. No matter how painful it was becoming.

And no matter how many times he told her that
she shouldn't trust him, she kept insisting that she
could. He wanted to believe her. Her faith in him
was endearing however wholly misplaced.

Tonight *she* crossed a line; *she* broke an unwrit-
ten rule by coming to his bedchamber in the dead
of night.

"I must say," he said, his words tight, "I am as-
tounded by your behavior this evening."

And he should really set her straight before she
got herself in trouble. He doubted he could keep
taking refuge in his imagination . . . The more he
denied himself, the more detailed his thoughts
became.

On a number of occasions, as she prattled on
about some silly hat she intended to redo or whatever it was that women did to their bonnets to
improve them, he found himself imagining her
perched upon his lap, wearing those spectacles of
course . . . and stockings and nothing else.

Damn. Must his mind veer off wickedly at
every turn? He was truly disgusted with his lack
of discipline. Apparently, his thought pattern was
identical to that of a farm animal.

Thankfully, she had no idea of the wicked thoughts churning about his depraved mind, which was a good thing. A great thing. For if she knew, she just might stride right out of his life.

He closed his eyes for a moment, blocking his rambling thoughts. "I must ask . . . You are known for your timidity, tripping over your words or unable to utter a syllable around men. However, you have never been so with me. Why?"

He knew the answer, but asked her just the same. It was because she had Absolutely No Romantic Interest in him.

She looked surprised by his question, but soon recovered. "Well, I suppose it is because I feel safe with you. Though I realize how absurd that sounds, for you come from a long line of scoundrels. But the truth is, I know you want someone else, and have for a very long time. And even before Lady Rosalind, you had asked my friend Madelyn to be your bride, or was it your mistress? I cannot recall." She gave her head a shake. "Either way. You are a direct sort. If you had entertained any desire for me at all, I reckon I would have known about it an age ago. Ravished in some garden or other." She paused, giving in to a quiet, husky laugh.

It amazed him that she had no apparent idea

just how provocative she sounded. And Lord, but did she have him all wrong.

"Can you imagine?" she asked through her laughter. "You and I? In a garden . . . in some passionate . . . embrace?" Her words slowed and sobered as she went on. Was she imagining it?

Hell yes, he could imagine it. And had. Numerous times.

"Come here," he said, more to see what she would do than due to a real plan.

After a brief hesitation, she took one small step in his direction.

For reasons unknown to him, the action made him want to grind his teeth. How many times did he have to tell her that he wasn't a man to be trifled with? That he hadn't a good side, no matter how adamantly she insisted that he had. Did she think him harmless because she had once seen him acting like a drunken fool?

Didn't she know how depraved he was? Hadn't she heard all the awful things he had done? Why had she come to his aid in the garden, when any other woman would have turned the other way, pretending she didn't see a bloody thing? And why *was* she still here? Hell, she might not know what was good for her, but Rothbury knew *he* certainly wasn't.

He would have never guessed that she'd do something so unwise as to visit him in the middle of the night. Friend or not. What could be so important that she needed to speak to him so urgently? Hadn't she a care for her safety? Didn't she realize the temptation she presented to him? Seeing her in the park, at Vauxhall, or sitting back-to-back at adjacent tables in a coffee shop in order to disguise that they were really there together was one thing. Having her in his room was an entirely different matter all together.

Standing, he clutched the sheet to his torso with one fist, his intent to finally show Charlotte how foolish it was to underestimate his self-control. Hell, to underestimate her effect on him. After all, he was only a man. And she was a lovely woman, albeit sorely lacking in basic judgment skills.

Heedless of his state of undress, mindless to the heat and tension thrumming through him, he stalked toward her, advancing so that she had no choice but to back up . . . or be overtaken by him.

Chapter 5

*A Gentleman's clothes are exquisite in cut
and fit, but inconspicuous in material.*

Pasting an innocent smile on her face, Charlotte tried desperately to appear cool and in control. Outwardly. Inwardly, she was ready to bolt.

She simply had no middle ground. She was either so incredibly shy that she couldn't manage a single sound to seep past her lips, or she did something so outlandish and hasty that she feared she was indeed ready to be locked up.

"Rothbury?"

She desperately tried to keep herself from glancing down at his bare chest. Embarrassment flooded heat through her cheeks. She thought he knew she was coming. And she hadn't meant to sneak into his bedchamber. According to the map, she should have been entering his study. Nelly must have reversed the directions.

However, she refused to back down. The old Charlotte would have taken one look at his lordship and scurried for the nearest exit.

Excitement and desperation had moved her, guided her behavior, she supposed. And if she was anything this night, it was desperate.

Rothbury's amber-flecked eyes glinted in the moonlight. Not for the first time that evening Charlotte thanked the Lord that the shadows hid her flushed cheeks. Whether he did it on purpose or not, his gaze perpetually held an air of both challenge and seduction, which resulted in some rather rampant babbling on her part. Not to mention his "look," as she liked to call it, which never failed to make her bones feel like butter left out in the sun.

Presently, however, suspicion swept across his lovely features. "State your business, Charlotte. And quickly too." He took another step toward her.

She slid a foot back and stepped on her ripped hem, which pulled the back of her dress tight.

"I have come tonight to ask for your assistance." His nearness was setting fire to her skin. The absurd thought that her spectacles were about to cloud over crossed her mind. There would be no denying his effect on her person then. "Whatever are you about, Rothbury? And must you stand so close?"

"What's the matter, Charlotte?" he asked, his tone mocking. "Are you suddenly having second thoughts on your decision to come here tonight?"

"A-Absolutely not. We are friends. We have no romantic interest in each other." Lord knew she had put herself in his path in the past numerous times . . . and came away with rather humbling results. She had known him since her debut. And for the past three months as his friend, he had not raised a finger even in the general direction of a possible seduction. She knew how he worked. When Rothbury wanted something—or someone—he struck like a viper; he did not hesitate.

"And besides," she added, "after you so stubbornly refused to answer my letters, I had no choice but to come here to speak with you. You very well know a lady cannot call upon a man alone, night or day."

"Have you no care for your reputation, then?"

" 'Twas why I thought to meet at night. It was the surest way to come and go undetected." Never mind the fact that the Greenes lived just around the corner. Her presence here tonight had not required a detailed mode of operation worthy of a naval captain. She hadn't even needed to hire a hack.

"And what of your mother and father should they wake to find you gone?"

"That's the benefit of having elderly parents. They sleep often and quite soundly."

"No thought to your safety?" With his free hand, he reached out to let loose a lock of hair that had coiled around her bonnet ribbon.

She batted his hand away. "I'm not a sap skull," she muttered, gesturing to the open window with a nod of her head. "I brought Ne— . . . I-I brought George."

"And he is . . ."

"Our burliest footman."

He turned his attention away from her to look out the window. And thank goodness for that. A lady could only take so much of Rothbury's undivided attention. Not to mention the fact that she was suddenly startlingly aware that he wore nothing but a sheet and was slowly inching his way closer to her. She tried to think of inane subjects to keep her mind from wondering what was under that sheet. Gardening. Yes, she liked to garden. Peonies, lily of the valley, chrysanthemums . . .

"Charlotte," he intoned, swinging those eyes back on her. "What you have down there is a chub by kitchen maid wearing a footman's costume."

She blinked and for a moment she was at a loss for words. "You have the eyes of a hawk," she admitted, astonished.

"I've been told."

"Despite what you might be thinking, Nelly is quite protective." He took another step closer to her. He smelled warm and clean and faintly like brandy. Her nerves taking a quick downward spin, she made to slide her foot back in retreat once again, but her heel met the wall with a clunk. "S–She can fight just as well as any man, maybe better," she blurted, nodding like a ninny when he lifted one tawny brow in question.

"Indeed," she went on, nodding. "Once, we had a thief trying to break in through the kitchen door. She waited in the shadows until he stepped inside, then clubbed him on the head with a leg of beef. Knocked him out cold, I'm proud to say." Lord, if she could only stop babbling.

"But your Nelly is all the way down there," he smoothly pointed out, his eyes briefly dipping, giving Charlotte's flushed figure a quick perusal. "What of the mischief that could happen right here . . . with me?"

She wanted to match his mood, show him she could be cool and unaffected by his nearness, unlike every other female in his company. Moreover, she knew he was only toying with her, which made her just a tad annoyed. However, that bit of annoyance gave her strength.

Thinking she could act just as smooth, she flicked her gaze downward, too. Straight away, her eyes seemed to lock upon his large, tan fist, which held the sheet tightly at his sculpted waist. Her face inflamed with her stubborn blush, so she forced her gaze back to his angular, beautiful face.

"How would you protect yourself?" he asked, smiling in such a way that she was sure he could read her mind.

"Well, I suppose if there came a need for me to protect myself against your lecherous advances, I'd use this parasol," she explained with a shrug, proud of the way her cool tone hid her anxiousness. "Besides, I am perfectly safe from you. I'm like a . . . a sister to you, I imagine."

"I don't have a sister." He leaned forward, resting his free hand on the wall behind her.

"Oh, well, if you did," she said nodding. She pushed against his chest with her free hand. He didn't budge.

"Let's forget all that, shall we? Instead, I'd like to prove my point. Let's pretend for a moment that I find you attractive. Let's pretend that your very virtue is sorely threatened at this very moment."

"Unlikely," she scoffed.

His warm gaze dropped down to the hand that rested against his warm, bare skin. Then he looked up at her, his eyes showing an emotion she did not recognize. "I want you," he said, then swallowed hard. "And every time you are near me, your scent, your voice, seeps into my soul."

"Oh my," she muttered with a giggle. "You're good at this. You almost sound as if you believe it yourself."

"I do."

Sighing, she supposed the only thing worse than being pursued by a sinfully attractive, manipulative rake, was having one for a friend. "Stop this, Rothbury. It's not funny."

Feeling flushed, she looked down at her hand with a start, realizing she was still touching his chest. She retracted it quickly, then made a great show of studying the tip of her index finger, where a tiny dot of blood had beaded. A thorn had jabbed her earlier during her perilous climb. She hoped it would draw his attention and distract him.

But it only made it worse. He covered her hand

with his own in a movement that could only be called a caress.

She swallowed. "Give me back my hand, you depraved hound."

"Mine." Slowly, he drew her toward his mouth, lips parted slightly.

Good Lord. Was he going to put her finger in his mouth? All her breath seemed to sink down to her knees, if such a ludicrous thing was possible. This had to stop. She thought to shove him away, only her muscles refused to respond.

"Now, what would you do?" He leaned down, his lips parting, giving her a tiny glimpse of his tongue.

Her heart tripped over itself. He was magnificent in the moonlight. But she wasn't going to stand for any of this teasing either. She brought out the parasol and pointed it at his chest. "Step back."

He merely raised a brow, his gaze flicking from her finger to the parasol and back again.

"I'm warning you."

Pushing his hand from the wall, he plucked the decorative umbrella from her slack hold and tossed it behind his back with ease. When it hit the carpet with a dull thud, he gave her a look that said, "So now what are you going to do?"

So much for her weapon.

"You can stop this now." She twisted her lips. "I see your point. However, I do have a very good reason for being here. And I am certainly not looking for your brand of mischief."

His eyes instantly cooled. Curtain closed, scene over. Thank goodness she was smart enough and strong enough not to fall for his rakish scheming. There was never any sincerity in his words. To him, playing the part of a rake was all an act, like a lever he turned on and off at will.

After watching her for a moment, he stepped away from her, disappearing into the dark room.

The air suddenly felt cold. She shivered, goose pimples spreading across her skin.

"What are you looking for, then?" he asked, his voice fading as he walked away.

A door opened in the distance, followed soon after by the sound of fabric swishing over smooth, bare flesh. She supposed he was getting dressed.

"Perhaps if you bothered to read my letters, you would know the answer to that question." She cleared her throat, eager to get to the point. "To begin, I've come to ask you why you failed to inform me that Harriet cried off. Tristan is free."

She nearly jumped when a door, which she hadn't known existed until now, was suddenly forcibly opened behind her, then slammed shut.

Rounding her like a stalking panther, Rothbury padded past, dressed now in a loose white shirt and a pair of tan breeches. He looked angry, his jaw tight.

A sudden stark awareness nearly made her shiver with apprehension. She was in his territory, of that there was no doubt. And if she were any other woman (a woman he truly found attractive, to be more precise), there was no doubt that her virtue would be in danger.

He lit a branch of candles sitting upon a side table, basking the room in a soft golden glow.

He wasn't lying. There weren't any chairs in his bedchamber. Or she supposed there weren't. For at that moment her mind could only focus on the huge mahogany four-poster bed crouching in the back of the room. The chocolate-brown coverlet sat rumpled in a heap at the end of the bed while a honey-colored sheet spilled halfway onto the floor.

Goodness, she thought, resisting the urge to fan herself. If his sheet was there, that meant that he had dropped it when he had walked away from her. Which meant he had walked to his dressing room utterly naked. Without the sheet. In this room. With her. For about five seconds, at least.

Crossing his arms over the broad expanse of his chest, Rothbury regarded her with a serious expression. In fact, he looked mightily irritated. Much like he was an inch from tossing her out the window, which, given her outlandish behavior this evening, might very well be justified.

"So your Tristan is free. What does that have to do with anything?"

"What does that have to do with . . . ? How could you ask me such a question?"

"Didn't I just?"

"You are very moody."

"Please. What does Harriet Beauchamp crying off have to do with the fact that you are standing in my bedchamber at . . ." he glanced at the mantel clock, ". . . at half-midnight, wearing a frock with a missing third button?"

"A missing . . . ?" She looked down at her dark green carriage dress. Sure enough, just where he said, a button was missing. "My, you do have re-markably good vision. The complete opposite of m—"

"Honestly, Charlotte," he muttered, shifting his stance. "Did it come as a shock? When he asked her, she thought she was marrying either the heir apparent to a dukedom or presumably giving birth to one in the future should Tristan's older brother live a long and healthy life. Think, Charlotte. Now that the duke married, she found herself engaged to a man who holds nothing but a courtesy title."

"Indeed," she said. "I understand. I just hadn't expected it, which brings me to my point for being here."

"Thank God."

She cleared her throat. "I will ignore your sarcasm."

"Wise choice. Proceed."

"Well," she said cautiously. "It seems you've forgotten a very special event. The Hawthorne Costume Ball. It's next week."

Rothbury hadn't forgotten at all. Admittedly, he had been avoiding Charlotte as the date approached. Knowing Tristan wasn't engaged any longer and knowing his friend would presumably attend the ball, Rothbury had no more desire to watch Charlotte blush and stutter in Tristan's presence than he would enjoy getting pecked to death by a flock of man-hungry seagulls.

He should have known this was coming. According to Charlotte, she'd been enamored of Tristan since the day he pulled her and her

mother from the mangled heap of their overturned carriage. Participating in the Bride Hunt
Ball had seemed like fate to her. And now that
the gossip columnists had recently reported that
the chit cried off the engagement, Charlotte must
be ecstatic, thinking this was her second chance.

"I received a letter from my cousin in the post
this morning," she went on, clearly warming up
to her point. "She said you had sent your regrets.
You simply must attend. You must. Tristan is
going to be there."

"That's nice," he muttered. "Have fun."

She started wringing her hands. "You simply
must come, Rothbury. As my friend, you must
support me. How ever am I supposed to with-
stand being in the same room with him after all
that has happened between us?"

"Avoid him, then," he offered with a shrug.
"It's sure to be a crush, packed to the ceiling with
guests. Shouldn't be too hard."

"But I need you. How else am I to implement
my plan?"

Momentarily speechless by her declaration of
"needing" him, his mind quickly scrambled to re-
focus. *Plan?* Rothbury stilled. "What plan?"

"Well, as you know, you owe me the sum of one
favor."

"Oh, Christ," he murmured, running a hand through his tousled mane.

"Wait," she said gently. "You don't even know what I'm going to say."

"I don't have to. I already know."

"You couldn't possibly."

"I am not a matchmaker, Charlotte."

"I'm not asking for you to do such a thing. You of all people know your friend better than anyone. Perhaps better than his own family."

"Perhaps not. Listen. You're close friends with the duke's bride. Why not pester them into helping you leg-shackle the man?"

She looked to the ground. "They're still in Wales, presently. Besides, they're against the match."

"Doesn't that tell you something then? His own family thinks he'll make you miserable."

"They don't understand," she said shaking her head. "*You* don't understand. He promised—"

"Men promise a lot of things when lust runs hot and steady under their skin."

"We've been through this before. I do not inspire such feelings."

And Rothbury knew she truly believed that. It was all there in her eyes. Open and sincere, anxious and hopeful.

"But I want to change that," she whispered, meeting his gaze hesitantly, "with your help."

Rothbury's jaw tightened as he smothered a curse.

She took a step toward him. He went to take a step back, but he found himself against a wall.

"Charlotte, I cannot help you." He shook his head, turning away from the hope flaring in her eyes, making them bright, making him wish . . . well, making him wish for things he had no business wishing for. "I have problems of my own," he muttered.

"All I need is your advice . . . on how to attract Tristan in such a fashion that he'll go mad for wanting me for his own. I want him to look at me again. But this time I want him to realize it was me he should have picked the first time. I want to make him jealous, Rothbury. Will you help me?"

He closed his eyes momentarily. What could it hurt? A few orchestrated trysts here, some advice there. A couple of days and she'd be satisfied. Or more likely, frustrated. Once Harriet cried off, Tristan finally admitted he'd proposed to the girl in haste. And now that he no longer needed to marry and carry on the family line because his older brother was happily fulfilling that obligation, Tristan was free to be the debauching, carousing, wastrel of a second son. Charlotte may have turned his head a time or two, but his friend wasn't interested in marriage any longer.

But what did he know. Rothbury didn't spend his days sitting in Tristan's pocket. Certainly, he wasn't privy to his friend's every thought.

Wait . . . She had said "jealous," hadn't she?

He jerked his head in her direction. "Did you say you want to make him *jealous*?"

"Quite."

"As in . . . *revenge*?"

"Yes," she said impatiently, widening those sapphire eyes of hers.

"So you do not want . . . you do not intend to win him now that he's free?"

"No," she replied in a small voice, her tone not as firm as Rothbury wanted it to be.

"Charlotte, you naughty little thing. Why, I ought to take you across my lap and—"

"Oh stop it, Rothbury," she said with a roll of her eyes. "Perhaps a decent amount of groveling will do."

"Groveling? Begging is better."

At her sigh of frustration, he chuckled. "All right. I'll be serious. Please, proceed."

"Of course, I don't intend for this to go on and on. I have other things do and I must work quickly. Time is of the essence. This is to be my last Season. I simply must ensnare another suitor before my mother makes other plans. Perhaps you could go over my list of proper husbands while we're there?"

A proper husband. Something inside him jerked with a stab of pain.

Quick as it came, he brushed the thought aside, thinking instead of the matter at hand.

So, he had misunderstood her. Good. He liked this version better. Now at least, he had an excuse to flirt with Charlotte to his heart's content. He didn't know if any of it would work, but it still sounded like fun.

Fun? Or torture?

He shook his head, sighing in resignation.

"Hullo?" She waved a hand in the general direction of his face as if to wake him from a stupor. "You didn't answer my question."

"I'll help you. But I cannot promise you the results that you seek."

She bounced where she stood, clasping her hands together. Rothbury couldn't help but smile. Was he such a bowl of pudding, then? Probably. But he suspected it had something to do with embracing an opportunity to spend more time with a chit who always made him bite back a smile, even while she frustrated him to hell and back.

"Oh, thank you! Thank you," she chirped, surprising him by bounding across the room and clasping him tight for a quick hug.

His arms hung heavy and loose at his sides during her gentle siege.

Rothbury had enchanted exotic opera singers into returning to his bed time and again. He had warmed coldhearted courtesans into confessing their undying love and he had seduced a number of beautiful, feisty women who were just as fickle in picking their lovers as he was. But Charlotte's hug unsettled him, knocked him off balance, one might say.

He didn't want her to let go. But he wouldn't dare bring up his arms to hold her either. Without a doubt he knew if he indulged himself, all he felt, all he thought, would be exposed in the warmth of his embrace. And then there would be no turning back. He would be bared, revealed, humiliated.

All too soon, she pulled away.

Leaving him, Charlotte started to flounce to the windows and then returned just as quickly.

"Yes," Rothbury joked, "do use the stairs to leave."

She shook her head. "I almost forgot."

"What's that?"

"My costume. With all those guests, how ever will you be able to spot me in the crowd?"

"You're not walking home," he said, deliberately changing the subject. Honestly, he didn't want to know what or whom she was going dressed as. It would only inflame his imagination, create more wicked fodder for his dreams, and cause him undue agony. "My carriage will take you and your burly kitchen maid home."

"You don't want to know?"

"I am certain I will be able to find you. Don't fret."

"Oh, I almost forgot to tell you." She gave him a small, knowing smile. "You'll be happy to know that Lady Rosalind will be there as well."

"Lady Rosalind, eh?"

"Indeed," she said with a wide smile. "Are you not excited?"

Oh, who the hell was he fooling? He was too tired to fake his interest in that woman right now. So he merely raised a brow and hoped it appeared sincere. "I can hardly contain myself, my dear."

Chapter 6

A Gentleman is welcomed by all.

The Hawthornes' Costume Ball
Northumberland

"**L**ord Rothbury is forbidden."

Charlotte gave her mother a dutiful nod, furrowing her brow for effect lest her mother suspect she wasn't paying attention, or worse, not taking the dire warning seriously.

"I realize we've become quite desperate," Hyacinth Greene stressed with all the maternal protectiveness she could muster, "but his lordship is not the answer."

"Yes, Mother."

"Pay absolutely no attention to him."

"Naturally."

As if any female with a pulse could possibly ignore Rothbury.

Perched on a gilded chaise lounge alongside her mother, a betraying warmth spread up Charlotte's neck and fanned to her cheeks. She had always been a deplorable liar, her skin forever turning splotchy pink and giving her away. Good thing for her that her mother was always too preoccupied to notice.

Hyacinth cleared her throat, apparently noticing Charlotte's flagging attention. "You wouldn't want to scare any possible beaus away by being seen consorting with that scoundrel, would you?"

Possible beaus? What were those again? Ah, yes. Elusive creatures, those.

Charlotte waved a dismissive hand in the air. "You may rest assured," she said wryly, "I am perfectly safe from him." Her mother worried needlessly. She wasn't a sniveling debutante. "If Lord Rothbury had any interest in me, I'd know. He'd make sure of it."

As when she so stupidly climbed into his room in order to make certain he would be attending this costume ball. And what a frustrating evening it was turning out to be.

Her mother had been watching her as if she were a pickpocket, making sure Charlotte never ventured anywhere near Lord Rothbury. Tristan arrived late and then proceeded to spend the better half of the rest of the evening in the card room. But she still held hope that her plan of inspiring jealousy would be implemented.

"He has a look about him tonight," Hyacinth remarked, worry evident in her tone. "Like he's on the hunt. It's quite unsettling. Quite."

"Please, do not worry over me. I'll be fine."

She conceded, however, that there was some substance to her mother's trepidation about Lord Rothbury. That is, if Rothbury suddenly acquired an appetite for spectacle-wearing wallflowers who wore hideous costumes to masquerade balls *per annum* in order to please their mothers.

No. She shook her head, disrupting the plethora of bows and ribbons adorning the frumpy contraption called a bonnet on her head. Highly improbable.

"You must admit," Charlotte said with an impish grin, anticipating her mother's animated reaction with her next words, "his lordship does look positively *tempting* this evening."

"Charlotte!" Her mother's cheeks reddened. Gently, she swatted at her daughter's lap with her open fan. "That fact should be of no consequence to you . . . or me." She cleared her throat. "Just promise your dear mother you'll stay clear of Lord Rothbury, will you? Don't do anything that would snag the rogue's attention. Your costume *is* rather beguiling."

Er . . . . right. With great effort, Charlotte refrained from twirling her eyes. She wasn't the type of woman to place wagers, but she'd be willing to drop a tidy sum on the odds that "shepherdess" costumes weren't lust inducing.

Next to her, Hyacinth yawned. Charlotte gave her mother one last reassuring smile, then sighed.

At two and twenty, Charlotte had come to that point in her life where she was beyond wanting to shed her wallflower status. She held no shame that she was more an observer of life than a participant, and that she would very likely someday become a spinster. A lot of women did.

With the exception of Rothbury, she often stammered her way into realizing she wanted nothing more than to fade into the background instead of being the center of attention. She knew who she was and what she desired in life.

And while she valued her mother's splendid eye-catching costume strategy, but not perhaps the costume choice, this particular evening Charlotte wanted nothing more than to be *invisible*.

Well, at least to one person in particular: the dreaded Viscount Witherby.

When it came to events such as these, bumping into him had been an ongoing worry in her life. He seemed to appear at every single event she happened to attend. Either he was stalking her like a deranged jungle cat, or her mother was supplying him with the information.

She shuddered. Who in her right mind would willingly wed an old man who perpetually smelled of stale cigars, had yellow teeth, and spoke directly to her bosom at every unchaperoned opportunity?

Unfortunately, Witherby was an old, trusted family friend of the Greenes. And incredibly wealthy. And incredibly tired of waiting for Charlotte to relinquish her dream of finding love with a gentleman closer to her own age.

Charlotte's mother rather hoped the aging widower would soon make an official offer for her daughter's hand in holy matrimony. Charlotte rather hoped that he would board the next boat to China.

True, each Season had been unsuccessful, and she had begun to feel the beginnings of a panic over her unmarriageable state, but she remained ever hopeful that she wouldn't have to marry Viscount Witherby, that one day soon she would find her love match.

Why, she even knew exactly what her true love would be like. He'd be kind and thoughtful, attentive, and trustworthy. He'd smile at her the instant she walked into a room and hang on her every word, her every syllable. And he'd never let his eyes stray to another woman. A true gentleman, he'd be. Someone her mother would undoubtedly approve of. Someone who made Charlotte sigh with pleasure just thinking about him . . .

She nearly groaned as the thought of Lord Tristan entered her mind. For years she had believed he possessed all those attributes and more. For years she had harbored a schoolgirl's infatuation with him. Whenever she had seen him, trotting handsomely on his bay in the park, buying a bauble for his sister in a shop, or driving his phaeton down the lane, he'd always tip his hat to her and smile. Unbeknownst to him, he was only encouraging her foolish hopes and wishes—the daydreams of a timid girl headed for nowhere but spinsterhood.

But that was all in the past. She was a woman now. And she'd never allow herself to entertain the idea that she could ensnare—and hold—the attention of one of the *ton*'s most sought after bachelors.

Men like him used words to manipulate women emotionally, which was why she wanted to exact her revenge.

"Oh, where is he?" she ground out the question between her teeth.

"Where is who?"

"No one," she replied innocently.

Hyacinth sat forward. "It sounded as if you asked, 'Where is he?' "

Charlotte pressed her lips together and shook her head. "No. Tea. 'Where is the tea?' I asked."

"Oh." Hyacinth settled back into the settee, satisfied.

Charlotte breathed a sigh of relief that her mother gave up her prodding before her skin stayed permanently scarlet from all the little fibs that were stacking up this evening. Truthfully, sometimes being friends with Rothbury was a chore.

She needed to speak with him. Right now. She wanted to find out what was keeping Lord Tristan and what their next plan would be.

"You've got that far-off look in your eyes again, my dearest." Hyacinth reached over and gently patted her daughter's hand. "Be a good girl and let us retire to our rooms above stairs. The evening is spent and I've grown tired. Besides, we should rest. Your father wrote that we've been gone long enough and he wishes us away from all manner of 'vice and impurity.' We must leave for London on the morrow."

Already?

Charlotte's shoulders slumped. Sometimes she wondered if her mother was, in fact, trying to *stop* her from marrying anyone other than Witherby. Inhaling deeply, she exhaled a long, weary sigh, the sound much like a muffled death knell marking the end to her deepest wishes.

She worried her bottom lip. "May I ask the Hawthornes if I could go up with Lizzie? You needn't worry–"

"Absolutely not. The last time I let her mother chaperone, you weren't returned to me until two o'clock in the morning."

She sighed. Older parents meant retiring earlier than everyone else, even if the evening was just getting interesting.

And this evening was no exception—Lord Rothbury's rare appearance was causing quite a stir.

She just needed to sneak away for a moment.

"Would I be permitted to take a stroll on the terrace before we leave?" She looked to her mother, but Hyacinth refused to make eye contact and instead fidgeted with the lace of her handkerchief, her jaw set.

The truth of the matter was, Charlotte had been born to parents late in their lives. The exuberant cost of a London Season aside, the hustle of city life and the endless stream of balls, dinner parties, and forays into the country were getting to be too much for her older parents. But what worried her the most was the fact that this Season was her last.

Her mother's enthusiasm for the marriage mart had waned considerably after the duke's ball. Charlotte suspected Hyacinth wanted her only daughter to cease fighting a losing battle and settle down with Witherby.

"He is a philanthropist; he is a lover of animals and birds. He has adored you since you were a child. He is your haven," her mother had said on many occasions, over and over again

He might be all those things, but he was also four decades older than she—more fit to marry her mother than herself, Charlotte thought cheekily—and the fact that she had known him since she was a child, and that he had adored her since, was not comforting in the least. The thought of marrying him or . . . she shuddered . . . *kissing* him gave her hives. He was practically her uncle.

A soft snore drew her attention. Glancing to her right, she realized her mother had, yet again, fallen asleep in full view of at least eighty people. Reaching forward, Charlotte blinked, pausing in the act of nudging her mother awake.

For the most part, she had become accustomed to her mother's impromptu naps, as had most of their acquaintances. At times—especially during church—it turned downright embarrassing.

Secretly though, Charlotte thought the habit wonderful. It allowed her a rare freedom, a breath of blessed fresh air, and a short-lived sense of independence. With her mother now dozing, Charlotte had every intention of slipping into the crowd. Oh, she would wake her mother eventually, she was a good girl after all, but for now she would seek out Lord Rothbury.

Their plan wasn't going to work. First of all, Lord Tristan hadn't poked his head out of the card room for nearly two hours now. More important: how in the world was Rothbury to help Charlotte if he wasn't allowed within three feet of her? Something had to be done.

Charlotte stood, her gaze instantly connecting with Rothbury's. A zing of awareness tingled down her spine.

Dripping with sensuality, the earl stood with

his back to the wall, his stance, as always, exuding a lazy confidence. The damp spring air in the crowded room caused his dark-blond locks to curl slightly where wisps had escaped the velvet queue secured behind his neck. He wore no costume, no mask, which of course wasn't required, therefore catching the eye of every warm-blooded female within a two-hundred-foot radius.

It wasn't an exaggeration. The sighs of feminine appreciation surrounded Charlotte. Though she found it slightly ridiculous, she could not find it in herself to blame them. He was simply that fetching.

His expertly cut dark gray coat hugged his broad shoulders, and his stark white cravat, frothy with elegant folds, emphasized his chiseled chin, gold with faint bristles. And his mouth—oh, that glorious mouth—both haughty and wicked, curving with his ever-present sagacious grin. Lord, what it must feel like to have those lips touch one's own.

Charlotte gave an appreciative sigh, drinking up the sight of him. For a masquerade, his plain evening clothes on any other man would have lent him to fade into the background. But not Rothbury. Dear heavens, no. It only added to his sinful, blush-inducing appeal.

She tightened her jaw, worrying her mouth had

gone slack while perusing him from afar. More-over, she despised the fact that she was starting to feel like a starved kitten being teased with a bowl of cream. "Good Lord, girl," she whispered, "he's just a man."

But that wasn't true. He was a *wicked* man. Sin embodied. A demon under the guise of an angel, his face and body designed to lure the weak-willed into temptation.

Lud, she really needed to stop reading all those Minerva novels.

But the truth was, Rothbury had the power to persuade a scorching blush from any woman, young, old, chaste or brazen, with just one lazy sweep of his heavy-lidded, whiskey-colored gaze. Any young woman, that is, except for Charlotte.

Without fail, in social situations such as these, he merely looked at her as if she were a pane of glass—aware of her, but with really no need to bother focusing on her, as there was a far more interesting landscape beyond.

And he was doing it again.

Husky feminine laughter trickled behind Char-lotte, prompting her to turn and look over her shoulder.

The dark-haired beauty, Lady Rosalind, stood ringed by a score of adoring beaus.

Charlotte nodded to herself, feeling mildly embarrassed, her neck and cheeks prickly with heat. Of course. Lord Rothbury wasn't looking at *Charlotte*; he was looking *behind* her, at the beautiful heiress.

Well, with that mystery solved, Charlotte heaved a heavy sigh, straightened the spectacles on her nose once again, and shouldered her way through the crowd toward Rothbury. And all the while she prayed she wouldn't find herself face to face with Witherby instead.

Chapter 7

A Gentleman obliges all who seek his company.

"**S**o, what do you think? Mother Goose or Perdita?"

A slow grin curving his lips, Rothbury flicked his gaze upon Charlotte. "Perdita, definitely," he answered, speaking of a character in a play.

"Ah, now I see," Tristan Everett Devine replied, having just sidled up to his friend after exiting the card room. "The shepherd's crook she's carrying gives it away."

With the ease of a man who could size up a woman and her worth within seconds, Rothbury's gaze raked the wispy-thin Miss Greene, from her pale ringlets dangling from a bonnet made droopy by too many lacy ribbons down to her silk slippers peeking out from under her frilly hem.

"She is more like a meek lamb than her costume suggests," Tristan remarked with a chuckle.

"Perhaps." Rothbury watched as she caught his smile and then looked behind her, apparently searching for what, or rather *whom*, he was looking at. "No, sweetheart," he murmured under his breath, "I'm looking at you."

"What say you?" Tristan asked good-naturedly. "She's pleasant enough, pretty and fair."

Rothbury responded with a careless shrug.

"Sweet Jesus," Tristan mumbled with disdain. "That's got to be dashed irritating, is it not? Following you around like besotted schoolgirls, watching your every move. "

Rothbury turned, raising a questioning brow.

"Over there," Tristan said, indicating behind Rothbury with a nod of his head.

Lifting his brandy snifter to his lips, Rothbury threw a negligent glance over his shoulder. A small group of young women were gathered behind him, fluttering their lashes, smiling coyly, and whispering behind their fans. He gave them a slow, polite nod of acknowledgment. As expected, their cheeks colored up in unison and they dissolved into twitters of maidenly giggles, guiltily looking away at being caught staring.

One corner of Rothbury's mouth lifted with a wry grin. He gave a careless shrug, then turned back to his friend. "Are you sure they are not looking at you?" He lifted his glass, tossed back the remaining contents, and set it down on a side table.

While Rothbury had grown accustomed to women blushing and gaping whenever he happened to walk into a room, he had the tendency to regard his uncommon handsomeness as an accident of nature. An everyday annoyance, if you will. Or put even more precisely: it was a blasted curse.

And it was getting to be bloody ridiculous.

A dour-faced footman approached. "Lady Gilton awaits, my lord," he muttered furtively, tucking a perfumed note into Rothbury's palm before slipping back into the crowd.

Rothbury's lips twisted in a faint smile as he tucked the note into an inside pocket of his coat. As eager as he was to quit this evening and enjoy a night of unmitigated lusty bliss at some secret location specified in the note, the lovely viscountess would have to wait. Tonight he had other obligations.

Tonight, Rothbury needed to find himself a bride. And fast.

But not just any bride. He needed her to be . . .

replaceable, for he didn't intend to keep her. Actually, he didn't intend to marry her either. He just needed to borrow her for a little while.

And so from the back of the room, he considered the unmarried female guests much as a methodical lion would peruse a herd of prancing gazelles. Looking for the weak and unguarded.

Somewhere in this god-awful congested throng there had to be at least one competent woman who could assist him. But alas, the night was winding down and his options were dwindling.

He hung back, giving every single woman careful consideration. His searching gaze was direct, thorough, and calculating. He had patience. He had the required instincts. He even had the necessary savvy of their various personalities and who could or who could not be manipulated to implement his behest. What he didn't have, however, was time.

"Just pick one," Tristan suggested, apparently reading where his thoughts were going. "Should be easy enough."

"If only that were true."

"What exactly are you looking for? Your usual? Gorgeous? Voluptuous?"

Rothbury gave a sardonic huff. "Hell, none of that matters, does it?"

"Why the bloody hell not?"

"She's only temporary," Rothbury said, leaning a shoulder against a marble column.

"Wouldn't you prefer a suitable one?"

"I'd prefer a *believable* one," he drawled.

"Hmm, let's see," Tristan murmured, tapping his chin in thought. "She would need to be an intelligent, crafty one, then?"

"She needn't be very clever," he answered, his attentive gaze focusing on another small group of young women and their chaperones across the room. "In fact, I prefer her to be rather dim and unobtrusive. Under my thumb, so to speak. I can't have her plotting to trap me into a true engagement or have the capacity to think to blackmail me for the rest of my days for recompense."

"Ah, I see," Tristan remarked. "Quite an amusing predicament you've placed yourself in, old friend. I escaped the hangman's noose and here you are looking for an invented one." He chuckled to himself, then cleared his throat, instantly sobering at Rothbury's cutting glare. "Perhaps your grandmother has already forgotten that you claimed to have a fiancée?"

" 'Twas what I had hoped, but it's not the case."

When Rothbury had arrived at Aubry Park three days prior, he had found his grandmother sobbing in the garden. It took a great deal of patience on his part, but he had finally worked out what had made her so sad. It seemed she was having a lucid moment, her memory and sense returning at least for a short spell. But in that small, precious moment she had realized that she had grown old, her mind oft confused. And, she realized, that she might not ever get to see her favorite grandson (and only grandson) get married, or even meet his wife, the future countess.

Rothbury had assured her that he would . . . eventually, which wasn't a lie, but instead of calming her, his assurances had made her angry and she slipped back into confusion. She had stormed up the stairs, demanding the presence of the steward. A short while later, in the presence of her weak-kneed, overpaid monkey of a solicitor, she was having the papers drawn up to sell Aubry Park and the twelve-hundred-acre horse-breeding farm with it. Unless Rothbury found a bride, and quick.

The park wasn't an entailed estate, but land that her equestrian mother had handed down to her. And it would, presumably, be handed down to subsequent female relations thereafter. What the dowager didn't understand, however, was

that the bulk of the revenue upon which the earldom of Rothbury was built resided in that horse-
breeding farm. Without that income, even if the
earl was frugal, the earldom would become desti-
tute, unable to support its other, entailed, properties and the families of farmers who depended on
them for repairs, and upkeep.

So then he *did* lie. He had no choice. He told a
whopping clanker. He told her he was recently engaged and had even promised to bring his fiancée
to visit Aubry Park so that she could meet her.

He told her all this, thinking she'd never remember a word of it fifteen minutes hence. However,
she seized upon the information like a wolf catching the scent of a plump hare jumping through a
field.

He was just grateful that he managed to keep
her from attending this ball. Her behavior was er-
ratic at best. Lately, she refused to speak in any
language but her native French and was prone to
tantrums and bouts of weeping.

Which meant he had one miserable option: to
find his aforementioned, unwanted, entirely fic-
tional bride.

"Would it be possible to hire someone from the
village near Aubry Park?" Tristan asked, stalling
his thoughts.

"Ah, you're forgetting I do not possess the luxury of time," Rothbury said, fixing his vigilant gaze upon the crowd of partygoers before him. "What I need is someone desperate. Someone easily manipulated. Someone . . ."

Whatever he was about to say fell away from his lips as his intense focus homed in on a pile of white lace and ribbons amidst a sea of people.

Miss Charlotte Greene. Docile. Incredibly gullible.

This whole bloody affair was her fault, wasn't it? True, she hadn't forced him to lie, but the truth of the matter was, if she hadn't broken into his house, batted her eyelashes, and asked him to attend this ball, he wouldn't have left London for Northumberland. He wouldn't have gone to Aubry Park. He wouldn't have lied to his senile grandmother.

Yes. As far as he was concerned, all of this was her fault.

He followed her progress across the ballroom, almost forgetting himself and shouting a warning when she nearly whacked a footman in the back of the head with her crook. To his surprise, she turned on her heel, deftly escaping that tiny catastrophe only to find herself tumbling onto the lap of Lord Asterley. Jumping off the old man, she smiled down at him, spilling over with apologies while splotches of crimson grew on her cheeks and neck.

In the last two years she hadn't received a single offer of marriage. The closest she had come to impending nuptials was when she was invited to the Duke of Wolverest's Bride Hunt Ball last August.

It was a great compliment to her family that she had been included in the most titillating event of last Season. However, the wave of interest so soon created had eventually gathered flotsam, leaving her to settle back into her quirky, timid demeanor, overlooked and easily dismissed.

And with the Greenes' estate and accompanying blunt entailed away, making a good match had surely become the deciding factor in whether Charlotte and her mother ate or starved following the death of her father.

For the first time that evening, the corners of Rothbury's lips curved into a slow, authentic grin.

"You can't possibly be thinking of using Miss Greene," Tristan said with surprise, perceptively guessing where Rothbury's gaze had focused.

"Why not?"

Not a single soul knew that Rothbury and Charlotte were friends. Not even Tristan. They had managed to keep it secret for this long, and there was no doubt they couldn't keep . . . other secrets.

"For the simple fact that she's . . . well, because she's friends with my brother's wife. And she just happens to be my *almost* fiancée."

Rothbury raised a sardonic brow. "You're *almost* fiancée, is it?"

"I don't think she should be involved. You risk trouncing her heart."

Ah, yes. You took great care of her heart, didn't you?

Tristan shook his head. "Sure, she's quite naive. And too sympathetic to try manipulating you into a true engagement. But she's quite a good sport, nice—"

"She's perfect," Rothbury replied. And they were friends, more than Tristan could claim. Surely, she'd need a bit of coaxing, but he was sure they could pull off a fake engagement without a hitch. After all, it would only be for one day.

"I think you're making a mistake. Charlotte comes off a touch . . . impulsive, but I would not underestimate her if I were you."

Rothbury's mind was made up. The tension in his shoulders eased and he immediately thought to go and pull Charlotte off to some secluded spot to explain his plan.

"I wish you luck," Tristan replied, shaking his head. "You'll need it, especially with your rather wicked reputation backed by all the ribald tales of the Rothbury males in your past. Hawthorne tells me that you, specifically, are not allowed anywhere near her."

"And has that stopped me before?"

"Hell no. But you haven't met her father. Irksome man. He fancies himself a man of strict moralistic values. He'll have a rapscallion such as you at the execution block before you can touch a single lock upon her head."

"Shush, Tristan. You're getting to sound like an overprotective mother hen. Besides, if my memory serves me, I've tugged one of those curls already." He slid a side glance at Tristan, remembering his blasted promise to Charlotte. "You're coming to Aubry Park tomorrow?"

Tristan nodded, muttering under his breath.

"It will work, I assure you. In fact, I probably won't need to tell her a goddamn thing. I'll just invite her and her mother for luncheon. She won't understand a single syllable my grandmother says, and then she'll be on her way back for London, none the wiser."

"You could just tell your grandmother the truth."

And take the risk of her going through with her threat? Not bloody likely. He needed to bide his time in picking his bride. It wasn't something he wanted to rush into. But his grandmother's insistence left him no choice. It had to be Charlotte. She would never expect it to be a serious engagement. She'd laughed uproariously the one time he mentioned it.

However, before Rothbury could take a step in her direction, a slender, warm hand settled on his wrist. Narrow, almost catlike green eyes smiled invitingly up at him, effectively snatching his attention from his intended prey.

"Didn't you get my note?" Lady Gilton asked with a pout.

"Indeed," he answered, his eyes still on Miss Greene.

Apparently sensing his inattention, Lady Gilton maneuvered herself in front of him, smoothly blocking his line of vision. "We were to meet in the library," she crooned. Bold as ever, she reached up to cup a hand over his ear and breathed a suggestion only a eunuch would refuse.

Though it had been over a year since he had last sampled the viscountess's charms, the pair always seemed to fall easily into their old routine.

"Down the hall," she whispered without looking at him. "Turn right. Second door on your left. Lord Gilton is in the garden with the buxom harpist. We have at least an hour." She skirted past him then, giving the appearance, at least to the rest of the ballroom that she was simply walking off.

Rothbury didn't follow straight away. He lingered, his gaze unerringly snagging on Miss Greene as she tried to weave through a particularly copious throng of people only to nearly slam into Miss Hawthorne.

Despite his ill mood, he chuckled low in his chest. Perhaps he had been wrong in suggesting she wear her spectacles. At least with blurry vision, she took care in crossing a crowded ballroom instead of plowing through at top speed.

All at once his muscles tightened as an odd surge of apprehension rose within him. Surely not from the prospect of tricking his grandmother with Charlotte's assistance. She'd agree.

Wouldn't she?

But what if she refused? What would he do then? Break his grandmother's heart? Even he couldn't do that.

No. He couldn't take the risk of Charlotte refusing to go along with his ruse. He was going to have to trick her into visiting Aubry Park under the pretense of meeting his grandmother. He could do it. Manipulating women was his forte.

So then, why did he suddenly feel like the lowest of cads?

He pushed the thought away, thinking instead of the bounty that awaited him down the hall. Yes. That's what he would do. A little tumble with Cordelia and he'd enjoy a bit of temporary relief from the quandary he got himself into. Soon he'd forget all his troubles.

However, as he sauntered down the dark hall leading to the library, he couldn't help but wish it were Charlotte waiting for him in the library instead.

Chapter 8

*A Gentleman always grants a Lady his
undivided attention.*

"I've decided to allow the Earl of Rothbury
to seduce me."

"Allow?"

"You are forgetting that in order for one to be seduced, one must be, at the very least, mildly resis-
tant. And we all know you are hardly opposed."

A symphony of giggles ensued.

Charlotte, not by any stretch of the imagination an active participant in the conversation surrounding her, considered it a personal triumph
that she refrained from rolling her eyes. Not that
the Fairbourne twins nor Laura Ellis would have
noticed if she had. They were all too busy ogling
Lord Rothbury.

After a rather embarrassing spill onto the lap of an eighty-three-year-old man, Charlotte had entered an area thick with shoulder-to-shoulder guests, which had slowed her progress across the room to a near standstill. The trio of young women continued to talk, unheeding of the ears that might overhear them. Charlotte tried to move past them, inch by aggravating inch.

"Well then, you should make your move soon," Belinda Fairbourne warned, "before I have a go at him first." She straightened her feathered swan mask with a proud sniff.

"Would you like to place a wager?" Laura Ellis asked. The jewels sown onto her dark blue bodice, which elegantly made up the pattern of peacock feathers, winked in the candlelight.

"Perhaps," replied Bernadette Fairbourne, dressed as a snowy-white dove, replied. She raised her dainty nose at the peacock in a challenging manner. "I daresay, the upper hand is mine. His lordship seems utterly distracted this evening and I believe I know why."

"Indeed," Charlotte muttered, finally finding the courage to speak up. Really, there was nothing else to do, as yet another person blocked her from breaking free. She might as well join in. "Lady Ros—"

Charlotte's next words died on her tongue as the Swan, the Peacock, and the Dove suddenly swung their heads in her direction. As if only now noticing she stood next to them, listening.

And by the pinched set of their faces, they weren't happy about her participation. Their eyes narrowed on her. Charlotte refused to shrink back, though they intimidated her all the same.

"All I meant to say is that if he seems distracted it's highly probable that he's watching—"

"We know who he's watching, you little widgeon," the dove remarked. "And it certainly could never be you."

That, Charlotte mused, was undoubtedly true. Lord knew she had been in Rothbury's path in the past numerous times before, but he never acted upon a seduction, a flirtation, or even a single bone-melting stare. Oh, now that they were friends, he teased her, but she was smart enough never to take him seriously.

She cleared her throat. "'Twas not what I was suggesting . . ."

The swan gasped, pressing her fingertips to her lips and then turned an alarming shade of crimson.

"He's looking this way," she whispered excitedly.

Charlotte sighed, resisting the urge to follow the gazes of the three silly birds.

Suddenly the crowd shifted as a large group of men made for the terrace, presumably to smoke. She hoped Witherby was among them. She had gotten this far and would hate to bump into the viscount now.

Quickly, she made for an opening.

Without warning, another peacock stepped directly into Charlotte's path. But unlike the other bejeweled bird, this particular one was quite short.

Charlotte's feet skidded to a stop in order to keep from slamming into Miss Lizzie Hawthorne.

"My word! He is a walking dream," Lizzie pronounced, eyes widened for emphasis.

Charlotte lifted her chin. "I'm sure I do not know who you're talking about."

"Oh, don't be such a ninny. You know who I'm talking about."

When Charlotte shrugged innocently, Lizzie nodded toward the earl, the tall blue feathers spiked through her auburn locks giving a twitch. "He is simply divine, do you not agree? Perhaps we should go over there under the pretext of talking to Lord Tristan."

"*That* is a grand idea."

"Oh, but look, Lord Rothbury's already walking away." She gasped loudly, a hand thrown to her throat. "And he's following Lady Gilton! Can you imagine?"

Quite suddenly Charlotte's stomach gave a painful twist. What in the world? She knew what Rothbury was. She knew he was a true rogue. Surely, she was not jealous.

"Oh! I almost forgot to tell you. Kitty said that her mother-in-law told my mother that her footman told the cook that last week Mrs. Breedlove, his last mistress, threatened to throw herself in front of a moving carriage unless Lord Rothbury agreed to renew their arrangement, but apparently he refused despite her claims. Can you imagine?"

It took all Charlotte's strength not to groan aloud. She liked Lizzie. Really she did. They were the same height, of the same age, and suffered the consequence of having mothers who insisted on choosing the most ridiculous costumes for events such as these. But the similarities ended there.

Charlotte was the shy, quiet sort, an observer of people. And Lizzie was loud, spoke at an alarming rate of speed—all gossip and speculation, of course—and possessed the most horrible habit of trying to drag Charlotte into situations that she would much rather avoid.

Lizzie threaded her arm with Charlotte's as they walked past a group of giggling debutantes who were busy making calf-eyes after the earl.

"You cannot deny how handsome! Are you not happy your mother permitted you to come instead of trolling about those ancient pathways and caves looking for spirits?" She wobbled her head in a gesture of disbelief, which looked quite comical considering her costume. "No doubt your mother hadn't counted on the earl to attend. My mother and I can scarcely believe he's here. Perhaps Tristan talked him into it. He and his grandmother are invited every year, but never come. I can't imagine why he would come this year. Can you?"

"Actually, yes," Charlotte muttered, smiling pointedly at Lady Rosalind, who returned the friendly gesture as they walked past. "Everyone knows the reason he is here. And *she's* it."

"Yes, well, that may be true, you know, but insofar that I know . . . and I am in the know as you well know . . . "

"Lizzie, you may very well hold the record for using the word 'know' the greatest number of times in a single sentence."

" . . . she doesn't have any apparent interest in the man."

"She's simply abiding by the duke's wishes," Charlotte offered with a lift of her shoulder.

"Oh, that's right! You're close friends with the duchess. How could I have forgotten? How are the newlyweds?"

"Brilliant," Charlotte answered with a grin. "Though they are hardly newlyweds any longer. They're traveling again. Wales now and then on to . . . Ireland, I think."

"Now that she has married, surely you don't see her as often. You must miss her."

Charlotte smiled wistfully. "Quite. But she's happy and that makes me happy. She has written, but I fear they're never in one place long enough for me to respond in kind. We'll catch up when they return." She wondered what Madelyn would say if she knew of her friendship with Rothbury.

Actually, she did know what her protective friend would say. She'd tell her she was absolutely mad and should stay far, far away from Lord Rothbury. And she would be right, of course.

As they rounded a marble column, the tall, stiff collar of Lizzie's costume accidentally slapped a glass of punch out of someone's hand.

"I say!" the man protested.

Wide-eyed, Charlotte blinked up at her cousin, but Lizzie continued prattling, oblivious to the havoc unfolding behind her.

Charlotte cringed. Thankfully, a footman bearing a towel happened by. Giving the guest an apologetic smile, Charlotte quickened her step to catch up with her cousin.

"Hmm." Lizzie tapped her finger on her chin. "Now there was something else I was going to say, but I've forgotten." She turned her head, nearly toppling the entire contents of a tray of full wineglasses. Only the deft hand of another footman saved the tray teetering in his grasp from dumping on another guest.

"Lizzie, perhaps we should find somewhere to sit," Charlotte suggested. "Your costume . . ."

" . . . is hideous. I know. And these awful feathers make my nose itch."

"Well, at least *your* mother didn't insist you dress as a shepherdess," Charlotte muttered with a rueful smile. "I don't think there's a person in this room that I haven't accidentally whacked on the back of the head with this dashed shepherd's crook." She eyed the thing crossly, then glanced at her cousin and her wide collar. Between the both of them, they could very well obliterate the entire ballroom. The idea had merit.

"Indeed," Lizzie murmured. "But you do look adorable, really."

"'Adorable' isn't the word. In fact, I can think of three more-appropriate words right off the top of my head. 'Absurd.' 'Ridiculous.' And 'mortifying.'"

"You *do* stand out," Lizzie offered weakly, with a hesitant smile.

Well, that much, Charlotte mused, was undoubtedly true.

She stole a glance at the couples swirling about the dance floor. Most of the young ladies wore bejeweled half masks and diaphanous white gowns, which floated teasingly about their ankles, drawing the appreciative glances of many gentlemen.

Charlotte's frock, however, had a stiff petticoat underneath, which made her feel quite like an overstuffed pastry puff. And on Charlotte's small frame, it undeniably gave the appearance that the dress wore her instead of the other way around.

At least she could find comfort in the fact that she had miraculously avoided the dreaded Viscount Witherby this evening.

"Charlotte," Lizzie whispered a clear warning

in her voice. "Don't . . . turn . . . around. In fact, you should just run."

She closed her eyes on a slow blink, then mouthed, "Witherby?"

Lizzie nodded, worry evident in her gaze. "Just go," she said without moving her lips.

Charlotte stepped forward only to have her cousin grab her by the shoulders and thrust her in a different direction. "Go hide in the library. We're redecorating. No one's allowed in there."

Trusting Lizzie blindly, Charlotte charged forward into the dense crowd, dragging the shepherd's crook along with her, of course. For once she was glad to have the dratted thing. Its reputation for bodily harm must precede it, for those who happened to spare it a single glance veritably jumped out of the way, which sped up the normally lengthy process of crossing a crowded ballroom.

In no time at all, she reached the corridor that led to the sanctuary of the deserted library. She hurried onward, paying no heed to the fact the hall grew quiet and substantially darker the further along she went.

Lizzie had said the library was in the process of being redecorated and was off-limits to guests. It made sense that there weren't any people milling about the hall.

A cloud of white seemingly emerged from an intersecting hall right before Charlotte's eyes. There was no time to stop or even slow her momentum. Before she could utter a squeak, she slammed directly into Lady Gilton.

As both women collided, Lady G remained upright, steadying herself with an elegant hand braced on the wall.

Charlotte, however, wasn't so lucky. She tripped over what she would have sworn was m' lady's own dainty foot, and found herself and the stupid shepherd's crook flying to the floor. She landed on her hands and knees with a jolt.

"My word," Lady Gilton said with a soft chuckle. "In a terrible rush, are you?"

Easing back to her haunches, Charlotte breathed deeply while she waited for the throbbing ache in her jarred knees to subside. "Pardon me," she breathed, "I didn't see you."

"Funny, that," Lady Gilton said with a smirk that Charlotte couldn't see as much as she could hear. "Do you not agree? I mean, considering that for once in your life you were actually wearing your spectacles inside a ballroom."

Good Lord, her spectacles! They must have flown off her nose when she fell. Never mind the beautiful woman with the tart tongue who was now slinking back toward the ballroom without so much as a by your leave.

She patted the floor frantically, sighing in relief when she found them. Hurriedly, she put them on, thankful that they hadn't been broken.

Taking care to stand, Charlotte retrieved her crook and continued down the shadowed corridor, albeit slower and with a noticeable limp.

She jiggled the handle of the first door she came to, but it was locked tight. Ignoring the wild beat of her heart, she tried the next door. She gave a sigh of relief as it opened easily on well-oiled hinges, making nary a sound.

Silently, she slipped inside, surprised to find the cluttered room awash in golden candlelight radiating from the elaborate brass sconces set on the far wall.

Softly closing the door behind her back, Charlotte took a brief inspection of the cluttered room. A vast array of stacked chairs, settees, tables, tall armoires, and other unidentifiable articles of furniture sat covered in either dust or swaths of white sheets. Linens were draped along the walls of bookcases, presumably to keep dust or paint from reaching them.

Charlotte's brow furrowed. Why on earth would Lizzie's mother order such a room to be lit? She shrugged, dismissing the thought.

Stepping deeper inside, she nearly tripped over a plump, tasseled pillow leaning against the leg of a chair. Using her shepherd's crook, she poked it out of her way.

And that's when she heard it. A soft swish. Like that of someone adjusting their position.

A shiver spilled down her spine and the air felt heavy. She remained perfectly still. Perhaps it was a cat, she thought. Then she heard it again. And again, the swishing noise becoming more persistent and agitated like someone or something was struggling to free itself.

A grunt, definitely a man's grunt, came from the back of the room.

Her instincts told her to leave, to get the bloody hell out of the room. Now. But something else made her stay. Be it curiosity, or blatant stupidity.

With silent footsteps, she crept around a tall, wide armoire blocking her view from the full length of the room.

And what a view there was to behold. Her

mouth dropped open and she quite forgot to breathe.

There, on a spindle-legged chair positioned against the far wall under the warm glow of the twin sconces, sat Lord Rothbury, blindfolded with his own cravat, his hands tied together, secured behind the back of the chair.

In vain, she tried to swallow, only it felt as if her throat had been doused with sand.

Good Lord! Why on earth was he tied up?

His shirt lay open, displaying the tawny skin of his broad chest, his flat nipples, and the sparse golden hairs that brushed the plane of his muscled stomach. Her greedy eyes remained fastened on that sleek, bare stomach, mesmerized by the rise and fall of each breath he took.

A voice in the back of her mind told her she should look away. After all, he was sin embodied. But what a sight he was for her starved eyes.

His dark blond locks lay in splendid disarray and he gave his head a quick jerk, tossing away the hair that fell across his forehead. He was unsuccessful, the silky strands sliding back into their former position. He blew out his frustration on a low growl.

Just what the earl was doing tied up, in an arousing state of undress no less, in one of their

hostess's spare rooms, Charlotte did not know.
She could only imagine it had something to do
with his amorous pursuits. But he had gone off
with Lady Gilton and Charlotte had just bumped
into the woman. Surely they couldn't have done
whatever it was they intended to do in such a
short time. Could they?

Well, what she did know, however, was that she
was an idiot for befriending a rake and then expecting him to behave properly and make good
on his promises.

She desperately needed to get out of this room.
If anyone should happen upon this room and the
picture it presented, her reputation would be utterly ruined. She turned to leave . . . no matter
how shamefully intriguing his position happened
to be.

"Whatever your little game is, count me out,"
Rothbury's cultured voice cut through the room.
"I've business to attend to. And you have no right
to be angry. Untie me now, Cordelia."

Charlotte gasped, clapping her hand over her
mouth. Why would Lady Gilton leave him here?

Her face and neck ignited with heat. "You *are*
shameless," she whispered heatedly.

Imagine, delving into risky love-play when
scores of people milled about down the hall in

the ballroom. She had never known, only wondered, of the games lovers played behind closed doors. Indeed, the Earl of Rothbury was a wicked, wicked man.

But still, she mused, looking at him with a thoughtful tilt of her head. He did look rather . . . helpless.

Rumpled and vulnerable. Like a beautiful, restrained beast, his bonds gave the illusion he was approachable, harmless, when in fact he was just as dangerous or rather even more so now because of his budding fury.

What if he was a victim of some trick? Who would have ever found him? Perhaps she should untie him.

No. She shook her head. She would not. His deviant, greedy mind got him in his current position and she didn't care what happened to the rogue. Shaking her head, she silently chastened herself for trusting him with her friendship. In fact, maybe he wasn't much of a friend after all.

Her parents were right to forbid her to be anywhere near Rothbury. He was depraved. Immoral. Irredeemable.

And he could bloody well keep the favor he owed her. She didn't want it any longer.

She turned to leave, tiptoeing toward the door.

Skirting around a pedestal table, she looked up at the door across the room and frowned, hesitating.

As soon as she walked out that door, everything would go back to the way it was before. She still would be shy Charlotte, sweet Charlotte, never-even-came-close-to-kissing-a-man-before Charlotte.

Tomorrow would come and she would still be unmarried, with no future prospects other than Witherby. At the end of the year she'd probably find herself unhappily married to him, forever joined. Good Lord, she most definitely would have to kiss him, wouldn't she?

Reaching the door, she placed her hand on the brass knob. She would never in her life forget the arousing sight of Lord Rothbury in such a scandalizing position.

Maybe just one more look. It's not at all like it was back in his bedchamber. He doesn't even know you're here. You can look all you want.

Turning back, she took one silent step toward him.

For quite some time Charlotte had felt like she'd been sitting life out . . . and she was getting dashed tired of it.

"No more," she whispered. Grabbing a nearby chair, she shoved it under the doorknob, effectively barring Lady Gilton, or anyone else for that matter, from entering the room.

Tonight, or at least this moment, she was going to do exactly what she wanted to do. Hang the consequences.

She was about to take matters into her own hands for a change. And right now, she wanted to find out what it was like to kiss a scoundrel.

"Who's there?" Rothbury nearly growled, straining against his binds, the muscles in his gloriously tanned arms bunching and tightening.

She didn't answer him. Instead, she took a deep breath and padded purposefully toward the earl, kicking another slumping tasseled pillow aside and tossing aside her shepherd's crook.

Tied up and blindfolded as he was, she would have her way and be out the door before he could ever guess who she was. Indeed, he might even think she was his curiously absent lover.

And once he'd returned to the ballroom, she would have herself a secret smile. He'd never know, he'd never guess his shy friend would dare to taste forbidden fruit. Besides, what damage could one little kiss do?

Chapter 9

*A Gentleman employs the library for
study purposes only.*

Rothbury inhaled the familiar lemon-tinged air wafting before him. He remained silent, ignoring the zing of awareness thrumming through him, and listened for the sound of foot-falls instead.

Whoever had entered the room, it was definitely a young woman. He'd bet one of his prized Arabians on it, but it wasn't Cordelia. She smelled perpetually of pungent roses, which he had been partial to in the beginning of their short love affair, but which now merely reminded him that the woman connected to it was just as clingy and thorny as the flower itself.

But this scent—he inhaled deeply as it now surrounded him—inspired contentment, which was a miracle in itself, considering all he wanted to do presently was break free, find Lady Gilton, and throttle her elegant neck.

"Who's there?" Rothbury demanded, his tone firm but quiet. He pulled at the twisted silk binds holding his wrists together behind him, noting they were finally starting to tear. "Come now," he said in a tone he used on skittish horses. "Tell me who's there."

Silence, but for the gentle rustle of a skirt. She was coming closer—he could feel it, hear it. The air changed, his senses telling him she now stood before him.

And she was trembling, he could hear it in her breath, almost feel it shuddering against his skin.

Who the bloody hell was in this room and why would they not reveal themselves?

Aggravated and growing impatient, he made a fist, the weakening silk tearing silently. In another minute he would be free.

Heat blossomed in front of him. He had the distinct impression that the woman was hesitating. He worked to remain virtually motionless as he tore more of the silk.

His cheek twitched as a strand of hair tickled his skin.

Her hair. She must be bending over him.

His lips parted, but before he could form a single syllable, tightly pursed lips pressed over his.

Evidently, a puckering statue had kissed him.

Whoever the untutored woman was, she pulled away before his body could decide whether or not he would have liked to deepen the kiss.

Just then, one of his hands finally slipped through the torn binds. She gasped. Quickly, he pulled his other hand free, his first thought to rid himself of the tight blindfold. But he didn't want to take the chance that she'd get away before he could take it off.

So instead he swiped blindly in her direction. He found nothing but air.

She was getting away.

With no time to react, he stood, rolling his stiff shoulders. He lunged toward the sound of her flight . . . and then promptly whacked his knee on the corner of a table. He howled in pain.

The woman in the room, strangely, crooned in sympathy. In fact, it sounded as if she was torn between the decision to continue her mad dash out of the room or run back to assist him.

Unfortunately for her, the sound of her voice told Rothbury exactly where she was in relation to him. He found her, grabbing her around the waist and pulling her back solidly against him.

"Oompf!" Charlotte couldn't believe her luck. Or lack thereof. She screeched, spinning in his hold. Clearly, Lord Rothbury wanted her to be still so he could remove his blindfold and discover just who had the gall to kiss him, but she didn't plan on affording him the opportunity. She twisted fitfully, hoping her jerky movements would require him to use both of his arms to subdue her.

It became apparent, however, as she pushed against the wall of his hard, bare chest, that he was equally determined to have his way and needed only one arm to hold her tightly against him. As she squirmed and pushed at him, he stood perfectly still and solid, his grip on her waist like a velvet manacle.

Still, she managed to jar his elbow just before he could push up the blindfold.

"Damn it, woman. Hold still!"

"Let me go," she ordered between her teeth.

Amidst their scuffling, Charlotte's feet became entangled with part of a sheet that had been draped over the table his lordship had banged his knee on. She toppled backward, the tasseled pillow she had kicked out of the way earlier thankfully making the fall on her rump less jarring.

Rothbury followed her down—not because he lost his footing, Charlotte suspected, but for the simple fact he wasn't about to let her get away.

Tangled up in sheets and pillows, Charlotte scrambled rearward on her back using her elbows and heels. But the earl was too quick—even with the blindfold still in place.

"Oh, no, you don't," he said with dark amusement. He crawled stealthily toward her, like a stalking panther, his tousled dark blond locks completely loose and hanging in his face. "You're not going anywhere until I find out who you are."

The muscles of his chest rippled with his movements. For a second Charlotte felt paralyzed by her fascination. He was mesmerizing. Hesitating, she had to remind herself to keep moving backward, for some wicked part of her wanted to do nothing more than wait for him to catch her.

Unerringly, his large hand clamped down on her ankle to keep her from scooting away while his other hand tried to lift the wound linen from his eyes.

In vain, she attempted to shake her imprisoned ankle free, but Rothbury's gentle hold was unflinching.

What a fool she was to think *he* was helpless! Her instincts spurred her into alternate action. Using the heel of her free foot, she kicked him in the shoulder.

He grunted in pain. "Why you little . . ."

And then in a swift, calculating move, Roth-bury sprang forward, covering her body with his own.

For a second her breath felt trapped in her chest and she was instantly immobile underneath his weight. His warm, hard thigh sat heavy between hers.

Panting from exertion, a shameful lick of heat ignited deep in her belly. Effortlessly, he joined her wrists together, holding them above her head with only one hand while the long, blunt-tipped fingers of the other trailed a silky path down her cheek.

"Who are you?" he whispered.

Her breath hitched at the explosion of feel-ing and thought thrumming through her. He looked so dominant above her, so beautiful, like he was created specifically for seduction. None of her wicked imaginings had prepared her for the plethora of sensations he sparked with only his fingertips upon her face.

Belatedly, she realized her body refused to listen to her mind. She had quit squirming. In fact, she had begun to relish the intoxicating feel of his long, lean-muscled body atop hers. His warm, bare chest pressed onto her bodice, his solid thigh planted firmly against her sex.

Her eyes dipped to his mouth, which was partially open, baring his straight white teeth. All she would have to do was arch her neck and her mouth would fasten to his.

She shivered, surprised and ashamed at the way her body reacted to him. She needed to escape before he discovered her identity.

But her mind warred between what was right and what felt wonderful. In the end, years of dire warnings from her pious father about the sins of the flesh returned at least some of her good sense.

"Get off of me," she demanded, albeit weakly.

"Absolutely not," he growled, his breath feathering hotly against her mouth, her cheek, her neck. "I'll not let you get away now. Not before I find out who you are. Wanted a taste, did you?"

His dark words spurred a thought to flit through her mind. Would he take her? He could if he wanted to, she realized with growing concern. Suddenly she regretted all those gothic novels she had read in the past. Tales of titillating horror, passionate embraces, men on the verge of losing their self-control, some of them succumbing to their base needs.

Part of her thought to tell him it was only she, his friend, but Charlotte was too embarrassed by the stolen kiss to admit her identity. She simply had to get away.

She twisted her wrists. He was so heavy atop her and at least ten times stronger. With only his weight he pinned her beneath him, with only one hand he held her two wrists together. She was utterly helpless.

Thankfully, he had stopped causing shivers to streak down her spine just by the inquisitive brush of his fingertips. Now, he was using those fingers to busily work his cravat from the cover of his eyes.

Just wait, Charlotte's conscience reminded her. *Just wait till he sees who you are.* Could anyone truly perish from mortification alone?

He'll spring off of you as if you were nothing but a bramble bush. And that's what she wanted. Wasn't it? Dear heavens, what was wrong with her? Didn't she *want* to get out from under him? Hadn't she been *trying* to escape from him barely moments ago?

With a grunt, Rothbury shifted his weight. All he wanted to do right now was remove the damn blindfold. One-handed, it was a surprisingly difficult thing to do. Especially if there was a mysterious woman panting beneath him.

No sooner had that thought entered his mind when the woman bucked beneath him, throwing him off balance. The movement allowed her a small space to bring up her knee and catch him in the groin.

He grunted and collapsed off to the side, curling into a ball. "I suppose I deserved that," he squeaked out at an octave higher than his usual.

Sounds of tripping and scuffling ensued. The door was thrown open and then slammed shut behind her. His little kiss stealer was, regrettably, getting away.

Rothbury waited for the radiating throb of pain to dull into an ache. He then wildly tossed off the blindfold with frustrated, impatient hands.

What the devil was that all about?

He stood, hands on hips, catching his breath and staring at the door for several moments. Shaking his head, he decided to dress and see if he could find her, though all he had to go on was a scent and pair of tightly pursed lips.

His face pulled into a scowl as he buttoned his

shirt. What he should do right now is seek out Lady Gilton. But really, why bother? He knew why she tied him up and left him there.

When they had started their little game in the library, he was an active participant, but once the blindfold went on, an image of a Charlotte flitted through his mind. He didn't expect her to be there lurking amid his memories and was certain all thoughts of her would simply vanish when the viscountess placed her greedy hands on him, but they hadn't. The images grew brighter and vibrant.

And suddenly what he was doing with Cordelia, what he was *going* to do with her, wasn't so stimulating any longer. The viscountess had sensed his rather obvious waning interest, had become angry—most likely a little worried she'd lost her touch as well—and left him there to rot.

After creating a loose knot in his cravat, Rothbury crossed the room. Just as he was about to grasp the door handle, the toe of his boot nudged something that clunked. He looked down, astonishment washing over his face.

The light scent of lemons.

As he stood there staring down at the damning shepherd's crook, a myriad of feelings coursed through him. He was bewildered. Shocked. Mystified. In a state of disbelief. And, he might as well admit, incredibly aroused.

His mouth quirked with a lopsided grin as he bent to pluck it from the floor. Sweet Lord, he had found his mystery woman.

Chapter 10

A Gentleman eschews all forms of duplicity.

Breathless from her dash out of the library, Charlotte forced herself to a more sedate pace so as not to draw undue attention.

Besides, it was unlikely Rothbury would come charging out of the library half dressed, bent on chasing down the fool who had thought to steal a kiss. Even someone as wicked as he wouldn't do something so shocking. Or at least she prayed he wouldn't.

Hoping to blend back into the crowd, Charlotte decided to return to her dozing mother.

How foolish she had been, she thought, shaking her head. Clearly she had stepped over an invisible boundary into a world she had no business sticking her nose into. Or her lips for that matter.

And really, she could push aside her compulsion for daydreaming about Rothbury. The mystery was gone. She had kissed him, she thought with a shrug, and there was nothing remarkable about it at all.

The earth didn't shift under her feet, her knees didn't buckle, and she certainly didn't feel like swooning. Surely, she could even discount the pulsing heat she had felt when he threw himself atop her as the effects of being jarred by her fall.

This revelation only further assured her that she was indeed safe from the rogue and his sinful wiles. Just why she had to keep assuring herself of this, she had no idea.

Rounding a grouping of chairs, she decided it would take forever to push her way through the throng of guests, so she decided to turn down a short corridor that would open to the other side of the ballroom. The air was cooler here and the shadowed floor stretched out empty before her, free of people. She breathed a sigh of relief.

Unfortunately for Charlotte, her relief was premature.

She was only about five feet from the opening when she felt cold, thin fingers give the flesh on the back on her arm a revolting squeeze. Revolting, because she knew exactly who stood behind her.

Whirling around, she smothered a groan.

Dressed as a Roman god, Viscount Witherby displayed more pale, tissue-like skin than she'd thought she'd ever care to see in her lifetime. He came up beside her and waggled his white, bushy eyebrows at her in a gesture he no doubt thought was charming and friendly, but in actuality caused Charlotte to shudder in aversion.

"You look so very beautiful, Miss Greene."

"Thank you," she muttered.

His probing gaze swept over the white, frilly layers of her dreadful frock, finally coming to a stop at the crisscross lacing of her bodice. "Are you . . . are you a milkmaid?"

"I'm a shepherdess, my lord." She took a deep breath and remembered she had a weapon. The shepherd's crook. Silently, she vowed to whack his knuckles with it should he raise a finger in her direction . . . Wait. . .

Her heart leaped. She turned her head from side to side, searching. "Oh, no," she groaned. "Wherever did I leave it?"

"Leave what, poppet?" Witherby nearly crooned.

A jolt of panic ran down her spine. She spun in a circle, searching the floor about her in vain.

"What have you lost?"

She swallowed and forced herself to take a calming breath.

Surely, there was no need to worry over the whereabouts of the crook, was there?

"Oh, never mind," she rushed out.

"Are you well?" Witherby asked, cocking his head to the side.

"Yes. Yes, I'm fine." But she was not fine. Her mind raced to remember where she left the dratted thing.

And then it felt as if all the air in her lungs sank to her knees, if such a thing were possible, when realization dawned.

I must have left it in the library.

Would Rothbury find it? She prayed the answer was no. But if he did find it, would he know it belonged to her? There was a chance he wouldn't.

There was also a chance he was still rolling around on the floor from a kick to the groin. She grimaced and hoped he had recovered. It wasn't her intention to hurt him so terribly.

Witherby drew her attention by reaching into his pocket and pulling out his monocle. With the lens crammed in front of it, his eye appeared twice its normal size as he boldly studied her bodice. "Would you do me the honor and dance with me this next set?" he asked her bosom.

"Well . . . I, ah . . . that is to say . . ." Charlotte threw a desperate glance about the room.

"I believe it is a waltz . . . the last of the evening. And there is something of utmost importance I've been waiting to discuss with you."

And then Charlotte knew, just knew, that if she went off with Witherby, he'd make an offer for her hand in marriage.

Good Lord, she did not want to dance with this man. She didn't want to *marry* this man. All she wanted to do was grab her mother and race back into her room to hide from Rothbury. She didn't even care where the devil Lord Tristan had gone. But what excuse could she use that she hadn't already used a hundred times before? She'd already exhausted every excuse imaginable in the past. She needed something fresh. Her mind scrambled for a solid reason.

Perhaps she *should* dance with him, her mind rebelled. Perhaps then, if his lordship should spy her, he might think she had been in the ballroom this entire time.

But then she ran the risk of encouraging the viscount. And that was something she wanted to avoid even more than Rothbury's probing gaze.

"What I mean to say, sir, is that I . . . " A curious heat spread across her back. She ignored it.

"Yes?" Witherby inquired, his eyes flicking above her head for a moment, making her wonder if her bonnet was in a horrid state after the tumble in the library.

Lord, the heat spreading over the span of her back made her feel quite like she stood too close to a coal stove.

"I cannot dance with you because I . . . well . . ." She cleared her throat. " . . . That is to say . . ."

"Miss Greene cannot dance with you," a deep, smooth voice rumbled behind her, "because she has already promised the next to me."

She swallowed a lurch of dread, instantly recognizing to whom the sultry, lazy drawl belonged.

Witherby recoiled at the intrusion. "I say," he replied, looking up at Rothbury with distrust, "no wonder the young lady hesitated over my offer. I know for a fact Miss Greene is not permitted to dance with you."

Rothbury only chortled, low and deep. Charlotte could feel it thrum through her spine and down to the soles of her slippered feet.

Turning, she stole a sidelong glance at him. He stood with his feet braced firmly on the floor, his hands behind his back. His burnished gold hair was swept back into place but for a thick lock that hung low on one side of his forehead.

His hooded eyes stared down Witherby as he gave a lopsided grin that on any other man, she supposed, would appear utterly charming in a boyish sort of way. On Rothbury's handsome face, however, it looked watchful, lethal. Quite like he was silently daring Witherby to touch her just so Rothbury could have the pleasure of breaking his fingers.

And, Charlotte was happy to note, he did not have her shepherd's crook in his possession. This of course meant that he hadn't found it in the library, so he couldn't have any idea she was the one to steal a kiss.

His gaze flicked briefly to her before settling again on the aging viscount. "Why don't we ask *Miss Greene* where her interest resides?"

A shiver brushed over her skin. They both knew that in public he couldn't address her informally, should someone overhear. However, no matter how formal "Miss Greene" might be, when it rolled off Rothbury's tongue it always managed to sound decidedly improper. Like he knew a wicked secret and wanted to share. However, she feared that this time it wasn't an act. He had a secret—her secret. And he meant to expose her.

The viscount puffed out his chest, evidently thinking she would make the correct decision. The easy decision. The safe decision.

Across the room, the sweeping chords of the violins signaled the waltz.

At Charlotte's hesitation, Witherby frowned with disapproval, dragging the wrinkles framing his thin lips downward. "Might I remind you, my dear Miss Greene, that your mother sits just a few feet away? She is *watching* this entire exchange."

So her mother had awakened already. In that case, she must keep her back to Rothbury and not acknowledge his presence. Should her mother realize Rothbury was attempting to keep her from having to dance with Witherby, there was no doubt Charlotte would find herself torn away from Rothbury's side once again.

But what was she to do? As distasteful as it would be, dancing with Witherby would save her the embarrassment of having to talk to Rothbury after what she had done, what she had seen. Although he couldn't possibly know she had witnessed his *dishabille*, nor that she had kissed him.

And waltzing with Rothbury *would* save her from Witherby.

She hesitated. True, he would be saving her, but really, it felt more like escaping the jaws of a graying wolf only to step into the lair of a sleek, wily fox.

However, surely the fox would have eaten her already given that he had ample opportunity. She took a deep, fortifying breath, her mind made up.

"Indeed, sir. I have promised this dance to Lord Rothbury," she said, her tone firm.

"Very well, then." Witherby bent his head close, his lips hovering over her ear. "If I didn't know better, young miss, I'd think you were avoiding me. It's no matter. Good sense will prevail. And when it does, I'll be waiting. Good evening." Dropping his monocle back inside his pocket, he bowed deeply and turned to stride away.

She watched his retreat in silence, strangely grateful that Rothbury had come when he had. Though her shame over her uncharacteristic behavior in the library superseded that admission.

And there was something else nagging at her mind now that she had time to think on it. What sight would she have beheld if she had come upon Lady Gilton and Rothbury five minutes sooner?

Her stomach roiled, suddenly queasy. She swallowed, trying her best to suppress the feeling and whatever nameless emotion that caused it.

"Thank you," she whispered, turning her chin barely an inch so that she could discern in her peripheral vision that he yet stood behind her. Although really, the heat emanating from his body onto hers was proof enough.

Though she liked to dance with Rothbury, his offer was meant only as a way to save her from Witherby. They both knew they couldn't dance now. Not here. Not now that her mother took it upon herself to guard Charlotte's heart with the ferociousness of an alley cat. For once she was glad for it. She suddenly didn't want to be in his arms; her reaction to his body in the library frightened her.

She cleared her throat. "Is that the second, third, or fourth time you've come to my rescue? If you don't watch yourself, you'll be bound to turn yourself into a gentleman. With or without my help."

Closing his eyes for a moment, Rothbury inhaled her light lemony scent. At this moment there was nothing in the world he wanted more than for every single guest in this ballroom to disappear so that he could pull Charlotte against him, rip off that silly bonnet, and sink his hands into her hair while sinking his mouth onto her throat. Christ, why did she have to smell so damn good?

Silently, he cursed himself for not realizing just who exactly it was that he had caught in the library when he had her squirming beneath him. Damn, he would have relished the moment, however brief it would have been, had he known it was Charlotte.

He did concede however, that it was a good thing for her that he *hadn't* known it was Charlotte writhing beneath him at the time. He would have been decidedly, and happily, obliged to expound, in lavish detail, upon the intricacies of an authentic kiss.

"Oh, I doubt I'll turn into a gentleman anytime soon," he drawled from behind her, "if at all."

All around them, guests started to traverse the corridor, some on their way to join the dance, some leaving the ballroom to wander elsewhere. The milling crowd afforded a bit of privacy as her mother's view was now, undoubtedly, blocked as people passed them by. And even if her mother sprang out of her seat to put an immediate stop to their conversation, it would take her at least ten minutes to cross the room. They could talk for now. Even if for a moment.

"Are you enjoying yourself this evening, Miss Greene?"

She nodded, thinking it safe now to face him.

"Good," he said, offering her a wicked grin when her eyes lifted to his. "I believe all young women, especially those timid and retiring ones like yourself, should embark on new horizons . . . try new things, if you will. I undoubtedly approve and, in fact, encourage, you to indulge your most wicked fantasies. Speaking of which, did you happen to lose something?"

Familiar pricks of embarrassment, not to mention dread, scattered over her senses. "Ah. N-no, no I haven't."

"Are you certain?"

"Absolutely."

Suddenly, he brought forth her shepherd's crook from behind his back.

Her heartbeat felt as if it tripped over itself. She swallowed, determined to admit nothing and think clearly. There was a chance she could convince him of some other story.

She forced a look of surprise. "Oh, look at that! I put that cumbersome thing down, oh . . . must have been an age ago. Forgot all about it, I did. Thank you, my lord. How silly of me to misplace it."

His laughing eyes sparkled with mischief. "Misplaced it, eh?"

"Mmm-hmm." She nodded, pressing her lips together. That, at least, was the truth.

"Tell me, I cannot help but wonder . . . where do think you happened to leave it behind?"

She lifted her shoulders.

One side of his mouth curved upward. "What's the matter? Have you suddenly become tongue-tied? I find that hard to believe, given that the few times we have been in each other's company you have never failed to find words."

A telltale hot blush began to creep its way up her neck. "I-I suddenly find I no longer wish to talk, or dance for that matter. If you'll excuse me, my lord." She made a grab for the crook.

Smoothly, he leaned it away from her reach, which caused Charlotte to stumble forward. Her chest pressed into the solid wall of his chest. He didn't move an inch to help her set herself back from him. He only stared down at her with that half-amused, half-seductive grin of his.

"Well," he said darkly, his rich, deep voice intoxicating her as it lured her in. "Would you like to explain why you kissed me, Charlotte? Couldn't control yourself, I imagine?"

Gaining her balance, she shoved herself away

from him and took a deep calming breath, before glaring at the crook still in his grasp. Secretly, she wished she could trip him with it.

"Hardly," she said with a sniff. She refused to be one of those females who contributed daily to the size of his ego. "It was a simple case of curiosity, 'tis all."

"And has your curiosity been appeased?"

"Quite. I no longer wonder what kissing is like," she added, batting at a drooping loop of ribbon that hung close to her eyes. "Truly, I found it rather . . . mundane."

His expression turned contemplative. "How interesting."

"Why is that interesting to you?"

"You see," he said, dragging a hand over his jaw. "I find that my curiosity has increased tenfold by your actions."

"Really?" she asked, realizing with a start that she sounded incredibly engrossed in his confession. She cleared her throat. "Really?" she repeated again, this time injecting a cool indifference.

Nodding slowly, he shifted his weight, moving closer to her by only an inch, but his body heat seemed to engulf her. Whiskey-colored eyes seemed to devour her, making her feel like she was being drawn toward him though her feet remained unmoved. "Evidently, I have greatly underestimated you."

She swallowed hard. "If you keep looking at me like that, we're sure to draw attention. Can we just forget about the entire affair and move on to a different subject?"

"And which subject would that be? Lord Tristan or Witherbottom?"

"Witherby," she stressed.

"Whomever."

"And no, I definitely do not want to talk about *him*."

"Am I to understand that old frump intends to marry you someday?"

She said nothing, only sighed. It was all very obvious.

"And your mother and father, no doubt, encourage his intentions?" he asked, his tone incredulous.

"Perhaps," she said with a shrug. "He has been a friend to my parents since I was a child. It's really none of your concern."

"Well, it damn well should be someone's concern."

Viscount Witherby, renowned in the underworld of society for having a secret fascination with very young girls, had undoubtedly set his sickening sights on his Charlotte long ago. Though much older than Witherby's usual fare, Charlotte on occasion looked a lot younger than she really was. Perhaps that was what drew the viscount's twisted attention.

But Rothbury couldn't very well march into the Greenes' town house in London and point a finger at their longtime acquaintance. Who would believe him? He imagined it would be quite like hiring a man-eating lion to protect her from a hungry bear. He might kill the bear, but what would stop him from gobbling her up for himself afterward?

"Come now," he said softly, redirecting his thoughts. "You can tell me. I'll listen. I could even make certain Witherby never bothers you again if you should wish."

"And why would you go to the trouble?"

"We are friends."

She lifted her chin. "No. I've decided to renege my offer."

"That's not very sporting of you."

"I find I don't care," she answered, coolly.

"I do."

"Perhaps you should go find Lady Gilton, then," she blurted, now finding interest in the lace of her glove. "She seemed to be up for sport of some sort."

He stilled. Was she jealous? He wondered if she would believe him if he told her that even though his intentions were quite wicked, he had quickly lost interest in what Cordelia was offering him. That he thought of her, Charlotte, so much that he simply couldn't continue.

No, she wouldn't believe him and he couldn't blame her. He still wasn't sure he believed it himself.

The idea that she was jealous was ludicrous. Besides, she had been studiously trying to help him find a suitable bride for the past six months.

No. She wasn't jealous. Charlotte had no interest in him other than friendship. Although, he mused, she really needed to cease sending him contrary signs. Just why had she kissed him anyway? Was it a dare? A joke? She kept insisting she felt that she was safe from him, but did she honestly believe that? Perhaps she was testing him.

"Tell me, you've decided to take back your offer of friendship based on what grounds?'

"On the grounds that you are a despicable rogue, sir."

"Despicable? Haven't I just saved you from the hands of that disgusting lovesick goat?"

"Where is Lord Tristan?" she asked, purposely ignoring him. "He was to come." Charlotte watched him for several moments, the heat in his gaze slowly evaporating at her mention of his friend's name.

A footman passed with a tray laden with goblets of claret. Swiftly, Rothbury plucked two glasses, offered her one, and at her decline, tossed them cleanly down his throat one after the other. "Delayed in the card room once again, I imagine," he said through a grimace, setting them down on a side table.

"What are we going to do?" she asked.

"Do you speak French?"

What? His question bewildered her for half of a second. Focusing again, she opened her mouth, thinking to explain that while she understood most French with the exception of some country dialects, her pronunciation was below average and she always had trouble conjugating her verbs.

But upon further contemplation she hesitated. It was quite an odd question for him to ask her at such a time. Just what was he about?

"Well?" he prodded softly.

She gave her head a tiny shake. "No, I do not speak French." It wasn't a lie. He asked if she could *speak* French, not understand it.

"Very well," he said, the corners of his lips turning downwards in contemplation. "Does your mother speak French by any chance?"

The more questions he asked, the more she was certain that it was a good idea for her to keep her little secret. Just why did he need her assurance that neither she nor her mother spoke French?

"Ah, no. She doesn't speak any French at all." That, at least, was the perfect truth. Hyacinth Greene didn't understand it, speak it, or even bother to partake of the drawing room French that was so popular among the *ton*.

"Perfect," he drawled.

"I wonder . . ." her eyes narrowed with suspicion.

"Seeing as your mother is determined to waste you on that disgusting pig of a man, I have decided to offer you a solution to your quandary. Provided you help me with something as well."

"What do you mean?"

"Simply this. My grandmother was invited to attend this ball this evening, but her health prohibits her from enjoying such events that once gave her much pleasure. It pains me to say that it causes her some distress."

"Understandably," Charlotte replied. Having older parents with a plethora of older friends, issues of health were often a topic of conversation, warranting her sympathy.

"She hasn't many visitors," he said, staring intently into her eyes, "and has become lonely. Come to Aubry Park tomorrow for tea and a late luncheon. Visit with her and in return I shall help you finally free yourself from Witherby."

She pressed her lips together, eyeing him dubiously. "And how to you propose to do this?"

"Compile a list of available men that you would rather marry, bring it to me at Aubry Park tomorrow afternoon, and I shall help you win a man on your list before the Season is out."

"That doesn't seem like a fair trade, my lord. Meeting with your grandmother is quite simple, the task that you've assigned yourself could very well be impossible."

"I don't believe so."

Her lips parted, but she hesitated to speak. His eyes had taken on an inner light, effectively causing heat to pool low in her belly.

He tossed a lock of hair from his eyes with a quick turn of his head. "And of course, there is always the possibility that Tristan will visit. He's got an eye on one of my fillies. Wouldn't he be surprised to see you at Aubry Park, with me? Might make him regret his choice for a bride.

And didn't you want to make him jealous?" he whispered the question. "He deserves a little distress for causing you such heartache, for misleading you. What say you, Miss Greene? I could issue an invitation to you and your mother, from my grandmother . . ."

Charlotte couldn't help but give a little huff of disbelieving laughter at that. The idea had merit but realistically, it would be impossible. Her mother would eat her hat, possibly Charlotte's as well, before pointing one foot even in the general direction of Rothburys' home.

"Thank you, but it wouldn't work, I'm afraid. You must remember, my mother has forbade me to be anywhere near you . . . indefinitely."

"But if we could think of a different way . . . "

She shook her head sadly. "Your offer is tempting, but I fear there isn't a single thing that could entice her to agree."

"There is a bit of supposedly haunted forest in my garden . . ."

She tried to conceal the astonishment from her features. "I can scarcely believe you remember me telling you about her obsession with the metaphysical."

One broad shoulder lifted in a shrug. "I pay attention, Miss Greene, to every single syllable that passes over your lips. Perhaps you should add that to your list of required attributes in potential husbands."

One hand on her hip, she tapped her foot, thinking. Could her mother be tempted by his suggestion that the forest on his estate was infested with spirits? Possibly . . . Her lips parted as another idea suddenly popped into her mind. A better solution. A strategy that could not fail.

Her gaze swept the length of him before returning to his face. He didn't look the part, but certainly she could sway her mother into believing . . .

"Very well," Charlotte murmured. "I will take you up on your offer to visit Aubry Park . . . and delve into this plan of yours."

His brow quirked. "Shall I issue the invitation in person?"

Charlotte laughed. "Oh, no. Don't bother, my lord. You had better leave the convincing to me."

Chapter 11

*A Gentleman leaves vigorous work to
the laboring classes.*

There was something to be said about the allure of a man's backside, Charlotte mused, as she watched Rothbury ram a muscled shoulder into the back of the Greenes' carriage with manly vigor.

Though there were many discerning females who remarked upon the importance of the symmetry of facial features, a pair of fine eyes, a strong jaw, and broad shoulders, Charlotte believed that a nice, tight, athletically toned backside was equally as significant an attribute.

"Can you believe all this mud? Indeed, we don't have nearly as much mud in Coventry." Hyacinth sniffed from her perch atop her portmanteau, her umbrella shielding her from the misty rain. " 'Tis a good thing Lord Rothbury insisted he escort us to Aubry Park *and* bring three outriders or else it might have been you and I, my dear, pushing the carriage out of the mud."

Standing under her own umbrella off to the side of the heavily rutted road next to her seated mother, Charlotte tilted her head as she continued to watch Rothbury push roughly at their carriage, his booted feet sliding as he tried, along with two other men, to release the back wheels imprisoned in the thick, sucking mud.

Their driver shouted encouraging orders to the horses while the men worked hard. Another man had been ordered to ride ahead to Aubry Park, to have a fresh conveyance sent in the chance that the Greene's carriage should need repair, or their horses a rest.

"Oh, I doubt that would be true," Charlotte muttered distractedly. "We would have simply sent our man along to fetch help."

Hyacinth snorted. "And wait helplessly until some Knight of the Road came along and accosted us? I think not."

Her mother's words barely penetrated through Charlotte's imaginings.

Unlike the other men, who wore their long

coats, Rothbury had recently shrugged off his carrick coat and had handed it to Charlotte to hold. She clutched it now to her bosom, enjoying the delicious warmth left in the fabric from his body. The cool mid-morning air smelled damp and fresh and—she discreetly dipped her face into the collar of Rothbury's coat—like a clean, warm man. Closing her eyes, a foreign but rather pleasant feeling vibrated through her. She caught a sigh before it escaped and changed it into a cough to disguise it.

Hyacinth clucked her tongue. "I do hope you're not catching an ague. We are only to stay one evening. This was supposed to be a quick trip, Charlotte. "

"And indeed it will be."

"I had no idea the roads would be so impassable with such little rain. We've been waiting here for at least a quarter of an hour. All this pushing, pushing, pushing, and still nothing will budge."

"R—Lord Rothbury has assured us that another carriage is on the way."

"Oh, I do hope he is right." She shook her head slowly. "His fine clothes are surely ruined."

"Indeed."

At that moment, all action ceased as the exhausted men stepped back to take a much needed break. Taking a step farther back from the carriage than the other men, Rothbury bent down, resting his hands on his knees, in order to catch his breath.

Charlotte slid a glance down to her mother, who, she was happy to note, sat staring down the lane looking for the carriage from Aubry. Now with Hyacinth safely preoccupied, Charlotte decided to indulge her curiosity, allowing her gaze to roam freely over Rothbury. After all, his back was to them; he'd never know.

Splatters of mud stained Rothbury's fine lawn shirt, which clung slickly to the broad expanse of his back like a second skin. Having rolled up his sleeves at the onset of his task, his muscled arms were now streaked with mud and rain as were the tall boots and tight black breeches that hugged the sinewy muscles of his long, undoubtedly strong legs.

Her admiring gaze alighted upon his golden-brown hair, which now looked more brown than golden as it was wet with perspiration and mist. A few locks lay plastered to his neck in wispy whorls.

Charlotte suddenly felt overly warm. Seeing him . . . wet . . . somehow embarrassed her. It felt dark, intimate. Truly, if it weren't for the mud—

and clothes—she rather thought this would be what he looked like after a bath.

A shiver ran down her arms as her eyes drifted to the dewy trails of rain droplets that ran over his slightly bristled jaw and neck, disappearing in the nest of his loosely tied cravat.

And then her hungry gaze raised . . . and connected with Rothbury's. All thoughts flew straight out of her head.

Looking at her from over his shoulder, he straightened, his smile twisting with arrogance.

Despite the chill in the air, her cheeks felt as if they were on fire. How long had he been watching her in-depth perusal? Long enough, she supposed, if the heated gleam in his eyes was any indication at all.

She blinked, shaking her head hurriedly, hoping by that action she was silently telling him, "No, I definitely was *not* looking at you."

He answered her gesture by nodding slowly, telling her that he knew *exactly* what she had been doing and that he had caught her in the act.

She gave her head another insistent shake.

Still looking at her from over his shoulder, he sauntered back to the carriage, his smile broadening. He lifted his shoulder as if to say, "I don't care. Look all you want."

She shook her head again, tightly.

He winked.

She gulped.

And then he set back to work with the other men to free the carriage.

Charlotte turned away, almost jumping with a start when she found her mother staring strangely up at her. "What in the world is wrong with you?"

"What?" Charlotte asked.

"What's with all the angry head shaking?"

"Oh, that?" She shrugged. "A raindrop in my ear."

Rothbury's laugh sounded from the back of the carriage where he worked with the other men. If her mother heard him, she made no mention of it.

The distant sound of a carriage rumbled down the road. Hyacinth jumped to her feet. "Oh, splendid. Splendid! Your lordship, it's come."

A gleaming black coach equipped with four matching grays rounded the bend in the road ahead of them. The Rothbury heraldic arms, a lion and a sword entwined with a thorny rose vine, proudly proclaimed the owners' aristocratic lineage on the doors.

"What an elegant set, my lord," Hyacinth remarked, standing.

Charlotte put out an arm so her mother could

grab it. Chilly wet weather made her mother's bones ache fiercely, and she knew that sitting in the same position for long periods of time made her joints feel so stiff it was if they had frozen.

"Allow me," came Rothbury's deep voice, coming up from behind them.

Charlotte had no idea where it came from, but the earl suddenly had a stark, white handkerchief draped over his arm, protecting her mother's white gloves from his soiled shirt as she grabbed his arm.

Slow and steady, Rothbury crossed the bit of lawn to the road with her mother by his side. Charlotte trailed behind, holding her mother's umbrella above them while still holding her own.

The coach had circled around and come to a stop on a stretch of road that had more rocks and spiny gorse than mud. Steps were brought down and Rothbury assisted Hyacinth inside.

"I shall see you both at the manor house," he said to her mother. "Forgive me for the delay of your carriage, madam. Once it is free, I'll have someone inspect it for damage."

Hyacinth nodded, settling her small frame into the cushy squabs. "I feel so terrible over the state of your fine clothes." She yawned. "I know how your sort can be about the state of your clothes."

When she started to rummage around in her reticule for something, he turned to Charlotte.

"My sort?" he asked, bending low so Hyacinth couldn't overhear. "Charlotte, you must tell me what she means. The woman would clobber me if I should do so much as stand next to you and now she tells me I have a fine coach and frets over the state of my clothes? What in the hell did you tell her to gain my acceptance?"

With as innocent a look she could muster, Charlotte met his gaze. "Don't you worry. It's working, so what does it matter to you?"

He gave her a skeptical look, then helped her into the carriage after assisting her with the closing of their umbrellas.

Once ensconced inside, Charlotte noted her mother was already snoring softly. A brow raised, Rothbury poked his head inside. "Does she always fall asleep so quickly?"

"All the time."

His golden eyes held a smidgen of suspicion for a moment.

"It's the laudanum she takes for her achy joints," she whispered.

He nodded, hoping her mother wasn't nurturing a budding addiction.

Though there were many who used the opium-based liquid for alleviation of pain or inducement of sleep, there were many who overused it, spurring wild hallucinations. Some misused it to the point of certain death.

Although, Charlotte's mother didn't seem to be traveling on the path of destruction, he still felt the need to inform her. Who knows, perhaps he could find an alternative medicine in one of his books in the library at Aubry Hall.

"See you in a bit, then?" His tone was casual, but his eyes fairly smoldered with warmth.

It was probably just suppressed mocking laughter, Charlotte told herself. In the last two days she had stolen a kiss from him and now he had caught her looking him over. Goodness, did he think she was a wanton woman? She shook the thoughts right out of her head. If she dwelled on any of them for too long, she'd probably jump out of his carriage and walk all the way home.

What could he be thinking? She was attracted to him, of that there was no doubt. However, to let him know about it would be futile indeed. Firstly, he had no interest in her and even if by some strange shift in the heavens he did hold a genuine attraction to her, it would be for lust and lust alone. He was completely unmarriageable, a terrible rake, incapable of knowing anything other than physical love—the details of which she knew little about.

Her parents' marriage was a love match and had been a perfect example of how a good marriage could work. With affection, mutual respect, and admiration. And devotion. She wanted that for her own and thought she could have had that with Lord Tristan.

Passion was a sin. Or so she had been told again and again. Giving in to it was like eating a forbidden sweet, her father had warned her. After it was all over, one would be filled with nothing but misery and shame for their lack of self-control. But for all Mr. Greene's dire warnings, Charlotte couldn't seem to stop Rothbury from sliding into her imagination.

Her attraction to him was getting to be a difficult thing to hide and she feared Rothbury had an inkling as well. But what would he do with that knowledge? Mock her? Laugh at her?

Seduce her?

She sighed, settling back inside his elegant coach, her gloved hands sliding over the bloodred padding. Expecting Rothbury to simply step back and close the carriage door, she nearly jumped when he poked his dripping head back inside.

"I had meant to tell you . . ."

"What?"

"You've got something on your nose."

"I do?"

Reaching out, he gently brushed the tip of her nose with his finger, leaving a smudge of mud.

"My lord!"

"Shhh. You'll wake your mother. And besides, mud never looked so good."

And with that, he closed the door, his muffled shout ordering the driver to move along.

"Shameless flirt," she muttered, refusing to give in to the smile that wavered upon her lips.

With a lurch, the well-sprung carriage rumbled away.

She was starting to warm to him. True, she considered him her friend. He had danced with her when no one else would, talked to her the year of her debut when she could not (because of an awful, albeit temporary, stammer). He had never tried to seriously take advantage of her, even though he'd had more than one opportunity; he had saved her from Witherby, offered to help her find a new suitor, and agreed to help her exact revenge on his best friend, of all people. He had been nothing but kind to her. Sometimes going out of his way to be kind to her. Perhaps there was more to him than she thought.

If she wasn't careful, her mother would be right. Her heart would be in danger once again.

Yes, it was safer to think of him as a friend. A general acquaintance. Her project. She could easily keep him at arm's length this way. Flirting was his nature, she reminded herself. It was part of his character. She'd be a fool to start believing something was growing between them. But . . . could love grow from passion, she wondered? Or would it be doomed to end in nothing but misery and shame like her father had always told her? She had no idea and her head was beginning to ache, so she decided to shake the perplexing notion away.

And besides, she would see Lord Tristan today. Hyacinth had relented, agreeing to meet the dowager and stay for a short jaunt into their famed gardens. Surely, that was enough time to implement her plan.

A giddy excitement bubbled inside her. Rothbury had promised to flirt with her like mad, and by the looks of things, he was already getting into the spirit.

Aubry Park was a glorious Elizabethan manor, lovingly restored in the last century and equipped with numerous gothic undertones—enough to send Charlotte's mother into a ghost-seeking frenzy.

The massive, cream-colored stone house sat hidden in a forest like some romantic woodland folly. Upon first approach, it seemed rather modest, enclosed in a small courtyard, the upper floors timbered and gabled, but after one ventured a look past the facade, the manor sprawled onward, connecting to a myriad of wings, towers hidden by tall trees and climbing vines and private walled gardens.

"Enchanting," Charlotte murmured, running her fingertips along the soft bristles of an ivory-handled brush.

She sat at a dressing table in a beautiful room she was to call her own during their short stay. Cozy, but by no means small, her appointed rooms had an air of welcoming and warmth.

The walls were covered in *toile de Jouy*, a blue-and-white print depicting a charming rural scene, which complemented the deep mahogany furniture. The coverlet on the daybed was soft blue and white with a matching canopy overhead. A tri-sectioned mirror hung above the alabaster fireplace and there were three very comfy looking chairs grouped together near a door that connected this room to her mother's.

A long case clock ticked in the hall, a bird twittered prettily outside, and if Charlotte strained, she could just barely hear the soft drone of her mother's snore. But for all the inducement to rest as well, Charlotte could barely sit still. In an hour they were to meet Rothbury's grandmother, the dowager countess.

When they had arrived, standing in the expansive front hall, Charlotte's head thrown back as she stared at the elaborate, gilded oval ceiling, a curious warmth spread through her.

Her chin dropped down and she found Lord Rothbury staring at her with an unguarded expression. He looked . . . almost regretful.

"What is it?" she had asked softly, suddenly feeling like she had made some grave error in judgment by coming here.

He blinked, giving his head a slight shake. "Nothing. I hope your short stay at Aubry Park is enjoyable."

"I cannot see why that shouldn't be so."

A butler appeared, taking their cloaks.

"I daresay, my lord," Hyacinth remarked while peeking into a shadowed room, "your sense of decoration is remarkable. Cozy and country without losing a noble air. I'm duly impressed."

He turned to Charlotte, a brow raised.

She shrugged. Looking down, she turned her attention to a porcelain vase painted with a chain of daisies around the rim.

He cleared his throat, his deep voice vibrating in the small but elegant foyer. "I cannot take the credit, madam. My gr—"

Charlotte shook her head hurriedly, hoping he'd get the signal to quit while he was ahead.

"Why?" he mouthed.

She widened her eyes.

His golden gaze narrowed for a moment, then relaxed. Thankfully, he didn't press Charlotte for an explanation.

After that, he quickly explained to them that they should expect odd happenings, as the dowager was getting older—affectionately joking that she was a hundred if she was a day—and senility was fighting for possession of her mind.

He then said that he would catch up with them later, as he was off to visit a tenant who was having ongoing problems with some marauders stealing his prize sheep.

But before he left, he winked at Charlotte . . . again. She'd give her left boot to know what he meant by the gesture. But then she reminded herself not to get too excited about winks. He was simply flirting. Just teasing. They were friends. They were going to help each other.

Bright sunlight beckoned her to the window. Putting the brush down, Charlotte crossed the room, her feet swishing across the plush of the rug.

A light yellow chaise lounge crouched under the window and she trailed a fingertip along the arm before sinking her knees into it in order to peek outside. Leaning toward the glass, she rested her arms on the sill.

Directly below her window, the dark waters of a pond reflected the bruised clouds scuttling across the clearing sky. Next to it crouched a pair of willow trees, their melancholy branches hanging low as if daring to disturb its placid, glass-like beauty.

Beyond the pond sprawled an expansive garden maze with walls of towering yew bushes, expertly clipped. From her vantage point, the maze appeared quite simple to solve, though she suspected that once one was surrounded by the labyrinth of hedges, all sense of direction would contort.

Suddenly, thoughts of Rothbury flitted through her mind and she wondered if he ran inside that maze as a child. He probably knew every nook, every turn. She wondered if he'd thrown rocks in the pond or perhaps sailed a toy boat or two.

Aubry Park seemed a magical, secret place. A lovely place. A place its mistress's beauty would complement in gentle accord. A mistress like Lady Rosalind, she thought gravely.

She shook her head and told herself to perk up.

After all, Witherby was nowhere to be found—unless he was hiding in the woods. And most especially, Rothbury was going to help her. And she was going to spend a whole marvelous day in his splendid manor. In fact, while her mother slept and Rothbury was away, she saw no reason why she couldn't dash outside and slip inside that hedge maze. It looked like cracking fun!

It was pure hell.

For what had to be at least an hour now, Charlotte had traipsed amid the towering, intersecting hedge-lined paths of the maze. Every path, every corner, every blade of grass looked exactly the same as the ones before it, or after it, or next to it. She wouldn't know. At this point she was so utterly, miserably turned about, the only direction she was sure of was up and down.

Bees darted at her (she suspected they had

made nests in the bushes), a bird dove close to her head (she suspected it had a nest somewhere around here as well), and an angry squirrel had bounded toward her with no apparent provocation on her part whatsoever, causing her to tear the lace hem of her favorite walking dress as she sped away from it.

Her enthusiasm spent, her limbs tired and aching, her only hope was that the gardener might find her whenever it was he next trimmed the walls of the maze. A day, a week, a month?

She paused, willing her nerves to calm. She would not panic. There had to be a way out of this godforsaken place and she was determined to find it.

Suddenly thinking of a plan, she pressed the heel of her palm to her forehead, silently admonishing herself for not thinking of it sooner.

Reaching out, she twisted a bit of greenery off the closest hedge and dropped it on the grass behind her. She did this, one after another, turn after turn, until there was no possible way she would accidentally retrace her steps—as soon as she saw the clumps of greenery, she would know that she had been that way before.

After several minutes, her confidence grew and she was soon clipping along. Shortly, she passed

what she assumed was the center: a wide expanse
of lawn, a white garden bench at each end, and
a circular pond enlivened with water lilies and
irises. Just like the rest of Aubry Park, at least what
she had seen of it, the center of the labyrinth was a
charming surprise. A place where she might be inclined to sit and read under other circumstances.

Quite pleased that there was only one other
exit, diagonally across from where she stood,
Charlotte trudged onward, dismally aware that
she was most assuredly late in her meeting with
Rothbury's grandmother and would have no time
to change her dress.

Skirting around what she hoped was the last
corner, Charlotte nearly shouted with absurd glee
upon seeing that she was indeed free.

A bit breathless, she stepped out of the maze,
her gaze instantly focusing on the elaborate ironwork of the arbor commanding notice from across
the lawn.

Rothbury was right. It did look like a giant
domed wrought-iron birdcage. Commissioned
from a local blacksmith, the garden sculpture was
exquisitely detailed. They all were to meet there
for tea, and by the looks of things, some individuals had already started to assemble.

Charlotte looked down, examining the state of

her pale pink frock. A good six inches of a grass-stained lace hem dragged behind her, perspiration dampened her bodice and sleeves, and her loosely pinned coiffure had undoubtedly come undone. She could feel the looping curls bouncing against the back of her neck and sliding upon the tops of her bare shoulders as she walked.

She cringed. How embarrassing. With no time to spare, she had to resolve herself to the fact that she was to meet his grandmother looking like an escapee from Bedlam.

Coming up behind her from returning from the stables, Rothbury's gaze raked Charlotte's state of dishevelment: hair mussed, tumbling down the back of her head in a cascade of curls, her dress a touch rumpled, a ripped hem.

"I must say, you look as if you've just come from a tryst in the garden. Have you?"

At the sound of his voice she spun around, her shoulders visibly relaxing once her eyes settled on him.

"Oh, it's just you," she said.

"Disappointed? Relieved?" He looked at her through hooded eyes. "*Delighted?*"

"Thankful."

"Thankful?" He raised a brow.

"Yes, *thankful*," she stressed. "Thankful that I've found another living soul. I've been lost in your hedge maze for the better part of an hour. I had started to believe I might not ever escape."

He tried to bite back a smile, gave up, and grinned fully. "Charlotte, what possessed you to try traversing that monstrous thing alone?"

"I spied it from my window and thought I'd give it a go. It looked easy enough from up there."

He smiled. "It does look rather simple from a higher vantage point."

He offered his arm and she took it without hesitation. That action alone managed to warm his heart. She was the only woman of his acquaintance who didn't stare down at his offered arm as if making some potentially life-altering decision.

She settled her hand upon his forearm and they strolled toward the birdcage arbor. "I reckon it's too late to tell you of a little trick that might have aided you had you known."

Suddenly, he felt nearly overcome with wanting to show her all his childhood haunts. The tree house his grandmother had ordered built to look like a scaled-down version of Aubry Park manor, his favorite fishing spot, the oak tree he had fallen out of not once but twice—and had not a broken bone to show for it—a tiny cave hidden in the dense woods that had a shallow creek running through it, the secret place where he had hidden from his father and uncles.

He wanted to tell her things about himself he'd never told anyone else.

"I reckon you're right," she said, giving a little laugh. "But tell me just the same. I'd like to know."

"All you have to do is keep turning right. Or, just put your right hand on the hedge wall, never stop touching it. You'll walk through every corner of the maze," he added, "but you'll escape eventually."

"I shall remember that."

"For the next time?" Why did he just say that? There will never be a next time.

She shook her head slowly back and forth. "Never. I'm not ever going anywhere near that place again, thank you very much. Unless of course, you are with me."

He swallowed, surprised to find that it was suddenly hard to do. Closing his eyes on a slow blink, something that others might call a conscience reared its foreign head and called him a soulless cad for bringing her here, for misleading her.

Taking a deep breath, he pushed the thought back to the dark, empty pit whence it came.

Chapter 12

A Gentleman admits defeat with dignity
and grace.

"*Sa poitrine est plate comme un flet.*"
By some miracle, Charlotte's polite
smile never wavered. It was a proud moment for
her. After all, it wasn't every day that a little old
lady told you right to your face that your bosom
was as flat as a flounder.

Bringing her teacup to her lips for a small sip,
she swiped at a pretend wrinkle on her gown with
her other hand. Remaining impassive was a must,
if only to keep Rothbury from knowing that she
did, indeed, understand every single syllable his
grandmother happened to utter.

Perhaps this was the reason he had asked if
she or her mother spoke his grandmother's native

tongue. He had warned them more than once that senility was slowly taking over her mind. That despite her grasp of the English language, she refused to speak it any longer. Still, her criticism was a touch startling, considering the comment had come out of nowhere.

Up until this point, Charlotte had thought that her meeting with the dowager countess was going along smoothly.

She had entered the arbor on Rothbury's arm, where she was met with much enthusiasm by a petite, gray-haired woman with kind eyes that showed absolutely no hint of her unstable mental state. She wore her tightly curled hair pinned up and tucked under a lace cap, with tiny ringlets peeking out. Her pink day dress was simple, no old-fashioned frills of unending lace, but the tiny pink bows sewn on the hem and frame of the bodice did give the impression that it was made from a design intended for a much younger woman. Her eyes were a clear, amber-flecked brown, much like her grandson's, and she smelled heavily of lavender.

Clasping Charlotte's hands within her wrinkled ones, she had kissed both sides of Charlotte's face and declared, in French, that today was the best day of her life. She insisted the Greenes call her by her given name, Louisette, and appeared, at least at the moment, to be in complete control of her mind.

And then things started to take a turn. She began to talk very fast and enthusiastically, and she asked many questions, mostly about Charlotte's family and upbringing. Rothbury patiently translated her queries, often with an apology in his eyes when the dowager asked another question before Charlotte had time to answer the first.

Hyacinth arrived a half hour later than Charlotte, still a bit groggy from her nap. Louisette seemed as pleased to make her acquaintance as well, and even spoke of the haunted forest near the pavilion, Rothbury translating, of course. Charlotte surmised that he must have told his grandmother about Hyacinth's fixation with the metaphysical.

Then Louisette had proceeded to go into great, horrific detail of a murder that had taken place there during the Jacobean Rebellion. Her mother couldn't understand a word Louisette was saying, but it didn't matter. Once the introduction and pleasantries were over, Hyacinth settled down on the bench next to the woman who had been sitting quietly near the dowager.

The tall, graying woman was Miss Drake, long-time nurse and companion to the dowager. And more interestingly, fellow specter enthusiast. While Miss Drake worked on her needlework, she and Hyacinth fell into easy conversation, often sounding like schoolgirls as they shared their experiences with the spirit world.

Charlotte slid a glance at Rothbury. Diagonally across from their little cluster, he lounged on an ornate garden chair that looked as if it was designed specifically for the dainty bottom of an English miss—not the long-legged grown man who was currently occupying it. Indeed, it looked in danger of crumbling under his weight.

Charlotte pressed her lips together, suppressing the need to smile. There was nothing like delicate furniture to make a man seem even more incredibly masculine than he already was.

In a manner that befitted a recalcitrant youth down from Eton, Rothbury leaned back in the chair, strong arms folded across his chest, eyes closed, lean muscled legs stretched out before him as he balanced the chair precariously on the back legs alone.

"You'll break my chair, Adam. Sit like a gentleman," Louisette ordered in the language of her family, getting up specifically to swat him in the leg with her fan before returning back to the chair positioned directly in front of Charlotte's.

Too late, Charlotte couldn't stop a smile from blooming. Both for his grandmother's use of his Christian name and for admonishing this grown man as if he were a child.

He didn't listen, however. One side of his mouth lifted in a grin. "But I'm not a gentleman, Grandmére," he pointed out cheekily.

"If you would have listened to me, and not that single-minded oaf you had for a father, not to mention your worthless uncles, you could have been."

Clearly growing agitated, Louisette shifted in her seat, turning her attention back to Charlotte. Unabashedly, she swept her gaze over the lower half of Charlotte's body.

"And where are her hips, hmm?" Louisette suddenly blurted.

Rothbury's chair wavered, his balance—and his impassive countenance—momentarily faltering at her bold question. However, he soon recovered, the balancing act of the chair restored, his face settling back into a devastatingly handsome expression of aristocratic ennui.

Charlotte had only blinked in reaction to the dowager's chosen subject matter. Although it wasn't what she expected, she must admit that Rothbury had aptly warned her.

"I cannot see them. Can you? How can she possibly bear children?" She posed the questions to Rothbury after casting Charlotte an innocent smile.

Rothbury muttered something unintelligible and then began rubbing his temples.

"Well?" she prodded. "Is she shaped like a stick?"

"*Elle est bien roulée*," he responded quietly. *She is nicely curved.*

Charlotte sat up a little straighter, the thought to thank him poised on the tip of her tongue. She tamped it down, bringing her cup to her lips for another sip.

"She is pretty," Louisette allowed quietly.

"She is beautiful," Rothbury disclosed, even quieter.

Charlotte turned her face away from them and acted as if she was engrossed with studying the landscape. An odd sting of tears burned her eyes. She didn't know if Rothbury meant what he was saying or was simply placating his grandmother. Either way, a blush was creeping its way up Charlotte's neck.

They are just words. He says these sorts of things to

lots of woman all the time. Surely, compliments just roll off his tongue with ease.

"I never thought you were partial to blondes," Louisette went on, "being one yourself. I had thought you preferred only the dark-haired ones. Feisty and somewhat wild. Like your horses."

He didn't answer.

"Do you like her family? Do they like you, Adam?"

He sighed. "It is impolite to speak in another language in front of guests," he replied instead.

"I am not speaking another language. *They* are. Now answer my question."

"You are in England," he pointed out, clearly growing agitated, but keeping himself calm.

"I know where I am. Now answer my question."

The foreign words tumbling from his mouth sounded alluring. His voice alone enchanted Charlotte. "I've only ever met her mother, and until recently, Mrs. Greene hasn't seen fit to allow me anywhere near her daughter. I don't understand how, but suddenly I have found myself in her good graces. It could be . . . interesting if things remain this way."

It seemed there were some advantages to being underestimated. Especially where Rothbury was concerned. Charlotte knew he thought her gullible.

Perhaps she was from time to time, but that didn't mean she hadn't a bit of shrewdness on her side as well. And she hoped that in giving the impression she couldn't understand what they were saying, she'd learn about some new facet of his character.

Even though she was marginally acquainted with him, there were many things she didn't know about him. And she wanted to. But he seemed to keep his thoughts locked up tight and often hid his true feelings behind a cloud of sarcasm and cynical remarks. When he did make a remark that seemed somewhat revealing, it was impossible to discern whether or not he was being serious. No doubt that was his plan all along.

Louisette reached out, covering Charlotte's hands with her own.

"You will not leave him?" she asked, her kind eyes beseeching.

Leave him? What was she speaking of? Charlotte wanted to ask, but kept her lips sealed tight.

"I don't think he could endure the pain a second time. It was long ago, but some wounds are cut so deep, they never heal. He is not like them. He never was. But without her guidance, he fell easily into their hands, into their ways. Tell me you'll not leave him."

Her eyes flew to Rothbury. His throat worked

and his jaw tightened, but his eyes remained shut. He looked angry . . . or uncomfortable. Maybe both.

"My lord," Charlotte implored, "please translate. Your grandmother is so earnest and seems to be awaiting my answer."

He opened his eyes a slit, training it on her. "Just smile and nod, Ch—Miss Greene. I told you she speaks nonsense."

That comment earned him a cutting glare from his otherwise loving grandmother. Quite suddenly, she whipped her fan at him, but it missed him by at least a foot, the ivory handle clattering to the stone floor.

"I guess it is of no significance," Louisette muttered, waving a dismissing hand in the air toward her grandson. "I have faith you will have her heavy with child by Midsummer Day."

Mid-swallow, Charlotte choked on her tea, sputtering into her cup at first, then standing in order to cough hard enough to clear her lungs.

"My word, Charlotte! Are you all right?" Hyacinth asked.

Charlotte nodded, using a linen napkin on the tea tray to pat her mouth.

"I'm fine," she rasped, glancing at Rothbury to gauge his reaction to his grandmother's prediction.

At the onset of her coughing episode he froze, watched her for a moment, and then went back to leaning in his chair.

Pursing her lips, Charlotte began to wonder if his grandmother's comments were truly only the babblings of a woman losing her hold on her sanity. Or was this some sort of ploy of Rothbury's that she hadn't figured out just yet?

Rothbury could feel Charlotte's studying gaze upon him.

Instead of opening his eyes fully, he continued to watch her, undetected, as he had been doing since the moment he sat in this ridiculous chair that made his arse hurt.

Christ, *he* was an arse.

He did not deserve her friendship, her kindness, her smiles. She had no idea why he had invited her here. But there she had sat, smiling at his grandmother, looking as if she understood every word Louisette said, which of course, he knew, she couldn't. If she could, surely his little ruse would have erupted.

The noonday sun had warmed the chilly nip in the air, but it had since returned, brought on by a swath of deep purple clouds creeping in on Aubry Park like a crouching beast.

Thunder rumbled in the distance and the wind started to pick up.

He opened his eyes, settling the legs of his chair properly upon the ground. Leaning forward, he rested his elbows on his knees, clasping his hands together in front of him as he stared at Charlotte freely as her back was now to him.

She was staring off at a far hill and he wondered what it could be that held her so entranced. And then it dawned on him, hitting him square in the chest.

She was waiting for Tristan.

He had forgotten. His ruse had been going so well, Tristan's absence had slipped his mind. He didn't know where the hell his friend could be. Tristan had either changed his mind about coming to Aubry Park or had chosen to wait out the approaching storm.

Just then he heard her take a deep breath, which sounded much like a sigh to his ears.

He gave his head a slow shake. She might not outwardly admit it, but Rothbury believed she wanted more, much more, than to simply make Tristan jealous. He suspected she wanted a chance to win him back.

For six years he had borne witness to her infatuation with his friend. He had watched her sapphire eyes follow Tristan across countless ball-rooms. Watched her alter herself, hide her spectacles, even stuff her bodice on occasion, all to gain Tristan's notice. All for naught.

He had watched her grow from an awkward duckling of a debutante into an alluring, willowy young woman who always had a smile for him despite the distraction of Tristan.

He did not hold his affection for Charlotte under the same scrutiny as he did her obsession of Tristan. Her fascination for his friend had burst forth from one lone incident of heroism combined with a dash of Tristan's charm.

Rothbury's admiration had grown gradually, steadily, despite his efforts to ignore her. Never quick to judge, she was kind, she was sincere, she was secretly funny, and quite observant. She was the only woman of his acquaintance, the only person really, to whom he had ever revealed even the smallest hint of what he was truly feeling.

Inviting her here was a mistake. Being in such close proximity to her, and for an entire day, just might unravel the threads of a disguise he had worked so hard to maintain. Soon, he feared, he would not be able to hide behind it any longer.

He might as well admit it . . . he'd every intention of tricking her into coming to his estate, posing as his bride-to-be. He was getting so good at disguising his feelings, he had tricked himself into believing that any woman at the Hawthorne Ball would do, and that his gaze had fallen accidentally on Charlotte.

But the truth was, it could have only ever been Charlotte. Pretend or real, it would only ever be her.

He never would have guessed it, but there it was. He couldn't help but wish he was a different man. That she was here for different reasons.

He wanted her to be here because . . . well, because she *wanted* to be here. Not because she wanted to make Tristan jealous, not because she considered herself his "friend," not because she wanted to show him some bloody list of men she'd rather marry. Lord knew he wouldn't be on the list. Hell, if he was lucky, she had forgotten all about the damn thing.

Tell her that you love her.

No. He couldn't. She would never believe he was serious. Never forget that when he had mentioned marriage to her in the garden at Wolverest, she had laughed in his face. Declaring his feelings might just make her quite hysterical again.

Miss Drake was now wrapping his grandmother in a thick shawl and helping her to stand.

He straightened, listening to his grandmother chatter on about the forest she wanted Charlotte's mother to see before they left, Miss Drake translating of course. Rothbury joined them and they all proceeded to exit the arbor, making plans to return to the house to wait out the impending rain for their ride to the pavilion for luncheon.

Rothbury offered his arm to Charlotte and she took it, her gaze cast down as they walked. She was thinking, mulling something over in her mind.

Miss Drake, forgetting her embroidery, dashed back to retrieve it, smiling warmly at Rothbury and Charlotte as they passed. His grandmother and Charlotte's mother walked side by side, several feet ahead.

"Miss Greene," she called as she returned on her way to catch up to the dowager. "I must offer my personal congratulations on the upcoming nuptials. I've known his lordship since he was fourteen. Never thought I'd see him so besotted. I wouldn't have believed it had I not heard it come straight from his own mouth. And you do make such a fine-looking couple."

Rothbury inwardly groaned. Hoping—no, praying—the comment would simply blow straight over Charlotte's pretty little head.

Straightening the spectacles on her nose, Charlotte cleared her throat delicately. "Pardon," she said, holding up a finger for Miss Drake to wait. But the nurse had moved quickly, practically running now to catch up to the dowager and Charlotte's mother.

Her breathing pattern changed. It was the first thing he noticed. Her chest rose and fell rapidly though their pace was slow. He couldn't tell if she was about to scream at him or—God help him—cry.

She came to an abrupt stop.

"I knew it! I knew you were up to something!" She turned on him, her pale pink lips in an angry line, her delicate winged brows knitted in a frown, her sapphire eyes narrowed and accusing.

Lord, she was beautiful when she was angry. An odd thought popped into his head. He started to compose a list of things he could do to make her angry just so she would look at him with such passion in her eyes. Of course, lust-induced passion was better than anger-induced passion, but he'd take either at this point.

"You tricked me," she whispered. "You invited me here to pose as your betrothed. That's why you asked if my mother or I spoke French. You wanted to be sure we wouldn't understand a word your grandmother said!"

He held up his hands in supplication. "I am guilty."

"Was Lord Tristan even to come?"

He swallowed, reminding himself that he shouldn't be surprised she mentioned Tristan straight away.

"Yes, he is. He was, that is. I have no idea if he has been delayed or changed his mind."

She stared at him, looking as if a thousand thoughts were rambling through her head. Her lips worked, but no words emerged.

Perhaps this was the extent of her anger? He hoped. Maybe? He flashed her a devastating roguish grin, hoping it would offset her anger. It had worked for him before . . . albeit not on this particular woman.

"How dare you smile at me," she bit out. She pushed at his chest with all her might. It didn't move him an inch.

She kept trying, grunting with the effort.

"Charlotte, what are you trying to do?"

"Push you down, you selfish, self-absorbed, egotistical man!"

"You could have stopped at the first adjective. I'm quite sure they all mean the same thing."

"What are we to do?" she asked desperately, giving him one last push that did absolutely nothing but wrinkle his shirt.

"We don't have to do anything," he assured her quietly.

"What do you mean? Of course we have to do something! Now we have to get married!"

He shook his head slowly, his mind again coming to grips with the fact that this woman would never, ever, want to marry him.

"I can't marry *you*," she said, sounding as if she would cry.

His jaw hardened. "I am well aware of your preferences in men, sweetheart. Now," he said, stopping himself just short of reaching out to brush a silky curl from her collarbone, "do not worry. My grandmother will not hold us to it. In fact, there is a chance she will forget all about it before she even reaches the house."

"But what of my mother?"

"Your mother has no idea. And it will remain as such."

Her gaze searched his. "But why? Why did you need to do this?" she asked, her voice barely a whisper.

It occurred to him then just how dark the sky had become. Indeed, it looked almost like dusk. "Come, I'll explain as we walk."

They were halfway to the house and he was

halfway through his explanation about his necessity for haste in finding a temporary bride when the sky opened, pelting them with heavy drops of rain.

The closest shelter was the small covered porch of the back door. Shrugging off his coat, Rothbury handed it to Charlotte to hold over her head. They were running now, slipping in the mud that seemed to form instantly on the path.

His hand sought hers, hoping she'd take it so he could be sure she didn't fall. She batted it away.

"Why me?" Charlotte shouted the question over the roar of the rain and ensuing thunder. "Out of all those women at the Hawthorne Ball, why did you pick me?"

"Because I . . . Because I . . ." *Because I love you.* "Because I knew that out of anyone there, you were the easiest to persuade, the easiest to fool."

He hated the words.

She stopped cold. So did he.

The driving rain drilled down on them. He turned to face her. Ready to receive whatever punishment, whatever scathing looks or words she wanted to give him. He deserved it all.

At first he thought all she would do was stand there and glare up at him, her spectacles dotted with rain. But then her chin lifted and hardened.

Reaching out with one hand, she pushed him as hard as she could.

This time, however, Rothbury was not on steady ground. His leather boots were encased in slippery mud and her puny shove did him in.

He fell backward. He didn't even fight it.

Ironically, Charlotte didn't wait to witness the successful result of her shove. He reckoned she didn't even realize what she had actually accomplished.

As he lay there in the mud, watching Charlotte as she marched away from him holding his coat over her head and shoulders, he felt he was exactly where he deserved to be.

Well. It was done. Tomorrow, after they visited the haunted forest, Charlotte and her mother would be on their way back to London. And rightfully so. He didn't know what bothered him more: the fact that he had hurt her or the fact that if she didn't find a suitor quickly enough, she'd find herself married to Witherby before the year was out.

He needed to ride. To hell with the rain. As soon as he changed, he'd ready his horse himself and set out to God knows where. In fact, why bother changing? In fact, why bother staying in England? Perhaps he'd go abroad. Visit his sprawling villa in Italy, pay a return visit to the sunny paradise of Cyprus, reintroduce his senses to the exotic spices of the Orient.

Slowly and sloppily, he rose up enough to lean on his elbows, his eyes settling on Charlotte's retreating form.

And then the oddest thing happened. She stopped and spun around.

Shaking her head, she strode back to him, nearly slipping a couple of times, but managed to catch herself before she joined him in the mud.

She extended her hand. "Come on," she said, holding back a laugh. "Get up."

"No," he said. "I think I'll stay."

"Don't be ridiculous. Grab my hand."

"Charlotte, go into the house. It's freezing, you're wet, I've got mud in places I didn't even know I had . . ."

"Rothbury . . ."

"Oh, all right. I'm coming. But you're not helping me up. Right now, you're just wet. I, however, am covered with five pounds of mud. If I touch you, I'll ruin your clothes."

Gingerly, he stood, shaking his head to dislodge water and mud that had found its way into his ear, then followed her to the covered porch.

Walking through the painted columns, they

paused to catch their breath. Just being out of the driving rain felt like heaven.

Her sodden skirts were nearly plastered to her legs, but because of his coat, her upper half was almost completely dry. Well, there was a mist of rain upon the flesh of her exposed bosom above her bodice. And a scattering of droplets upon her face. He watched as one ran over her cheek and dipped down to the corner of her mouth. He wondered if it was a rivulet of rain or a damn tear that *he* had caused.

"I forgive you," she said, breathlessly. "You've helped me in the past. But I still think you should have asked me instead of tricking me."

"I agree," he said, just as breathlessly.

Her eyes dipped to his mouth as he spoke, igniting a scorching heat in his blood.

Surely, he was misjudging where her eyes were cast. Her spectacles were streaked with rain. He could be mistaken. He had to know.

Slowly, he reached out, gently pulling them from her face. She did nothing to stop him. And damn if her sapphire gaze was yet fastened to his mouth.

He swallowed hard. "Charlotte, are you all right?"

She nodded. "I realize why you did it, but I'm . . ."

"You're what?" She needed to stop looking at his mouth.

"I'm quite sure . . ."

"Charlotte?" His heart thundered in his ears.

"Hmm?"

"I will replace your ruined dress," he stated firmly.

"But my-my dress isn't ruined. It's only rain."

"And mud."

"There isn't any mud," she pointed out, her brow quirking. "You're the one covered—"

One heavy hand at her waist, the other molded to the back of her head, he dragged her roughly against him. His starved mouth swooped down upon hers, smothering her next words with his kiss, changing her next syllable into a soft, feminine moan.

His coat lay forgotten on the floor along with her spectacles.

This kiss, this first kiss, was not subtle, soft or gentle. It was as if they were ravenous for each other. She opened so easily for him. He didn't expect this reaction from her. Truly, he hadn't expected to kiss her today. But as their mouths joined, their lips caressing, moving hungrily, steadily becoming more demanding, he wondered why he hadn't done this sooner.

"I could kiss you for hours," he drawled hotly against her mouth. "Possibly for days." It felt as if he was savoring heaven. Something Rothbury never thought he would ever even glimpse let alone taste.

She responded to his words by grasping at the sodden material of his linen shirt, her arms trapped in between their chests.

The feel of her lush mouth under him was intoxicating. She tasted sweet, wet, the rivulets of rain upon their faces making the kiss wilder, hotter somehow.

His lips moved hotly over hers. He had thought about this moment for so long, and now that it was actually happening . . . it was better than he ever imagined it could be.

She stumbled a bit, sinking further into him. Her hands now clutched at his shoulders, her fingers sinking into his muscles. Sweet Lord, she was kissing him back, a bit too eagerly, especially when the rhythm of his kiss slowed before picking up again. It was as if she was afraid that he was stopping.

Over and over she met his movements, surprising him with her fervor, humbling him with her unexpected enthusiasm. For a second he had to ask himself, just who was kissing whom here?

He broke the kiss for a moment, his lips a breath away from hers. They were both panting heavily.

"Still think my kiss is rather mundane, Charlotte?"

"Mun . . . what?"

Hmm. Kissed her senseless. He could live with that.

"Do it again," she whispered, tilting her head, offering her mouth to him.

Staring down at her swollen bottom lip, he gave it a little lick.

A small, soft moan sounded from the back of her throat.

"Ask nicely," he whispered.

"Please." She gave a lock of hair at his neck an impatient tug.

He came undone. Delving his tongue inside her sweet mouth, he walked her backward until her back met one of the pillars. With one hand cradling the back of her head for protection, his other hand held her hip immobilized, under his control. Rhythmically, he sank his tongue into her honeyed depths, mimicking the motion of making love.

She whimpered, the sound a desperate plea. Her fingers threaded through the damp hair at the base of his neck; her other hand clutched at his forearm.

He squeezed her hip, his long fingers digging into her soft bottom as he rocked her into his arousal.

For several moments, she ground her hips against him as he plundered her mouth. The kiss was no longer enough. He wanted to take her. Right here, right now. His fingertips trailed down the back of her neck to caress her shoulder, her arm, her breast. His breath hitched when she pushed herself more firmly into his hand. She wanted his touch. He complied of course: he would never deny her. Gently he kneaded her through the fabric of her dress, purposely passing his thumb over the hardened tip. She made a small sound of pleasure that nearly pushed him over the edge.

The manor, the rain, the mud disappeared. Reason and practicality were momentarily suspended. Nothing mattered in those moments. Nothing but the ever-escalating power of their passion.

And then suddenly, everything seemed too quiet. The rain had stopped. The radiating warmth of sunlight spread along his back. Their movements stilled, their lips parted. The spell cast between them had broken.

A rhythmic sloshing sound, imbedded somewhere in the distance, grew closer. Someone was coming.

He set her apart from him just in time to spy Tristan rounding the far corner of the manor.

"Who is it?" Charlotte asked.

"Tristan."

"Did he . . . do you think he saw . . ."

"Undoubtedly, part of it at least." Truthfully, all he could have seen was when Rothbury set her apart of him. But she didn't know that. And given what she wanted to accomplish today, that just might be all that Tristan needed to see.

"Wh . . . why did you do that?" she asked, bringing up her hand to touch her fingertips to her lips.

His gaze swung back to her. He was such a damned idiot. He should have never brought her here. But he was weak. Years of self-imposed restraint, months of being close to her, it had all come to a tipping point once she stared at his mouth quite like she *wanted* to kiss him. But the idea was preposterous. She considered him her friend. She thought she could turn him into a gentleman, and if anything, his behavior just now only drove the point home that she was wasting her time.

Belatedly, he realized she wasn't wearing her spectacles. That's right. He had taken them off of her. They must have dropped. He scanned the ground.

"Did you know he was there? Did you know he was coming? Was that why?"

Hell, no, that wasn't why. But he couldn't tell her why.

No, she didn't want him for a husband, he wasn't good enough for her. But she sure as hell couldn't deny her response to him. He should be relishing the moment, but all Rothbury could think right now was how much he wanted her heart.

"Was that why you kissed me?" she asked through her teeth.

He grasped the excuse Tristan's presence presented. "That was your little plan, wasn't it?" he bit out. "Got a little swept away, did you?"

Bending down, he plucked her spectacles from just to the left of his mud-caked boot. For a second he mulled over the fact that there wasn't a stitch of clothing on his person that wasn't soaked with mud or rain. He couldn't possibly clean them. But he needn't worry about it much longer.

Angrily, she snatched them from his hold.

"Go inside," Rothbury said, "before he gets any closer."

Telltale splotches of red bloomed on her neck and cheeks. He knew why. It always happened when she was embarrassed or feeling shy. Right now, he reckoned it was both.

He met her gaze, giving her a lopsided grin. "I must say, you're quite the good little actress. For a second there I believed you were enjoying yourself."

She took a deep angry breath, then exhaled, trying to gather her wits and pull herself back together.

Halfway to them now, Tristan shouted in greeting, saying something about being holed up in the stables waiting for the rains to stop. Neither Charlotte nor Rothbury paid him any heed.

Patches of mud were smeared all down the front of her dress, especially her skirts. Lines of mud from his fingers branded her neck, throat, and hair. How fitting, he thought morosely. He had sullied her with his touch, figuratively and literally.

Rothbury opened the door for her, gesturing with his other hand for her to proceed inside.

She did, but not before giving him a long, scathing glare.

Chapter 13

A Gentleman always finds room in his heart to pardon a tiny untruth, especially if it was conveyed by a well-intentioned friend.

Tell me, what are your plans for her?"

"She's a little sensitive and immature."

"Yes, but is she a winner?" Tristan asked. He nodded to the stable lad who brought out his saddled horse. "I've noticed she often overreacts to every move you make with her."

"You have to move slowly with her," Rothbury suggested. "She's just beginning to get into the routine."

"Perhaps she's not ready and needs to mature naturally. You could be pushing her too hard."

Rothbury smoothed a hand over his jaw, staring across the field to where the three-year-old filly was currently being exercised. His mind was in another place. He hoped Tristan didn't notice. "She's ready. I believe she will only improve further from here."

"I don't know. Can't make up my mind."

"She's in great condition," Rothbury murmured. "Thought you wouldn't want to pass her up. We've had other offers . . ."

Tristan laughed. "If I didn't know your blood was so blue, I'd say you've peddler's blood flowing in your veins."

Rothbury scowled in mock offense. "A peddler's fare is often inferior. My horses are some of the finest in all of England. Prinny purchased a marvelous two-year-old last month. I should demand an affair of honor after your careless remark."

The friendly banter came to an end, both men becoming quiet, both well aware of the friction sparking between them. They had been friends since Eton, having much the same interests and a similar disposition, though Tristan was admittedly more carefree and less willing to settle down—yet many women duly felt he was the safer choice between the two of them.

They hardly ever shared a disagreeable word, each often guessing what the other was thinking before he said it, and had a long, happy history of drinking, gambling, hunting, and general carousing together.

They had never fought over a woman. And Rothbury didn't plan on starting now. Not that Charlotte wasn't worth fighting for, it was just that Rothbury wanted her whole heart. Could she ever love him? Would she always harbor a secret adoration for Tristan?

"My opinion is unwanted, I am sure," Tristan finally said, "but I think you should tell her how you feel. You might be surprised by her response."

Riding crop twitching at his side, Rothbury swung his serious gaze to his friend. "I don't think the little filly cares."

"You know whom I'm talking about."

Rothbury looked down, tightening his gloves. "I do. I'm her friend. And for that I am grateful. Men like me often do not have the opportunity to know a woman like Miss Greene."

Swinging up into his saddle, Tristan laughed. "Friend? Had I 'friends' who kissed me like that, I should never need a mistress."

Rothbury cleared his throat. Tristan might be his friend, but Rothbury hesitated telling too much. After all, he had no idea if Tristan was growing enamored of Charlotte. Hell, Tristan could be jealous for all he knew—could be the very reason he brought up the subject of Charlotte.

"If I cannot have her," he said tightly, with a coolness he did not feel, "then I will make sure, at least what is within my power to do so, that she does not enter into any union that she does not find completely agreeable."

"I see," Tristan remarked, eyeing Rothbury with a mischievous gleam in his eye. "Well, if I were you, I'd snatch her up before some fat, perfumed, loudmouthed deviant purchases her."

"And were I you," Rothbury countered, swinging up into the saddle of his favorite black Arabian, "I'd cease comparing Miss Greene to a horse, before you find a riding crop up your arse."

"Thank you, Nadine," Charlotte murmured to the maid who just finished redoing her coiffure into a loose bun, artfully arranging the curls.

Seated on the cushioned stool before the dressing table, Charlotte waited until the plump-cheeked young girl left before allowing the small smile etched upon her face to crumble back into a frown. Bending over the dressing table, she groaned, dropping her forehead onto her folded hands.

It was of no use. Try as she might, her mood would not change.

She had asked to take a bath, thinking the sting of the hot water against her cool skin would banish the feel of Rothbury's long, hard body pressed into hers.

But it only made it worse. The heat only served to remind her of the melting sensations she felt when he had touched her, squeezed her, kissed her.

Then, she had scrubbed her lips, hoping to banish the lingering feel of his lips moving hungrily over hers, but it only made her replay it in her mind. There could be no mistaking her enjoyment of the wicked act, she had thought, while gliding her wet fingertips over her mouth. Sweet Lord, hadn't she asked him for more?

And when she dressed, she had chosen a simple long-sleeved white muslin, its only decoration a pale pink ribbon of satin that banded the bottom of the skirt. Surely the primness of the day dress would dispel any erotic thoughts from her mind, wouldn't it?

However, all she kept thinking of when she looked down at herself were Rothbury's strong hands smoothing over her shoulders, grabbing her bottom, dragging her hips forward to cradle his . . .

She inhaled sharply, picking her head up to look at herself in the mirror. "Stop it, Charlotte. He must think you're just like every other eyelash-fluttering, brazen Cyprian more than willing for his ravishment."

Roughly, she pinched color into her cheeks, willing the discomfort to discourage her sinful trail of thoughts.

Here she sat, thinking, thinking, thinking. Reliving the moment over and over, and for what? No doubt Rothbury was off somewhere in the manor, sipping claret, playing billiards, out shooting up game, or whatever it was men did in the country, with not a single thought to what had happened between them today.

Sure, she was somewhat satisfied that Tristan may have witnessed at least a little bit of Rothbury's heated embrace. But getting kissed within an inch of losing her virtue wasn't exactly what she had in mind when she asked Rothbury to flirt with her.

Lord, she hadn't wanted him to stop. It was better than she had ever thought it could be. And her knees *did* buckle and the earth *did* feel like it shifted under her feet. It was wonderful. It was intoxicating.

It was all a game to him.

And he was so *good* at it, she thought with a groan.

She should have never come here. She should have never imposed herself on Rothbury and bullied him into attending the Hawthorne Ball. How could they continue a friendship after something like this happened?

Truly, it was not fair. It rankled her to the very marrow of her bones that she was so affected and he was not.

In fact, it was probably just an everyday occurrence for him. Who knows, she might have been the second, third, or fourth woman he kissed today.

And then he had the nerve to disparage her reactions. Telling her that she was a *good little actress*. He shook off the kiss like a wet canine shakes off rain, while she continued to shiver even now.

She groaned in frustration.

"Of all the arrogant, presumptuous . . ."

"I believe you are talking about me."

" . . . perceptive."

"Ah, yes. I was correct. You are talking about me, after all."

"Rothbury," she said tightly, catching his reflection in the mirror as he stood in the doorway. "What are you doing in my bedchamber?"

"Funny how things turn about, isn't it? It wasn't too long ago that I was asking you the very same question."

She turned on her perch at the dressing table to face him fully. Her breath caught in her throat. She swallowed it painfully down.

He looked achingly handsome. He wore an expertly cut black frock coat with tails over a buttercream-colored shirt and matching waistcoat with small silver buttons. His cravat was simple today, falling in only a few folds, but complemented his slightly squared jaw, faint with gold bristles. Nankeen breeches hugged his long, lean-muscled thighs, his polished boots folded over at the knee. His strong, very capable hands were covered in leather and he carried with him a riding crop.

His amber-flecked gaze followed hers to what he held in his hand. "I've run up from the stables. Your mother, as absurd as it sounds, sent me to fetch you. She wanted to know what was taking so long."

She watched as a muscle worked in his cheek.

"Her trust in me, Charlotte, is strangely profound, and I fear after what happened about an hour ago, utterly misplaced. I cannot fathom what you could have possibly said to warrant sudden absolution of my past sins."

She shrugged, too annoyed at this point to offer her explanation.

He looked both ways down the hall before stepping inside her room. With slow, measured steps, he sauntered to the foot of the bed and leaned his back on the post closest to her.

The light scent of sandalwood wafted over to her, mixing with leather, telling her that he had recently bathed as well. He must have a remarkable valet, considering the amount of mud that had covered him.

"But I'm glad for it, for I've come to apologize," he said softly, looking down at her with . . . with *tenderness*.

Tenderness? Surely, she was mistaken. She made a mental note to ask her mother to have new spectacles purchased.

No, what she saw in his gaze had to be pity. He didn't want her to think there was something more to that kiss.

Apologizing for a kiss was a bad thing, Charlotte realized just then. It meant that the giver of the kisses revokes all possibilities that true, honest, pure, passion had provoked the occasion.

It tagged it as a mistake, a blunder, an error in judgment, never to be done again. She mustn't allow him to know how it truly made her feel.

He was a rake, a wicked man born into a family of libertines. He couldn't know of anything other than lust, seeking his own pleasure without a single care for anyone else. For years he had chased one woman after another. To her knowledge he had never even properly courted a lady.

Why in the world did she keep reminding herself of these facts?

Rothbury stared down at Charlotte, willing the ability to erase the pain and confusion from her gaze. Undoubtedly, she was shocked by the strength of his ardor and feared she was his newest target.

"I realize I went a touch too far with our kiss," he said quietly. "I hadn't realized Tristan was so close."

"Yes. I agree, we were much too enthusiastic about it. In the future, perhaps, you could simply stick to gazing at me longingly, or smiling at me a lot."

"Indeed," he said, bowing his head slightly.

"There should be no more touching . . . of any sort. It is too much by far. And I am of the mind that a little mild flirtation goes a long way."

"No more touching."

She stood and swiped any wrinkles from her gown, pausing to pluck a minuscule thread from the tiny lace trim of her bodice. His eyes followed her movements. She looked up to find him watching her and instantly stiffened.

"And you should cease . . . *looking* at me like that."

He affected being taken aback. "You just said looking was fine."

"When Tristan's around, you big goose."

He smiled, glad to see she seemed to be acting a little bit more like herself now.

"But all is not lost," she said, with an adorable glint in her eye. "As a matter of fact, I have every reason to believe your . . . zealous display of affection might have worked to my benefit. Nadine told me he has decided to join us for luncheon."

"Indeed, he has."

Keeping her watchful gaze on him, she skirted around him, heading for the escritoire in the corner. She opened a drawer and pulled out a wrinkled sheet of vellum.

Padding purposefully toward him, she made him wish this was their shared chamber and she was about to push him back onto the bed and toss herself atop him.

"Here you are," she said, thrusting the paper at him.

"What is this?" he asked, taking it.

"My list of prospective proper husbands. I brought it with me."

"And why would I care to look at such a thing?" he said with a wry note in his voice, eyeing the paper crossly.

"You've forgotten already?" she asked, incredulously. And then she realized he was only teasing her. "You said to make a list. That you'd look it over and help me find a suitor from among the names."

He nodded, his eyes skimming the names. "Lord Beckham . . . Sir Nicholas Camden . . . the Marquis of Ravensdale . . . Mr. William Holt . . . Lord Fieldcrest . . . the Earl of Langley . . . the Duke of Goldings . . . Mr. James Cantrell . . ."

He gave his head a slow shake and settled his gaze upon Charlotte, who was now smiling, no evidence of the damage he had caused from that afternoon apparent in her blue depths. "Charlotte, I'm amazed."

"What is it? What's the matter?" she asked, innocently.

"These men . . . They are all my friends. Every single one of them . . ." His gaze returned to the list. "Lord Tanning, Mr. Thomas Nordstrom . . . all of them."

"Well, then, it should be easy, shouldn't it?

Finding one of them whom you think might be interested in courting me. After all you know them, right?"

"I don't want . . ."

At that precise moment, Rothbury was saved from explaining how torturous thrusting the woman he loved in the path of any of these men would be, when the sound of Charlotte's mother's voice echoed from down the hall.

"Charlotte! Where are you? Everyone is waiting," Hyacinth called out, her footsteps fast approaching.

Without a word he stepped around the bed and crouched down to hide from view.

Charlotte looked at him strangely. "What are you doing?"

He pressed a finger to his lips.

"Ah! There you are!" Hyacinth declared. "And looking pretty as a daisy, I might add."

"Thank you," Charlotte mumbled, self-consciously patting down her skirts again.

"Well, what are you waiting for, my dear child? The air is warm, the company is agreeable, and there are spirits afoot!"

"Are there?" Charlotte asked, none too enthusiastically.

"Why, yes. 'Tis why I wish you wouldn't tarry.

We are to picnic in the pavilion, and then tomorrow we are to explore a nearby patch of haunted forest. Miss Drake said that there is a cavern located there where one can hear the moans of a restless Scottish ghost. Once she claimed to have even heard breathing and footsteps."

"That's quite remarkable," Charlotte replied, not sounding impressed. "I wonder . . . did they hear the braying of a sheep, by chance? Rothbury said one of his tenants is having a problem with someone sneaking in and stealing his sheep. It is entirely possible that is who she heard, is it not?"

Still in his crouching position, Rothbury smiled at her deduction, making a mental note to post a guard at the cavern in the future, just in case.

"Oh, you're no fun. No fun at all anymore. Come down, will you?"

"Yes, I'll be right there. I just have to find my shawl."

Hyacinth sighed. "You seem a touch maudlin today, dear. Are you certain you're feeling well?"

"I'm fine. Just terribly hungry, is all."

"As am I! I hear we are in for a bit of a feast! I've been told the cook is quite famous here at Aubry. And we'll be having to break our fast here as well. It's good to travel on a full stomach, I say. One cannot depend entirely on coaching-inn fare. You didn't forget, did you? We are still going home tomorrow," Hyacinth reminded her. "This Season is to be our last. We—you—should make the most of it."

She nodded, turning her attention on Rothbury. Their gazes locked, though his ears concentrated on Hyacinth's fading footsteps.

"She's gone," Charlotte muttered, taking a step to snatch her list away from him.

He straightened, shaking his head.

"I don't know why you felt obligated to hide from my mother on behalf of my reputation."

"Old habit."

"Well, you can stop all that right now. She trusts you," she said, walking over to the armoire.

His jaw hardened. "Why, Charlotte? Explain this to me now."

She swung open the door of the closet, rummaged around a bit, then pulled out a light blue shawl. "It is of no consequence, I assure you."

"And I assure you that it is," he said gruffly. "Now tell me."

She sighed, settling her shawl around her slender shoulders. "It's really nothing of significance." Looking up from her small task, she smiled . . . a bit too sweetly.

He just stared at her, his riding crop twitching against his thigh.

"I simply told her you were just like my Uncle Herbert."

"Your Uncle Herbert?"

"Yes," she said, blinking innocently up at him. "He is my mother's twin brother. They are devoted to each other. Of the same mind, she has always told me. Sometimes they even have the same dreams. Isn't that remarkable?"

"It's extraordinary," he nearly yelled. "Now. Why would telling your mother that I am just like your Uncle Herbert have any effect on her trust in me? Is he an honest man? Forthright and amenable?"

"And well-liked all around. Can't say I've ever met a person who knew Uncle Bertie without having something nice to say about him. He's very popular."

Clearly, she had no idea just how aggravated he had become with her obvious hedging.

"So he's a bloody saint, is he? And your mother believes I hold all these commendable qualities?"

"No. Oh, goodness, no," she said with a small laugh. "Not at all."

A vein in his neck started to throb.

"Oh, all right," she acquiesced finally. "I shall tell you."

"Well, it's about damn time."

"Don't curse . . ."

"Charlotte . . ."

"Very well. My mother trusts you because I explained that you and my uncle happened to like—no *love*," she corrected, "the very same thing."

"What? Fencing, horses, cards, cricket, boxing . . . ?"

"Heavens, no," she said.

"Then, what?" he asked.

"Other men."

Chapter 14

*A Gentleman always sees to the needs
of the Lady seated next to him at the
dinner table.*

The path to the pavilion in the Aubry garden
turned out to be entirely too muddy. So,
Charlotte, Hyacinth, Louisette, and Miss Drake,
escorted by Lord Tristan and Rothbury alongside on horseback of course, all piled inside the
Faramonds' carriage for what Charlotte was told
would be a short ride.

It wasn't true. In fact, it was all a terrible lie.

When one who spends a lot of time in London—
where space is at a premium—hears the word
"garden," images spring forth of nestled flower
beds, neat rows of blooms, kitchen gardens, pad-
docks, and bits of forest and lawn.

When visiting the country, one might imagine a garden on a much grander scale: sweeping manicured lawns, intricately designed landscapes, curving walks winding through flowering shrubs, quaint ponds, strategically placed outbuildings set to inspire peace, wealth, and elegance.

However, the gardens at Aubry Park were composed of more than seventeen hundred acres of parkland. The size was immense. After riding along for nearly two hours, Charlotte was willing to wager they had to be at least in another county or maybe even Scotland by now. When she had voiced her beliefs, she was told by Miss Drake that they were not even anywhere near the end of the estate where the horse-breeding farm happened to be located.

They had arrived at the pavilion a short while later. Charlotte couldn't have been more pleased. Her stomach had growled very loudly four separate times in the carriage, prompting Louisette into asking if, perchance, an angry, growling barn cat had crept inside undetected and nestled himself under one of the compartments under the seats.

The pavilion was indeed breathtaking. Charlotte had toured enough country manors with her mother throughout the years to know that buildings such as these often had no other function than to draw the attention of one's eye. Designed as an object to be viewed rather than actually used.

Such was not the case here. The red-brick building had a curved roof, sparkling clean white-mullioned windows, and two wide entrances equipped with French doors. Tucked inside the pavilion was a long table covered with a red cloth.

A bevy of servants, who had followed in another, less ostentatious conveyance, charged up the steps carrying baskets of cold chicken and ham, sweetbreads, buttered lobster, potatoes, cheese, pastries, and various berries.

When they were done setting the table, Charlotte was so impressed, she had to stop herself from telling the servants what she thought, for it was considered bad form to make such remarks. But it was so artfully arranged, looking just as it should in the dining room proper at the manor house.

They all sat, Louisette at the head of the table, Miss Drake at her right, Tristan at her left. Charlotte sat next to Lord Tristan, Hyacinth across from her, which meant Rothbury sat at the other end of the table, closest to her and her mother.

With much interest for her welfare she watched him, noticing with alarm that his scowling gaze was presently alternating from his dinner fork to her elbow.

Was he thinking to poke her with it?

She hoped he would rise above his anger. She knew he was much displeased over her little fib to her mother about just what side of the fence his passions did reside.

He probably worried that word would leak back to Town. He needn't fear. There was a conspiracy of silence. People like Uncle Herbert were banned from living in Town if discovered. And if her mother had kept Uncle Herbert's secret from the wagging tongues of the *ton*, she would keep Rothbury's "secret" as well.

But she hadn't had time to expound on that in her room. Quite frankly, she hadn't wanted to spend another second with him after she saw the look of utter disbelief on his face change to seething anger. She had skipped out of her room, aware that his angry strides followed her closely all the way across the hall, down the steps, around the corner, and out the front door. There were a couple of times he called out for her to stop, his mouth close to her ears, but she ignored him, just as she was doing now.

Having been ravenously hungry, Charlotte ate heartily. Everything was simply scrumptious.

Well . . . everything . . . but *the scones*.

Miss Drake had explained that sometimes, when Louisette experienced anxieties, she enjoyed baking.

"Scones are her new specialty," Miss Drake said proudly, giving Louisette a reassuring smile.

"Ah, I see," Charlotte said, warily eyeing the scone set on her plate by a footman.

Miss Drake leaned forward whispering, "Sometimes she overkneads. Makes them a touch stiff."

Stiff? They were stones.

"Go on, try it," Miss Drake urged gently. "It will please her."

Slowly bringing the scone to her mouth, Charlotte couldn't help but notice how engrossed everyone else at the table seemed to have become with their food. No doubt they each fretted they'd be the next one singled out to break his or her teeth.

Next to her, Lord Tristan was dissecting a plum. Across from her, Hyacinth busied herself with cutting up an already shredded heap of chicken.

"Prendre une morsure," Louisette coaxed, her eyes wide and hopeful as she apparently anticipated Charlotte's praise.

"Go on, Charlotte," came a dark whisper from her left. "Take a bite."

She turned to see Rothbury smiling devilishly. Heat billowed up from her belly as she stared at his mouth. Images of their kiss swam into her vision. She blinked them away.

She licked her lips. He watched, licking his own. But it had to be unintentional. They were eating a late luncheon after all.

Her gaze alighted on his plate. "Where is your scone, my lord?"

His hooded eyes were still watching her mouth. "I ate it already," he said with a cold smile.

She leaned in a touch closer to him and whispered, "I don't believe you."

"You don't?" he asked, his voice a deep rumble.

"No, as a matter of fact."

"And why not?"

"Well, for one, it appears you still have all your teeth."

He sat back in his chair, a low chuckle shaking his chest as he watched her.

Grimly, she brought the thing to her mouth. There would be no way to take a polite bite. Perhaps if she had a cup of hot tea to dip it in, that would suffice, she supposed, but without it, she was simply going to have to chomp down on it. It was really just all too sad. She rather liked having all her teeth.

"She's not looking any longer, " Lord Tristan muttered from her other side. Without moving his head, he cast his azure gaze in Rothbury's grandmother's direction, then settled his attention back on his mangled plum.

She looked to him then. Really looked at him. Perhaps for the first time since he joined their party. He was a handsome man, she had always thought so. But for some reason, today his looks paled in comparison to . . . well, to Rothbury's. She didn't know why she was suddenly looking upon him differently, only that she was.

His auburn locks were clipped short, his dress impeccable as always . . .

"Hurry," he whispered, stopping her thoughts short.

Not quite believing him, she slid a side a glance down the table to see for herself. Miraculously, Louisette and Miss Drake were now talking in hushed tones. And apparently, they had forgotten about her taking a bite.

Charlotte seized upon the opportunity and tossed the scone over her shoulder. She never heard it fall, and it surely would have clunked on the floor, so it must have gone straight out the open doors. She hoped to God that it hadn't accidentally clubbed a servant.

"Thank you," she murmured to Tristan.

"You're welcome," he answered back.

Suddenly, Rothbury cleared his throat loudly, nearly making Charlotte jump. "Miss Drake," he called.

"Yes?"

"Would you mind passing down another of my grandmother's delicious scones to Miss Greene? She loved it so much, but was too shy to ask for another."

"Of course! Of course!"

Louisette beamed while Miss Drake placed another rock on a linen napkin and handed it to a servant to give to Charlotte.

Oh, that man!

Leaning back in her chair, Charlotte raised a brow, locating his leg.

He anticipated her move, however, and caught her foot before it met with his shin. Despite her anger, she shivered as his hot hand smoothed over the top of her stocking-encased foot. She thought he would simply let go, but he squeezed gently, meaningfully.

She gave a small gasp, jerking back her foot from his hold. Which was a mistake, because he held fast and her slipper dropped to the floor.

Her gaze darted to the others seated at the table.

No one seemed to notice what was happening at this end of the table.

"Dropped something, Miss Greene?" Rothbury asked.

"Um, no."

"Allow me to retrieve it for you."

But before he moved an inch, Charlotte abruptly rose from the table. "If yo–you'll all excuse me. I'd like a bit of fresh air."

Surprising her, Lord Tristan rose as well. "May I accompany you, Miss Greene? I must be on my way, and wanted to speak with you privately before I left."

She looked to her mother.

"Go on," Hyacinth said between bites of her chicken. "If you stay within sight, I should see no reason. Why not stand just across the way?" She gestured with her napkin toward a row of forget-me-nots and tulips just outside the window.

Charlotte nodded, suppressing the urge to look at Rothbury and judge his reaction. She wasn't even sure of her own reaction. She should be delighted, shouldn't she? Lord Tristan was here of his own accord and he wanted to speak with her privately. Whatever could he have to say? Had being caught in Rothbury's embrace worked that well?

But just before she turned away, she felt his warm hand heavy on her arm.

"Your slipper, Miss Greene."

Blinking down at it dumbly, she hoped no one would remark on why it had come off in the first place. She bent to sit, but Rothbury stopped her.

His hand at her heel, he gently slid it back onto her foot without taking his eyes away from her face.

"Thank you," she said, then pressed her lips together. She had to remind herself that she was mad at him. That he was angry with her.

She turned and left, Lord Tristan following her out.

Outside, the burst of sunshine made her eyes smart. She had to put a hand over her brow to shield them.

"Miss Greene?"

"Lord Tristan," she answered, not certain how she was to act, given that he so coolly had broken her heart just a few months ago.

Could she so easily forgive him?

Smiling, he walked toward her, grasping her hands within his and giving the knuckles of each a kiss in turn.

"Please," she said, pulling them from his hold.

"Too bold. I'm sorry. I did not expect to see you here," he said.

"Nor I you," she replied. "I-I mean I knew R . . . Lord Rothbury invited you to luncheon, but I had not expected you to come."

"I wanted to visit some of our old haunts," he said, his bright blue eyes nearly sparkling with an inner light. "Haven't visited Aubry Park in an age. Well, the manor house anyway. Nothing much has changed. Fishing spot still looks exactly the same."

"I see," she said all politeness.

"The maze," he lifted a sweeping hand, "is the same as well."

She nodded. "Yes, I became familiar with it as well, earlier today."

"Got lost, did you?"

"Quite."

He smiled in such a fashion that, had he not broken her heart months ago, would surely have made her sigh.

"And of course I wanted to visit the horse farm. Interested in an Arabian filly."

She nodded, plucking a purplish-blue wild-flower from the edge of the path.

He shifted his stance, looking nervous. It was so unlike him. He took off his hat and started smoothing the brim, turning the hat circularly. "And I wanted to see you."

She fought to keep her jaw from going slack. "Me?"

"Yes. The circumstance at which we parted left me no room to approach you. To explain the way of things."

Her spine straightened, determined to deliver her words with dignity. "There is nothing to explain. You told me I was a cut above the others. You told me you had always liked me. You told me I was the only genuine one of the bunch and that if you had to spend the rest of your life with any of us, it would be me." She swallowed, surprised at how calm she felt. "And then you chose someone else."

He shook his head slowly, those beautiful, beguiling blue eyes never leaving her face. "You and Harriet were the only women attending my brother's ghastly bride quest who were sincere in your regard of me. Though I believe Harriet's regard was hastily placed."

She remained motionless, her every nerve on edge for what he would say next.

"Believe what you want of me. I don't blame you at all. But I didn't want to marry. It is still my wish to remain a bachelor. And I meant everything I said to you. However, in choosing you, I knew I couldn't bring myself to break your heart. I would see that the deed was done. I would go through with the marriage, uphold my vow. But by choosing Harriet . . ."

A frown marred her brow. "Are you trying to tell me that you knew your brother was going to marry my friend, thus there would be no need for you to marry and carry on the line?"

He nodded solemnly.

"And by choosing Harriet . . ."

"And by choosing Harriet, I knew she would cry off as soon as she realized she wasn't going to be marrying the heir apparent or possibly giving birth to one eventually."

"So you picked her because you knew she'd release you?"

"Precisely."

Raising her brows, she shook her head. "I don't know what to say." Did he want forgiveness? This had all turned out very neatly for him, hadn't it?

"You don't have to say anything. I only wanted you to know that I meant what I said."

What was she to do now, she wondered? Thank him? Offer him forgiveness? Go skipping through the tulips in a burst of joy that could not be contained?

However, she was saved from making any sort of decision when everyone began descending the steps and making their way back to the carriage, the servants staying behind to straighten the mess.

"I see you are going to be off as well," he said.

She gave him a small smile. "Are you not to return to the manor along with us?"

He looked down at her, his expressive mouth curling with a rakish grin. "No, I'm off to take another gander at the filly Rothbury keeps promising will be ready for the three-year-old-filly race this summer. But I'll see you again, I'm sure. Your best friend seems to have stolen my real brother and replaced him with one who smiles, laughs, and jokes. But of course, only for her."

"Of course," she said, smiling genuinely now, thinking of how happy Madelyn and Gabriel were together.

Taking her arm, Tristan draped it over his, ushering her down the row toward the carriage.

The others were still some distance away. Rothbury, strangely, was not with them. Where had he gone?

Coming to the carriage, Tristan bent his head low. "Miss Greene," he whispered in her ear. "Regarding Lord Rothbury . . . you would be wise to remember one little thing."

"Hmm?"

"Lord Rothbury is rarely what he seems." Tipping his hat, he turned on his heel to offer a brief but charming good-bye to the others.

Charlotte didn't know what he could have meant by that, but it sounded ominous indeed.

"Did you have a nice little chat?"

Charlotte nearly jumped as Rothbury's deep, sultry tones sounded behind her.

She suddenly felt nervous, jittery. "We had a nice chat. Yes. We did." Tristan's warning rang in her ears. Just what did he mean?

The others now joined them, Miss Drake and her mother talking animatedly about a patch of haunted woods nearby. Rothbury helped the women into the carriage and then turned his amber-flecked gaze on her.

Schooling her features into a composed expression that she did not quite feel, she twirled the little flower she still held between her fingertips.

"And where did that come from?"

She looked down at the bloom she had plucked while talking to Tristan. Hmm. If she didn't know any better, she would swear his question had a definite jealous ring.

"It came from the earth," she said sweetly.

"That's not what I asked."

"Indeed. It is exactly what you asked."

His eyes changed, taking on a sudden vulnerability that stunned her.

"Did he give it to you?"

It was on the tip of her tongue to say yes, but she decided against it.

"No," she said. "I picked it myself."

He gave his tawny head a shake, the vulnerability she saw disappearing so fast, she rather thought she must have imagined it.

"You know," he remarked, his teasing lilt returning to his voice once again as he helped her into the carriage. "The lord of the manor considers flower plucking on his property to be a capital offense."

"He does, does he?" she asked, smiling. "And what is the punishment for my heinous crime?"

"Oh, I don't think you'd like my manner of chastisement at all."

"I wouldn't?"

"Not at all," he murmured, shaking his head slowly, his hooded eyes skimming ever so slowly down her body and back up again.

"Wh-Why don't you tell me?"

Barely perceptible, he moved his head, gesturing her to venture near the open door of the carriage. When she was close enough, he whispered, "First, I'd take you inside my library . . ."

"And?"

" . . . bring you over to my desk . . ."

"And?" She swallowed, held her breath.

" . . . sit you upon my lap . . . and feed you all of my grandmother's left-over scones."

She straightened, her lips twisting with playful aggravation. "Oh, Rothbury," she admonished in a whisper. "You are an awful, awful man." Laughing, she settled herself back into her seat.

Once they returned from the pavilion, the women returned to their chambers to rest and change for dinner. Charlotte busied herself by writing three letters, one to her cousin Lizzie and the other two to her friend Madelyn.

Dinner proved to be a quiet affair, as Louisette decided to forgo eating, choosing instead to stare blankly at a portrait of a horse hanging on the wall across the room until a very tired-looking Miss Drake bid Charlotte good evening, then ushered her charge up to her private chambers. Which left Charlotte quite literally alone. Her own mother had complained of an ache in her back and requested to dine in her room. She was now sleeping.

Rothbury hadn't even come to dinner.

To Charlotte's dismay, Miss Drake had explained that he was needed in the village to assist a family whose barn was in need of repair and on the verge of collapsing. He would most likely return after they had all retired. The news left Charlotte in a whirl of confusion. Just why did she feel so disappointed that he wasn't going to be able to join them?

Dear Lord. Did she miss him? How could she miss him? She had spent more time with him in the last two days than she had in the past year. What in the world was wrong with her?

Perhaps she needed to relax a bit. A book. Yes. Perhaps she would find a book to read before she retired for the evening. Indeed, it was a splendid idea.

And then perhaps she'd quit lying to herself and just admit the truth—that she was going to wait up for him in the hopes he'd kiss her again.

Lamp in hand, she moved down the hall leading from the dining room. The manor was quiet and dark. Except for the footman who had come to clear away the dinner dishes, she hadn't seen or heard another servant.

She turned the corner, spying the library door, which was open a crack. Quietly, she slipped inside. It was an odd-shaped room, quite like a giant letter *H*. Books lined the walls along the longest sides, each aisle ending with a window seat. A small fire crackled in the grate in the wide center; a deep blue settee crouched before it, a white blanket folded over the back.

Holding her lamp aloft, she perused Rothbury's stock of books. Taking her time, she read the titles, her fingertips gliding down the leather spines. Pleased to find one of her favorites, *Sense and Sensibility*, Charlotte padded over to the settee and sank onto it with a contented sigh, placing the lamp onto a nearby table.

After about an hour she became chilled and told herself that she ought to leave. Rothbury might not return until morning. But she was just so comfortable. Bringing up her legs, she covered herself with the blanket and sank further into the plush settee.

Her mind could not concentrate on the beautifully woven words of the book, for she wanted nothing more at that moment than for Rothbury to stride through the library door and kiss her senseless again.

With that thought, she snuggled into the cushions, indulging herself in her sinful daydreams.

A scarce three minutes later she was fast asleep.

* * *

There was a small bear in his library.

Returning from the village and the horse-breeding farm, Rothbury froze in the act of shrugging off his frock coat as soon as he heard something akin to a snort. *Just what exactly was that sound?*

He strained to hear. A minute ticked by on the long case clock on the landing above. Nothing.

Hmm. Well, whatever it was, he must have imagined it.

"Must be tired," he muttered, placing his coat on a chair in the hall, then adding his cravat and waistcoat to the neat pile.

He'd have a drink in his study and then head up to bed.

He froze. There it was again. Was that a snore coming from his library? Choosing to investigate, he crossed the hall, stepping inside the shadowed room.

Once his eyes adjusted to the darkness, he moved deeper inside, following the soft snoring sound. If his butler hadn't answered the door a second ago, he'd have thought Norton was sleeping in here. But if it wasn't Norton, who . . .

He smelled the lemons a second before he saw her. Curled up on his settee, an open book facedown on her chest, her glasses askew, lounged Charlotte.

His hand still on the doorknob, he pulled the door to the library shut behind him and then locked it, not wanting anyone to disturb this moment. She looked like a slumbering angel.

Crossing over to her, he gently removed the book and glasses, setting them down on a small nearby table where a long-extinguished lamp sat. He should go, his conscience shouted. This was too much of a temptation.

The floor creaked under his feet and her gentle snores ceased. He held perfectly still, relaxing only when he was sure she wouldn't waken.

Dropping to his knees before her, he reached out a hand to touch her cheek, but stopped himself before he could caress her downy skin. He pulled back as if burned. Would he dare?

Perhaps he could manage to refrain from the danger of touching her with his hands, but certainly there was no harm in raking her with his gaze.

His eyes slid over her sleeping form instead, taking in the turn of her hip, the gentle slope of her neck, the achingly luscious swell of her breasts peeking above the square neckline of her light blue dinner gown. She wore tiny pearl earrings that matched the pearl-tipped pins arranged in her hair. At once he regretted having to leave the manor today. How many other times would she be at Aubry Hall? How many other times would he be able to spend an entire day with her?

Sitting back on his haunches, he watched her sleep a few moments longer. After several moments, he moved to pull her blanket up to her chin. As he did so, the backs of his fingers brushed the tops of her hands. She was chilled.

"Blasted idiot," he muttered at himself. He'd been so engrossed with watching her sleep, he hadn't even noticed the fire had nearly gone out. Pivoting on his heels, he worked on building a fire. Soon, it roared with new life, heating the area before the hearth immediately.

"Hullo," came a husky feminine voice from behind him. She poked him in the back when he didn't immediately twist to face her.

He turned to her, his lips tight and flattened together as he struggled with the budding spark of lust that instantly ignited at the sound of her voice.

"I'm sorry. I was just so tired and this really is a cozy room." She yawned.

"You needn't apologize, Charlotte. You are welcome in any room in this house." He sighed, rubbing his temples, suddenly feeling overly tired. "I apologize for not being here for dinner. After I helped the McNeillys, I was needed at the horse-breeding farm. A mare became spooked by an overly excited stallion and injured herself.

"How is she?"

"Calm," he said, quietly. "Mended and resting." He inched closer to her, still on his knees.

"And the barn?"

"Complete."

"It was very nice of you to help them."

"It is partly my responsibility. And with Jake's son at sea, he's short a hand . . ."

"Do you know what I think?" she asked, rearranging the blanket to wear around her shoulders like a shawl.

"Not this again."

"I think there's more to you than you let people believe. I think you actually do care what people think. Oh sure, it's fun having everyone think you're dangerous and cold, but inside, where it matters, you're just warm pudding."

"Warm pudding?"

"Quite," she uttered confidently, with a firm nod.

The things that came out of that woman's mouth never failed to astound him. "Well, I'm going to . . . to leave now," he said slowly, as if he thought her the strangest creature on earth—just to tease her. When she laughed at herself, he smiled and muttered, "Good night, my sweet Charlotte." Fists on the edge of the couch, he made to push himself up.

"Wait," she said. And he froze.

Slowly, she sat up more fully, swinging her legs down. Which put her knees between his planted fists.

He couldn't help but give a low chuckle. "Charlotte, if I didn't know you better, I would venture to say that you are deliberately tempting me."

"Tempting you to what?" she asked, her tone utterly oblivious.

He had had enough. "Remember that little problem I forewarned you about? The one about a man and a woman never being able to become friends because lust gets in the way? That eventually, one or both of us would end up wanting something very intimate from the other?"

She nodded jerkily.

"Well, I'm there. I've been there. For years."

And with that wicked declaration hanging between them, he arose, then strode out the door.

Chapter 15

*A Gentleman never underestimates a
Lady, no matter her age.*

After breakfast the following day, they all
piled into the carriage and headed for the
haunted forest. Rothbury led the way on his glossy
black stallion, Petruchio. He had spoken not a
single word to her since last night in the library,
hadn't even looked at her. Conversely, Charlotte
couldn't seem to stop looking at him, studying
him as if he were some new species of animal.

She had believed for so long that he had no interest in her, that he had thought of her only as a
friend. Her world tilted.

They travelled for almost an hour, passing a
broken section of an ancient crumbling wall. Finally, they stopped near a break in the veritable

sea of pines. A path sliced between the trees, looking like it led deeply into the woods.

Alighting from the carriage, Louisette pointed to a stone bench situated next to a tumbledown building of some sort. After Charlotte helped her over to it, she shooed her away.

Stepping back, she took in the breathtaking scenery. They were in an emerald glen surrounded by a forest of tall pines. The path ahead must open to the "haunted" forest everyone kept speaking of. She thought nothing of it when Miss Drake linked arms with her mother, both of them atwitter as they clambered toward the path. She supposed if she wanted to, she could have followed behind. Perhaps she was supposed to do so, but she wasn't in the mood for scaring herself needlessly.

With nothing to do but wait for them to return, Charlotte thought to go for a little walk herself. She needed to think.

Rothbury desired her. And had for years? Somehow she couldn't quite believe it. And it seemed to make him angry. But why? And if he desired her so terribly, and had for so long, why had he not acted upon it? Why had he refrained from a seduction? It just didn't make sense.

Grabbing her skirts to keep the hem from dragging in the mud as she rounded a puddle, she wondered, why her, of all the women he had pursued, conquered, rejected? Why did he hold himself back from her?

It wasn't long before she heard footfalls. She turned to find Rothbury coming up behind her. Her heartbeat increased twofold. Wordlessly, they strolled through a field dotted with the long sprigs of cowslip and foxglove.

Rothbury was quiet, his mood contemplative. She looked at him a couple of times, but he never returned her gaze. Instead, he stared out at the flower-rich meadows toward a river that zigzagged through the grassland like a crack across a frozen pond.

"Did you fish there when you were a boy?" she asked.

He smiled tightly and nodded once. "Trout. Salmon too."

"Really?"

He nodded curtly once again.

"Did your father teach you?"

He stiffened, ever so slightly. "No. My mother. She loved to fish. Well, she didn't like baiting the hook, which is why I think she started taking me along with her in the first place, but she loved to be out here. We always had fun."

"And did your father come along as well?" she

asked tentatively, hoping she'd be able to keep prying him open, at least for a little while.

"Never. I never did those sorts of things with my father."

"What did you do with you father?"

They came to a rocky outcrop, and he took her hand to help her around it.

"Oh, the usual. He took me to my first pub and got me drunk when I was a lad of nine, stole my allowance from me under the guise of showing me how to play cards, whipped me when I tried stealing it back, tried to drown me in a thinly disguised attempt to teach me to swim, introduced me to the concept of whor—"

"Are you jesting?"

"Not at all," he said, a sad note in his voice.

Climbing the gently sloping hill now, he guided her along, her hand tucked within his.

"It sounds as if your mother was the only light in your days."

"She was," he said quietly.

"What happened?"

"She left. I was eight."

Was that who Louisette was referring to when she asked if I would leave him?

Charlotte wanted to ask more questions, she wanted to know more, she wanted to grab him to her and squeeze him tight. His voice had sounded so desolate. But she held her tongue, resisting the urge to pry further.

Suddenly he turned to her, his whiskey eyes warming her from the inside out. He might desire her and she may desire him, and that should frighten her, she knew. But what scared her more was the fact that she could feel herself slipping.

It was colder up here and Charlotte trembled.

"You're shivering," Rothbury said, grabbing both of her hands now. Cupping his large hands around hers, he brought them to his mouth and blew air, hot and welcoming, into them. "Let's return to the carriage. Your mother and Miss Drake will be returning soon, I imagine."

"Just a little longer," Charlotte murmured, casting her gaze along the wide, open, velvety expanse surrounding them. Here the grasslands seemed to go on for miles in either direction, except for the bit of dense forest behind them. It was a place she imagined one might go to clear their mind, be alone with their thoughts. Alone . . .

She spun around, looking down the hill to the stone bench where Louisette had been sitting. But she was gone.

"Rothbury! Your grandmother! Where has she gone?"

Together they raced down the hill. While Charlotte questioned the driver of the carriage, Rothbury mounted his horse in one swift motion.

"Stay here," he ordered her, pulling on the reins as the beast snorted and pranced, feeling the impatience and agitation of its rider.

And then Rothbury was off, searching for Louisette.

Charlotte went off to look for her as well. After only a short while she found her, talking to an older gentleman with a Scottish accent standing by a small footbridge. They seemed to know each other and it wasn't until Rothbury happened by that she realized that the older man was a priest. His name was Robert Armstrong and he lived in a small cottage just down the lane from the footbridge.

Rothbury was thankful that Louisette was found, but he gently admonished her about wandering away.

And then the afternoon turned for the worst.

Louisette started talking so fast, so angrily, Charlotte could not understand her, despite her knowledge of the language. Her wrinkled hands in tight fists at her sides, Louisette stamped her foot like a child, her eyes taking on a wildness that bespoke of the battle against senility Rothbury kept warning was going on in her mind.

Rothbury's patience clearly at its end, he still managed to speak quietly, gently, but his words were spoken quickly as well, rolling off his tongue. Charlotte could only pick up bits and pieces.

From what she could discern, Louisette was adamant that Charlotte and Rothbury marry. Right now. Right there.

He tried reasoning with her. He was so gentle and patient, but nothing would soothe her. In the end, Charlotte had placed her hand upon his sleeve and quietly asked him if she could speak with him privately.

"Where are we?" she asked once they had stepped away.

Rothbury worked his jaw. "I don't see how that is of any significance. I apologize for inviting you and your mother here. I should never have dragged you—"

"You did not drag me. Where are we?"

"We are near Berwick, I imagine."

"And Berwick is . . ."

"A border town," he stated, running an impatient hand through his tawny, windswept locks.

"And it's an English town?"

He blinked several times, obviously trying to

drag long-forgotten information to the forefront of his mind. "Yes, it is. Though it's changed hands with the Scots some thirteen times."

"But it's English now?"

"Quite. Since the fifteenth century, if I remember my history correctly."

"Good," she said. "Let's do it."

Clearly, she had lost her senses, but in that very moment all she wanted to do was help him. Besides, as long as they were on English soil, the marriage would not be legitimate. As it so happened in England, one needed either a special license (expensive and given by the Archbishop of Canterbury by his discretion), or the banns would have to have been read for three successive weeks in their parishes in which they belonged.

He froze. "Do what, Charlotte?"

"Get married."

"What?"

"It's not going to be legitimate, Rothbury, so you can stop looking at me like I just told you I sleep on the moon when the inclination strikes me."

"But Charlotte . . ."

"It'll be fine. No one will know. And it will not be real. Now go tell her. But not before you ask the priest if he'll play along."

Dragging a hand over his jaw, Rothbury hesitated, making Charlotte think he would refuse. But in the end he strode back to his grandmother and gave her the news.

She instantly sobered. Looking down at her hand, she pulled a ring off her finger, and thrust it at her grandson. "Take it," she said. "I do not want it back. It's hers now."

Rothbury looked down at the ring, studying it. "I've never seen this ring before," he muttered, holding it up to examine it further. "Is it new?"

Louisette beamed, saying nothing.

Tilting his head to the side, he cast his gaze on Charlotte and held out his hand. Smiling, she went to him.

Louisette beamed throughout the quick ceremony, her temper only flaring when the priest insisted they speak English, and then once again when she insisted Charlotte and Rothbury cross the footbridge to say their vows. It was a small request and they did so to mollify her, though the reason for doing so perplexed Charlotte.

At the look of confusion marring Charlotte's brow, Louisette chirped in her native tongue, "Adam's grandfather and I were married at that exact spot. I am a superstitious woman, ma belle. We had a blessed union and many happy years. I wish the same for you." Rothbury shook his head at her explanation; Charlotte pretended not to understand.

Not more than two minutes later, Charlotte and Rothbury were married.

Well, not precisely, she supposed. But vows were spoken, troths were pledged, and the ring was placed on her finger.

It all seemed so fast. And, strangely, genuine.

There had been a priest, two witnesses (Louisette and a sweet young lad who was cutting through the field with his collie) and when it was all over, she had been kissed. First by Rothbury (a quick, warm press of his lips on the apple of her cheek) and then by Louisette (roughly, and on both sides of her face).

It felt real, but empty somehow. She supposed it shouldn't matter. Officially, they were not married.

None of that seemed to matter to Louisette, who clasped Charlotte to her bosom afterward and proclaimed her to be the most beautiful bride she had ever seen.

It was all so very, very odd.

After it was done, they returned to the carriage to find her mother and Miss Drake already ensconced inside. The dowager chattered happily, telling Hyacinth of the joyous news all the way back to the manor. Her mother nodded and smiled politely, even though she didn't understand a word. They returned without further incident.

Thankfully, the damage to the Greene's carriage from the previous day had been minimal, and they could soon head back to London.

Looking down at her hand, Charlotte twisted the tiny gold ring on her littlest finger—the only finger the ring would fit—and read the inscription: VOUS ET NUL AUTRE. *You and no other.*

Rothbury insisted she keep it, then briefly pressed the back of her hand to his slightly bristled cheek. "You are a dear friend," he said. "And so kind to my grandmother. Thank you. "

"I like her. I do."

"And she likes you."

But what about you? she wanted to scream. *What is going on in that austerely handsome head of yours?* Would she ever find out?

"Are you coming to London for the Season?" she asked, leaning forward from inside the carriage in order to talk to him. "You did say you would help me find a husband."

"Didn't I?" he joked, meaning himself.

She grinned. "A real one."

"Good-bye my wife," he said, one side of his mouth lifting, a roguish gleam in his eye.

"You are coming?" she persisted. "You promised to help me." She felt suddenly desperate. Not for finding a suitor before she found herself shackled to Witherby, but for Rothbury. Desperate to know what he was thinking.

"I don't know," he said. "I was thinking of coming to Town for a slightly different reason."

"And that is . . ."

"To seduce my wife." And with that he knocked on the side of the carriage, signaling the driver to go, leaving Charlotte with a curious feeling deep in her belly, a flicker of heat.

It wasn't fear, however. It was anticipation.

Chapter 16

~~~~~⌒◯◯⌒~~~~~

*Riding, fencing, or say, throwing oneself
off a jagged cliff, are healthy ways for
a Gentleman to deal with burgeoning
frustration.*

Two days later

"**I**t wasn't I who needed to speak to you,
dear," Lady Rosalind was saying, pacifying Charlotte's bemused expression with a soft
smile. "My brother claimed the need to impart
some sort of information. He couldn't call upon
you next door without raising suspicion, so he
asked that I send a note, requesting your presence
in our drawing room instead."

"I see," Charlotte murmured, sitting straighter
as Tristan turned his azure gaze upon her.

Grabbing her embroidery, Lady Rosalind lifted her chin. "So now I shall turn my attention to my needlework and pretend not to listen to a word either of you say."

"Thank you, sister," Tristan bit out, not sounding appreciative at all.

"No need to thank me. That's what sisters are for."

His eyes narrowed. "To henpeck and annoy . . ."

Lady Rosalind clucked her tongue. "We have a guest. A lovely guest, I might add. I heard you were recently at Aubry Hall, Miss Greene. Did you enjoy your stay?"

"Very much," Charlotte said, noting that Tristan was now grasping the arms of the leather chair he sat in as if growing vastly impatient at his sister's attempt at conversation. "We've only just returned yesterday," she added.

"Really? How were the roads—"

Tristan cleared his throat loudly, gesturing to the clock on the mantel with his chin.

Ignoring him, Rosalind continued, "Miss Greene, I hope you do not mind my saying so, but you seem to grow more pretty each Season."

"Me? Tha—"

"May I get to my point?" Tristan interrupted.

Lady Rosalind narrowed her eyes on her

younger brother, sticking her needle in the tightly bound fabric quite like she envisioned she stabbed him with it. "And *you* get more obstinate and rude each Season."

"I wouldn't want to disappoint you."

Returning her attention back to her embroidery, Lady Rosalind harrumphed, a dimple creasing in her cheek as she tried to hide a sisterly smirk with a grin.

Tristan sat forward. "Miss Greene, you are no doubt wondering why I needed to speak with you."

She nodded, casting a look at the doorway leading into the hall. She was eager to find out why she was here—so she could leave. Rothbury was to accompany her and her mother on a shopping trip this afternoon.

"You seem anxious, Miss Greene," Tristan asked. "I hope I'm not keeping you from something. Or someone."

"Not at all," she assured him, as she didn't want to be rude. "It's just that . . . Roth . . . I mean Lord Rothbury is calling today and I—"

"Lord Rothbury? Calling at your home?"

"Yes."

"Interesting. Well, I should get on with my point, then. I wanted to ask you, are you attending the Langley Ball this evening?"

Why in the world did he care? "Why, yes. Yes, I am."

"Good. Good." He cleared his throat again, throwing his sister a beseeching glance, which she ignored. "May I request a dance. Now."

"Right now?"

"For the ball."

Her brow quirked. "I suppose."

"Good," he replied. "I shall anticipate it until then." He glanced pointedly at the porcelain clock on the mantel again.

Was that her hint to leave? "Well . . . if that is all?" This was all so strange.

"Yes, indeed," he nearly shouted, sounding overly glad. "That's all."

Charlotte stood, as did Lady Rosalind.

Tristan just sat there. His sister widened her eyes meaningfully.

"Oh, right! Yes." He practically jumped up. "Well, may I walk you out? I mean, I'll walk you out."

She shook her head. "There is no need, I assure you."

"I insist." He motioned for the women to precede him out of the room.

Their butler opened the door, revealing a bustling street scene. Ladies walking in pairs, parasols clutched in their hands, shiny carriages rumbling down the lane . . . and Lord Rothbury standing at the edge of the Devine's walk.

Before Charlotte could utter a syllable, Tristan picked up her gloved hand and kissed her lightly on the knuckles.

"Good day, Charlotte," he said.

"Good day," she answered. She turned to bid farewell to Lady Rosalind, but she seemed to have disappeared.

Numbly, she descended the front steps toward a waiting Rothbury, who only had eyes for the Devines' front door, looking quite like he wanted to murder someone.

"Perfection, dear brother," Rosalind proclaimed, while peeking out the little window next to the door. "Utter perfection."

Slipping a finger inside his cravat to loosen it a bit, Tristan craned his neck from side to side, easing the building tension. "If he kills me, I'll see to it that you get hanged for murder as well."

"Pfft. How would you? You'd be dead."

"That's true enough, I suppose." He bent down to take a look out the window himself. "Rosie, why do you insist on playing matchmaker?"

She straightened. "Because I'm so good at it."

"So humble."

"Well, I was right about Gabriel and Maddie. I knew within seconds they needed to be together."

"And Charlotte and Rothbury?"

"Do you not pay attention at all when you attend balls? Do you not see the yearning glances of a man in love?"

He burst into a grin. "No. I can safely say that I do not notice yearning glances of men in love."

She waved away his teasing. "I think the wicked earl would have married her a long time ago if it wasn't for one thing."

"And that is . . . ?"

"If the woman he loved didn't fancy herself in love with you."

There was nothing quite like a London Season.

For a woman and her milliner that is.

And her dressmaker, and the person who designs her shoes, and the . . . ah, hell, and whoever else was responsible for making all the other things scattered all over the Greenes' morning room; evidence of their recent return from a shopping trip.

It was stunning, actually.

Bonnets, gloves, gowns, shawls, hair combs,

shoes, boots, coats, stockings . . . it gave him a blasted headache.

Up until now, Rothbury had no idea of the amount of clothing a young woman could possibly need for such a short period of the year. Three, four months, tops. Yet, as he surveyed the rather staggering wealth of fripperies draped over every available inch of the room—and himself, he thought grumpily as he lifted a lacey thing from his knee, examined it, deemed it a glove and tossed it to the floor—he came to the conclusion that there was enough material in this room to outfit an entire naval squadron in His Majesty's royal navy for a year. Should they wear such feminine attire, that is.

If he hadn't been an only child, if perhaps had he a sister, then maybe he could grasp the concept of just all that was involved with making a young woman presentable among her peers.

Well, he thought glumly, while he was here, he'd offer advice, gladly tell Charlotte what color suited her best, what gown complemented her pleasing frame, what bonnet brought out the utter beauty of her eyes. But he absolutely drew the line at holding up a gown under his chin simply because Charlotte had to use the powder room and Mrs. Greene couldn't wait for her daughter to come out to see if her new Spanish blue muslin would make her hair look even more flaxen than it already was.

"But, my lord, your hair is nearly the same color," Hyacinth said, looking at him hopefully.

"I refuse," he muttered, as gently as possible.

He liked Hyacinth. He liked her a lot. And he regretted that her acceptance of him into the sanctuary of her household was based on an untruth, for if the truth should come out and she should despise him, he would truly miss her motherly doting. It was something he never had. Or had once, but only briefly.

After their visit at Aubry Park, Rothbury told himself that it was better for all involved if he stayed away. He didn't trust himself around Charlotte any longer; his restraint had slipped and he knew it would do so again. Only, he couldn't stay away. It had lasted all of half a day.

So it had come to this, this compromise within his own mind. He forced himself to believe that it was enough, simply enough, just to be her friend. To come to dinner on occasion, perhaps to play whist with her and her family every now and then, to grit his teeth as a wave of longing swept through him when Charlotte stood too near. But then he had seen her at the threshold of the town house Tristan resided in with his sister. He had kissed Charlotte's hand. And she looked . . . bewildered. Damn. She was probably in raptures.

He shifted in his seat, bringing in his long legs so as not to trip any of the maids bustling about the room as they worked to take some of the boxes upstairs.

Taking a deep breath, he balanced the ankle of one leg on the knee of the other and asked himself what the hell he was doing here today. Why wasn't he at his club or at Jackson's Rooms, using his fists to clear his head? Why wasn't he drinking himself into oblivion at some bachelor's private house party with some nameless, faceless trollop perched on his lap, instead of this wide-brimmed bonnet, adorned with a hideous big red poppy?

"Rothbury," Charlotte called as she waltzed back into the room, tapping him lightly on the knee with her pointing finger as she passed.

Oh, yes, he suddenly remembered. She's why.

Abruptly, she snatched the bonnet off his lap, making him jerk in reaction.

"You never answered me. Are you coming to the Langleys' soiree this evening?"

His eyes dipped down, skimming her bodice, the gentle swell of her bosom, and down further to her narrow hips and firm little bottom. Well, he couldn't really *see* how firm her bottom was through the fabric of her dress, but he remembered. Sweet Lord, he could almost still feel her in his arms . . . could almost taste her . . .

"Hasn't this been the most fun day?" Hyacinth suddenly proclaimed, an armful of frocks nearly blocking her face as she passed them to a maid. "How I miss being a young girl and having my brother help me pick out which gown to wear. And he was so good at it too."

Rothbury couldn't help but smile. After explaining to Charlotte the dangers of her mother's potential budding addiction to laudanum, he had pored over the few medicinal volumes in his library at his town house and finally found an alternative. It seemed that soaking raisins in—of all things—gin, and having her partake of eight of them each day, gave Hyacinth some relief. She was still quite stiff in the joints at times, but she was much more alert and awake than she had been in a long while.

"I shall have to send him a letter," Hyacinth continued, "and tell him what a good friend my daughter has found in you."

Rothbury looked up, his gaze meeting Charlotte's, soft and full of tenderness. Surely, he was mistaken.

"Are you coming?" she asked. "I heard at least three of your friends will be in attendance. Ravensdale, Cantrell . . . Holt too. And of course, Lord Tristan will be there as well. You could dance with me . . ."

He stood abruptly and growled, "I'm going home."

She blinked at his abruptness. "I'll walk you out," she said, watching him closely.

He suddenly felt very uncomfortable, quite like she could see through him and read his thoughts. Preposterous.

"There's no need," he returned mildly. "I know my way out."

He had said he was going to seduce her once they returned to London. Truly, that was all he had thought about since. But then he realized he wouldn't be satisfied. He was a selfish bastard. Hell, of course he wanted to claim her, to make her his own; his blood boiled for her, but he wanted her heart as well. Maybe even more.

Grabbing his coat from the back of the settee, he bid farewell to Hyacinth and walked out into the hall. Charlotte followed him.

"Wait," she cried out.

At the door, he turned, shrugging on his coat. Striding toward him, she reached out. Slipping her fingers in his coat, she brushed his collarbone and smoothed her way to his shoulder.

What the devil?

Her fumbling fingers nearly made him groan. A second later, she pulled out one of her stockings from the inside of his coat. The damned thing must have been lying on his coat when he picked it up. The back of the settee did look quite like an avalanche of clothes.

She smiled. "You certainly don't want to go home with this, do you?"

Well, actually . . . "Of course not." He smiled tightly.

"You've been in such a mood lately," she said with concern. She smoothed out the collar of his coat. "I have been remiss in my duties of helping you win your Lady Rosalind, haven't I?"

Rothbury merely grumbled, plunked his top hat upon his head, tipped it to her, and then left without saying another word.

He couldn't remember ever going this long without a woman before.

Striding down the street, Rothbury contemplated this while paying no heed to the sudden, thin drizzle that was slowly soaking him. Purposely, he had decided not to bring his carriage or his horse when he visited today, thinking the chilled walk to and from their town house might do well to discourage his burgeoning desire.

He walked quickly, his footsteps sure and determined, making short work of the pavement. Sooner than he thought, he arrived at his residence just around the corner.

As he stomped up the steps to his town house, the door flew open just as he would have walked through it. He shrugged off his sodden coat, told the butler he was not to be disturbed and strode directly to the brandy decanter in his study.

A small fire smoldered in the grate. He closed his eyes to it as he leaned back his head, downing a snifter of brandy in one gulp. He was so damn tense. He was getting bloody tired of being in a perpetual state of half arousal.

"Your lordship," came Summers' somber tones from the doorway a short while later.

Rothbury turned. "Yes?"

"You have a caller, sir."

"I do?"

"A lady, sir."

Charlotte, Rothbury thought with a sigh. Honestly, as much as he loved her, he did not want to see her right now. Not when they would be quite alone and she quite without a chaperone. He sighed. It sounded like a growl. Well, at least she was using his front door now.

"Show her in, Summers."

"Very well, sir."

Collapsing into his leather chair behind his desk, he resigned himself to the fact that he was indeed a cursed man.

A cloaked female slid into the room.

Confusion marred his brow before recognition dawned.

Lady Gilton, long-legged, raven-haired, and—she hesitated, opened and dropped her coat to the floor—completely naked.

"Miss me?" she purred, not a flicker of concern in her eyes that the door was still open behind her. She lifted her shoulders with a heavy sigh, causing her ample breasts to bounce. "I miss you."

He said nothing, his eyes dragging up and down her body. Yes, he was cursed.

"There are a lot of us who miss you. Me especially. Ever since you started paying attention to that mouse, you haven't paid any attention to me."

She placed her hands on her hips, then slowly sculpted them over her ribs and up further still to cup her breasts, holding them high in a gesture of offering.

"It's cold in here," she said in a husky voice. "Come and warm me like you used to."

Pushing away from his desk, Rothbury stood, took a deep breath, then crossed the room with slow, steady steps. He stopped directly in front of Cordelia.

Within reach, she clasped his hand in hers and brought it to her stomach. "Touch me," she begged.

But instead of his hand being poised to offer a caress, his fingers curled into a claw. Bending down, he picked up her coat, and whipped it around her shoulders.

"Go home," he said, coldly. "I am done. I no longer wish to live the life of my father, of my uncles. I am not them. I never was."

Cordelia's laughter held disbelief. "What are you talking about?"

"Leave."

"Oh no," she muttered, shaking her head. "No. No. No. You are not doing this to me again."

"Yes. I am. Now go."

"You cannot be serious!" she cried in disbelief as he guided her down the hall toward the front door.

"I am."

Summers stood there waiting. He opened the door as they neared.

"No. You cannot possibly be attracted to that odd creature? Witherby's to have her, everyone knows."

His jaw hardened, but he did not say a word.

"I cannot believe it," she cried, her voice shrill. "You are choosing *her* over *me*?"

"Believe it," he said, ushering her out the door. "You'll be a lot happier."

She spun to face him, her face—a countenance that at one time seemed exotic and beautiful—contorted with her jealousy, her hatred. Her mouth opened to spew more scathing words, but he did not hear them, for he slammed the door in her face.

Her frustrated scream sounded muffled through the door.

"Summers."

"Yes, my lord?"

"I will not be accepting any more female callers, unless of course, it is Miss Greene."

"I understand, my lord."

Rothbury turned on his heel, disgusted with what had just happened, but before he could return to his study, his butler spoke, stalling his strides.

"There was a missive delivered while you were . . . occupied with your caller, sir."

"Just put it on the salver near the door. I'll look at it tomorrow."

"Beg my pardon sir, but the young lad who delivered it said you must read it straight away."

Rothbury sighed, taking the letter from the servant. Striding into his office, he broke the seal with his opener and held it up to the waning firelight.

Dear sir,

I'm writing to inform you of a situation that occurred during your recent visit to Northumberland. The wedding that took place, though you and your lady believed it to be a forgery, was in fact genuine and binding. Once you crossed the bridge, you were on Scottish soil, the village Dirleton, the place of my birth and where I have lived all my life.

By Scottish law, you have been well and truly joined in a most blessed union. As much as I would like to say that it was accidental, your grandmother orchestrated the entire ordeal, purchasing the ring from my brother, a blacksmith up the road. She begged me not to disclose her trick, but I could not, as a Christian man, continue to withhold such information. I've enclosed the marriage certificate.

May God bless your union and the years ahead bring you both joy.

Regards,
Father Robert Armstrong

Dear God, what had his grandmother done?

Belatedly, Rothbury realized his hands were shaking. Wordlessly, he dropped into his chair.

He wasn't going to tell her. It would be his secret and his secret alone. He'd take it with him to the grave. He . . . he was only fooling himself.

He must tell her. Scoundrel that he was, he loved her. And it was the right thing to do.

What would Charlotte's reaction be? And how would he tell her? *When* would he tell her?

Now, he must tell her now.

His head jerked toward the mantel clock. Half past nine. She was most likely just now arriving at the Langleys' soiree. Smiling and dancing and flirting with his friends in the hopes one of them might be obliged to court her.

He had to tell her and soon. She was going to hate him, of that he was certain, it irrevocably took away any hope for her winning Tristan. That chapter of her life was done.

"Summers!"

His butler rounded inside the doorway from

the hall, making Rothbury suspect the man was hoping to find out what urgent message the letter contained.

"Send orders to have my valet set out my evening clothes posthaste and have my coach brought around. I'm off to fetch my wife."

Chapter 17

A Gentleman is in control of his temper
at all times.

It occurred to Charlotte, as she weaved within the steps of a lengthy quadrille along with her dance partner, that she should rather enjoy throttling Rothbury.

For the past two weeks, maybe longer, she suspected he harbored a secret affection for her. Maybe it wasn't quite love, but she was fairly certain it was more than friendship.

But whatever his feelings were, he was holding them back. Just as he held everything back. If he wanted her, he was going to have to reach for her. And she refused to make it easy for him. If he wanted her, he was just going to have to come and claim her.

And she would do whatever she needed to do to draw out his true feelings. It wouldn't be pretty and she might lose some sense of herself in the process, but she was ready.

Any lingering doubts evaporated when she spotted him clutching the balustrade of the gallery overlooking the ballroom. Out of the corner of her eye she noted how his predatory gaze skimmed the crowd, searching. Presumably for her.

When she felt his gaze upon her, warming her from the inside out, she lightened her steps, smiled wider at her dance partner, and laughed louder at his rather dull quips.

And when the dance had ended and she would have normally settled herself next to her mother, she instead walked across the ballroom, head held high as she relished the feel of his eyes following her every move.

She felt different tonight. Instead of pulling inward when she entered a room, she was expanding.

She had once thought that being shy and quiet allowed her to observe so much of other people's behaviors, little things that others would hardly notice—the slight change in tone of one's voice when one's feelings were hurt, the rush of excited breath when a young man asked a pretty young lady to dance, her heavily disguised disappointment when she was hoping his friend would have asked her instead. Things that wouldn't cause most other people to raise a brow.

However, she had come to find this evening that there was quite a lot to be missed when one's head was firmly buried in one's chest. For tonight she held her head high. And tonight *she* was getting noticed instead of being the one who noticed everything about everyone else.

Her newfound posture had attracted a Mr. Holt. A widower, he was in his mid-thirties, had thick russet hair and a rather pleasing smile. He was also one of Rothbury's friends and the man she had just finished dancing with.

She stood next to the refreshment table now, Mr. Holt having just kissed her knuckles and bid her good eve, when Lord Tristan appeared by her side.

"I say, Miss Greene," he said as he approached. "It is so nice to see you once again."

She inclined her head. "My lord."

"May I inquire if you have saved a waltz for me this evening?"

A surge of heat inflamed her cheeks. She had forgotten all about their strange visit earlier that afternoon. "I'm terribly sorry. I had forgotten and my dance card is full."

He looked . . . relieved. "Perhaps, then," he drawled, "I could bring you a glass of punch?"

Good. Punch was good. Well, Langley punch was in actuality a tepid, watered-down concoction made with questionable wine, but having Lord Tristan bring her a drink was a fabulous idea. She hoped Rothbury was watching.

"Of course," she answered. "After that last dance, I find I'm rather parched." Though honestly, she rather thought if she was stuck on an island with nothing to drink but Langley punch, she'd rather drink seawater and die.

Lord Tristan smiled, the brackets around his mouth the perfect frame for his sculpted lips. "Wonderful. I shall return."

"And I shall await you," she said, grinning.

A dead man just handed his wife a glass of punch.

Pushing off from the balustrade, Rothbury descended the stairs, his eyes still settled on Charlotte and Tristan.

The crowd seemed to part before him as he stalked across the room.

Upon reaching her, he stilled, bewildered by her beauty.

She wore a light blue gown with short cap sleeves and a plunging bodice; a band of lace stretched across the top was meant to disguise her bosom, but only served to tease him.

Another narrow band of lace was wrapped around her delicate throat, and her golden locks had been swept up neatly. Tiny pearls had been tucked here and there within the curls piled atop her head. She looked elegant and refined and . . . and all he wanted to do was strip her naked and lick her from top to bottom.

Remembering Tristan, he turned his gaze on him.

"Rothbury," Tristan said in greeting.

Rothbury only offered him a scowl. He turned his attention back to Charlotte.

"I need to speak with you," he growled.

"It will have to wait," she said, throwing a pointed look at Lord Tristan. "Cannot you see that his lordship was kind enough to bring me a glass of punch?"

Rothbury plucked it out of her hand, turned to a nearby potted fern and poured it in the dirt. "You can thank me later."

Charlotte gasped. "You are being exceptionally rude," she whispered.

"I don't give a damn," he muttered.

Out of the corner of his eye, Rothbury watched with satisfaction as Tristan's complexion turned a touch pale and he started to sweat. "Er . . . I just remembered, Miss Greene, that I have asked . . . that I have asked Miss Langley to dance . . . I think. Good day." And then he practically ran away.

Charlotte's gaze narrowed on Rothbury. "I don't know what's come over you."

"We need to talk now, Charlotte."

She started to protest, but clamped her lips shut upon seeing the ferocious look in his eyes.

"On the terrace. I'll go first. "

"Oh, very well. But how am I to find you?"

"I'll be waiting."

"Yes, but . . ."

He turned and headed toward the terrace doors, his long, purposeful strides so powerful, she was surprised the guests in his path had time to move before he plowed through them.

She waited several moments, growing uncomfortable because a country dance was to start within the next twenty minutes and she might miss it. Someone would come looking for her, and should they find her on the terrace, alone with

Rothbury, her reputation could be ruined. Good Lord, what if her mother found out and insisted they marry?

As was her old habit, Charlotte moved across the room by way of the walls. No one seemed to notice her as she slipped out the French doors, into the cool, black night.

A couple stood at the baluster, overlooking the garden, whispering and laughing. Shyly, Charlotte passed them and descended the steps into the deep shadow at the base. She had no idea where Rothbury was, if even he was out here.

Her eyes tried to adjust to the darkness, but she could barely see her hand in front of her face. Just when she was about to rush back up the steps, a large, warm hand settled at her waist. She turned, giving a jolted whimper as Rothbury's lips settled atop hers.

His mouth was hot, ravenous, intoxicating. She had no idea where his gloves had gone, but his hands were bare, sliding up and down her back, cupping her backside and holding her tightly to him.

Charlotte groaned at his glorious siege of her senses. She wanted to touch him as well, only it took extreme concentration to do something as little as raise her arms. Gliding her hands up his strong arms and then his neck, she sunk her fingers into his thick hair at his nape, pressing herself closer to him, needing him to touch her more.

He spun her around, pushing her back against the stone wall of the terrace. With a finger at her bottom lip, he easily coaxed her open, sinking his tongue inside to mate with hers. Surely, her bones were melting.

One of his strong hands molded around her hip, travelled up her rib cage and settled on her breast. She moaned into his mouth as his thumb plucked at her nipple through her dress. Impatient for more of his touch, she rose up on her toes, lifting her hips. She shuddered with pleasure upon feeling his arousal press against her belly.

Softly, now, as if he was reigning himself in, he trailed kisses along her neck, causing shivers to shimmer all over her skin. His movement slowed, little by little until it became apparent that he was stopping.

She squeezed his shoulders. "What are you doing?" she asked breathlessly.

"Charlotte, I'll not take you against the wall."

Why not? she wanted to scream.

She must gather her wits. He was right. They were in a garden, for heaven's sake. Anyone could happen by.

Placing her hands upon his chest, she gave him a little push. He didn't move.

"Today, when I saw you leaving Tristan and Rosalind's residence. . . Why were you there?"

He was rubbing her neck and shoulders. It felt glorious, but she had a hard time concentrating.

"He wanted to ask for a dance."

She couldn't see his face, but could tell somehow that he was scowling again. "Well, he's not getting one."

"Is that what you had to talk to me about?"

"No. It's something entirely more important."

Music poured from the French doors. The next dance had begun. If she didn't return to the ballroom, someone, either her mother or her dance partner, would soon be looking for her.

"It will have to wait. For the first time in the history of my life, my dance card is actually full! Can you believe it?"

"It cannot wait."

"Do you know . . . five men have already asked to call on me tomorrow?"

Rothbury looked to his feet, suddenly weary. He must tell her and it wasn't going to be easy. And her utter happiness garnered by the attention of other men, Lord Tristan especially, meant she wasn't going to be terribly delighted about it either.

He supposed he ought to let her enjoy her night. Let her bask in her well-deserved attention. She looked absolutely stunning this evening, and there was something else as well.

She moved differently now. Instead of hesitant steps, clinging to the walls, and downcast eyes, she possessed an air of subtle confidence. As if she had finally embraced her beauty instead of trying to arm wrestle it into mousy submission.

And by the looks of things, he wasn't the only male who had noticed.

"How many?" he asked, grimly.

"How many what?"

"How many more dances?"

She thought for a moment. "Four."

He dragged a hand over his jaw. "Christ, that could take all night."

She stepped into a strip of light shining from the ballroom. Just as she had so many times before, she looked at him in that assessing manner of hers, quite like she was trying to pinpoint one of his thoughts and read it aloud. "I guess I could claim a headache."

"No," he said, now resigned to his decision. "I'll wait. Enjoy yourself."

For it would be the last time he allowed any other man to touch her.

* * *

Four hours later, Rothbury thought he just might be in danger of losing his mind.

His mother was right. He was truly wicked. And he was paying for all his past transgressions by having to watch other men flirt with his wife.

For four hours.

However, he behaved. His hands remained at his sides, though balled into tight fists, and he even managed to smile. Once. And it was at Charlotte's mother.

Or more precisely, his shiny new mother-in-law.

Hyacinth had approached him to ask if he would mind taking Charlotte home. The hour was late and she was tired. He was surprised by her suggestion, but agreed very readily. Having her in a carriage alone should allot him ample time to tell her the news.

"Be discreet," Hyacinth had whispered. "No one must know."

He nodded, feeling a stab of guilt.

"She's having such a fine time. I've never seen her so happy, and I would hate to shorten her evening on account of my stiff knees and back."

Pain sliced through his chest. Charlotte may be happy, but he was about to squash it.

But perhaps not. Perhaps there was something he could do about it. Petition the Church of Scotland for an annulment. Truth be told, other than claiming they were brother and sister, he couldn't think of another way out of this predicament.

Unless of course Charlotte could convince the courts that he was unable to perform his husbandly duties. But who the hell would believe that?

And then of course, there was fraud.

Fifteen minutes later, Charlotte found herself ensconced inside Rothbury's elegant carriage.

Despite having had a wonderful evening—she had never danced so much in her life—a sudden anxiousness took over her senses. Her heart was racing, her limbs felt shaky, and her breaths were coming all too quickly.

She supposed it had nothing to do with the state of her health and everything to do with the clearly tense, devastatingly handsome man seated across from her, who, for whatever reason, found it perfectly acceptable to look at her as if he wanted to gobble her up.

Faint, gold bristles on his chin and jaw glistened every so often in the moonlight. He looked . . . a little tired, his eyes hooded as he watched her study him. A silky lock of hair hung down, partially covering one eye, just barely dusting the crest of his angular cheekbone. His golden locks appeared almost brown in the shadows, the wavy ends resting on his shoulders. His cravat was loosened, but the rest of his evening attire was impeccable.

She didn't think she'd ever get used to being in a closed carriage with the man. He was so long, his legs seemed to take up all the room on the floor. And if he brought in his legs to afford her more room, there was no way he could be comfortable. So, she scrunched her own legs and skirts off to the side, practically pressing against the door in order to accommodate his size.

She folded her hands upon her lap, forcing herself to appear calm. "So . . . my mother asked you to take me home, did she?"

He gave her one nod of his head.

"And your . . . your driver . . . I couldn't help but hear . . . You asked him to circle thrice before taking me home."

"Indeed."

"What for?"

"To make sure no one sees you exit my carriage without the benefit of a chaperone."

"Ah, well, that makes sense." Her voice sounded a bit shrill to her own ears, so she took a deep breath, hoping it would help calm her.

Shame flooded through her, making her cheeks feel as if they were aflame. Trouble was, despite having a grand time at the Langley soiree, she was most excited this evening by having Rothbury take her home.

She had practically begged her mother to ask him to. Hyacinth had hesitated. Though her mother still believed Rothbury was like Uncle Herbert, society did not. And she certainly couldn't be seen climbing into his carriage and not have her reputation utterly ruined in one fell swoop.

But Hyacinth had relented and Charlotte had inwardly rejoiced. For she had a plan of her own this evening, and that plan included kissing Rothbury again—and letting him stop.

Just how she was going to go about it, she didn't know, but she was confident that the situation would present itself on its own.

Delicately, she cleared her throat before saying, "You had said earlier that we needed to talk?"

Another nod.

"Well, what did we need to talk about?"

"This," he said, handing her a slightly wrinkled letter.

Unfolding it, she held it toward the window to make use of the moonlight. "What is it?"

"Read it."

Straightening the spectacles on her nose, her eyes skimmed the page, quickly at first, then stopping abruptly at the words "genuine and binding."

She looked up at him in alarm. "Rothbury, what *is* this?"

"Please," he said calmly. "Read on."

Over and over she read the letter, each time thinking she had missed something. It was a joke. It had to be a joke.

"Rothbury . . . this isn't true, is it?"

He closed his eyes on a slow blink. "I'm afraid it is legitimate."

Afraid, he said. So he was not happy about this outcome at all. "But . . . I don't understand. When did you receive this?"

"This evening."

"So I am . . . we are . . . we could . . ."

"Yes. Yes. And, I'm not certain exactly what you mean by 'we could,' but I'm willing to accommodate you."

"This is . . ." Her mind scrambled to grasp what had happened. "This is . . . a lot to take in. Does anyone else know?"

"Not yet, I imagine, but they will."

"But what are we to do?"

She watched as his throat convulsed when he swallowed heavily. "I've contacted my solicitor and he believes it is indeed a binding marriage. We could always petition the Church of Scotland for an annulment."

She looked down at the letter. That was not what she had been expecting him to say. Here she had thought, had hoped really, that what he had to tell her was an admission of love, or at least some sort of budding affection stemming from their deep-rooted friendship. But not only did he give her the shock of her life by telling her that they were truly married, he also had been, obviously, thinking of ways to get out of it. He contacted his solicitor, for goodness sake!

Which meant she had been wrong. Completely wrong. He wasn't hiding any secret feelings from her. All those looks he gave her . . . They meant nothing. How could she have let herself fall for the practiced charm of another scoundrel? She had fooled herself into believing there was more to their relationship than there truly was.

As she brought up her hands to rub her temples, the letter drifted to the floor.

Lifting her head, she looked at him, surprised

to see an odd mix of emotions glimmering in his amber-flecked gaze. But she dared not name them, not even to herself, for she could never trust that she was right.

She had thought by the end of the night she would have figured him out. And here she found herself more confused than ever.

"What would you like to do, Charlotte?" he asked, his voice a sultry whisper.

"Honestly, right now I would like for you to answer two questions."

He settled deeper into the squabs, sliding his booted feet forward. His knees now brushed hers.

"You've been so grumpy lately. Is . . . is it because you wanted another? I do realize I have been remiss in helping you win Rosalind, but now—"

"Charlotte," Rothbury drawled, shaking his head slowly. "I don't want her."

Her brow furrowed. "You don't?"

He shook his head again, his tongue darting out to moisten his sculpted bottom lip.

She swallowed hard, aware of a low heat building in her belly.

"Since when?" she asked, not sure if she should believe him or not.

"Since the beginning. Since before the beginning."

"But what of Madelyn? You had asked my friend to marry you once before."

"Charlotte, I have only ever wanted you."

Her breath whooshed out of her at his admission, but she tread carefully, not allowing it to go to her head. "Well, I suppose that brings me quite neatly to my second question."

"Yes," he coaxed, grinning like a devil in the dark.

Could he read her thoughts?

"Would you please kiss me again?"

Chapter 18

> *A Gentleman respects a Lady's*
> *reputation and would never, under any*
> *circumstance, encourage her to succumb*
> *to passion.*

Charlotte waited patiently. And then waited some more.

"Would you kiss me again?"

The first time she asked, he merely blinked at her in such fashion that she began to think he hadn't heard her. Or . . . hadn't he said that he was having his solicitor look into the validity of their marriage a minute ago?

Embarrassment prickled her cheeks. Perhaps he *had* heard her the first time. He just didn't *want* to kiss her.

But all such misgiving flew out of her head,

when he reached across the carriage, grabbed her by the hips and hauled her atop his lap.

"I believe I can accommodate your request," he whispered, his lips slowly descending to hers.

"Oh thank you," she whispered back, now into his partially opened mouth. "You are most obliging."

"You're very welcome."

And then his mouth brushed against hers, gently at first, their breath mingling. His lips were firm but soft and they moved upon hers with deliberate slowness.

The carriage rocked suddenly.

"First turn," he muttered between kisses.

"Hmm?"

He broke the kiss. With his finger he traced her bottom lip. "Two more and my driver will arrive at your town house," he drawled, his gaze steady on her mouth.

That's right. He had told the driver to circle three times. Which meant that they still had a little time. Perhaps enough for another kiss.

She opened her mouth a bit, her tongue darting out to shyly touch his finger.

"Take the tip into your mouth."

She did, suckling softly.

His sharp intake of breath told her that he liked what she did.

He trailed the moist tip of his finger down her chin, applying gentle pressure. And then his mouth swooped over hers, grazing gently at first and then increasing in intensity.

She moaned, running her hands over his jacket, then under his jacket. His lips moved hungrily over hers, stirring a hidden desire to the surface.

Though it was she who sat atop his hard thighs, she felt surrounded by his heat. One of his hands slid up her back to cradle her head as he continued to devour her mouth, while the other smoothed over the curve of her back, down to her bottom.

His tongue swept inside her mouth and she welcomed him, bravely mimicking his actions, though he was clearly more dominant, more demanding.

With a little coaxing and the pulling of much material, he soon had her straddling him, her skirts rucked up to her waist. Her stocking-clad thighs slipped softly against the material of his breeches. She moved restlessly against him, a need to touch skin to skin nearly overwhelming her.

She pulled impatiently at his jacket.

Without breaking their kiss, he nearly tore it off to oblige her. She ran her fingers over the hard plane of his chest, wishing he were free of his shirt.

She moaned into his mouth, asking for more, asking for something . . .

The hand at the back of her head curved around the column of her throat, shoulder, then started tugging at her bodice. His hot mouth pressed a trail of kisses down, down, then stopped to playfully nip at the side of her neck.

She shivered, her head dropping back.

And then he tugged her bodice down, her breasts spilling free, bobbing from the motion of the carriage.

He stared down at her momentarily. "You're beautiful, Charlotte," he said, his breath caressing one hardened tip.

Threading her fingers through the back of his hair, she pulled him forward.

Rothbury seemed all too happy to answer her silent plea.

He worshipped her breasts, licking, and sucking, brushing her aching nipples over his firm lips, flicking them with his tongue.

Glorious sensations spiked downward, connecting what he was doing to the exact spot where moisture gathered between her thighs.

He suckled at one breast while twirling the nipple of the other between his thumb and index finger. She cried out, and started to rock against him.

He grabbed her ankle with his other hand and then slid his palm slowly up and around her calf, knee, and over her garters to squeeze her thigh, his deft fingers massaging ever closer to her damp center.

The carriage lurched to the side once again. Second turn.

Charlotte gave a small whimper of disappointment as his other hand left her breast. A second later her entire body rejoiced as he cupped her hip and bottom, rolling her into his arousal, the rocking of the carriage helping them along.

A throbbing ache started to grow in her womb. She wanted more, wanted something . . .

"Rothbury, please," she begged. "Please."

And then his fingers were there, delving inside, spreading her moisture up and down and around her opening. Her hips circled and dipped along with his movements. She moaned, saying his name. He groaned, panting along with her. Expertly, he handled her. Rhythmically, sweetly, he tortured her.

"Open my trousers," he breathed.

She complied.

Soon he was freed, his hardness jutting upward, seeking her heat.

"Look at me," he bit out through his teeth.

As if through a haze, she met his heated, intense gaze.

"This is the only time in my life I will ever hurt you."

Her brow scrunched and it was on the tip of her tongue to ask him just what exactly he meant, when the tip of his manhood pulsed at the opening of her center.

"Hold on," he said, his voice strained.

Charlotte gripped his shoulders. Rothbury gripped her hips. Lifting her, he hesitated for a moment.

"Do you want it?"

She nodded and made some sort of noise, half whimper and half the word "yes."

He bent his head to suckle one of her breasts again. For long moments, he held her poised above him as he toyed with her nipples, flicking, lapping, and gently running the bottom row of his teeth against them.

When she startled to wriggle, he impaled her in one smooth, swift motion.

She cried out, nearly surging off of him.

"Shh. Shh." He kissed her eyelids, the apples of her cheeks. "Only this time, my angel. Only this time it hurts."

He kept very still, waiting for some sort of response from her, she imagined.

Where there was once only pleasure, she now felt a stabbing pain. It seemed to radiate around his arousal. Her breathing slowed. This couldn't be it. There had to be more . . .

And then she felt a sort of tickling. She looked down at their joined bodies to find Rothbury using his thumb to flick quickly against a tiny nubbin of flesh hidden in her folds. It felt . . . wonderful.

Like magic, her hips began to move of their own accord. Her breathing increased and the throbbing, damp pleasure returned. She rocked against him.

"There you are, Charlotte," he murmured against her throat. "Better?"

She nodded shakily, tiny shivers shimmering down her upper body as he nipped at her earlobe.

His large hands held her backside tightly against him, controlling, rolling her with him in a primal rhythm. He rubbed his slightly bristled jaw between her breasts, nipping at the sides and tips playfully as they bobbed from their movements and those of the carriage.

Charlotte groaned feverishly, a tension building within her core that begged for release.

Grunting, he lifted his hips slightly, expertly angling his body so that part of him pressed against the nubbin of flesh.

She called out his name, clasping his shoulders. Her hips pumped furiously now, a building, pulsing ache growing and growing, winding tighter and tighter still. Until it exploded.

And then they both cried out, surging upward and down, upward and down, their bodies shaking with pleasure.

Holding her to him, his face buried in her shoulder, they remained joined until their breathing returned to normal.

"That was . . . my goodness," she said, breathlessly. "Is it always like that?"

"Charlotte," he said, pressing a small kiss on the swell of one breast, "it was never like that."

The carriage lurched to the side, making their last turn. Soon they would be pulling up to the front of her family's town house.

He helped her right her appearance as best he could, then grimaced when he saw some chafing from his bristles where he had rubbed his chin between her breasts.

She waved away his concern, curling up next to

him on the seat. He held her so tight and secure. She sighed.

A few minutes later the carriage pulled to the corner.

"Stay," he whispered, his lips at her temple. "Come home with me."

"I can't"

"But you're my wife."

He had a point. But her parents didn't know that little secret, so she couldn't very well move in to his residence overnight.

Before alighting from the carriage, she turned to kiss him, hoping there was more than simple lust hiding behind the glint in his ever-jaded gaze.

Chapter 19

*A Wise Gentleman knows the
appropriate time to lay his heart down
at his Lady's feet.*

*T*ick . . . tick . . . tick-tack . . .

Charlotte rolled over, punched her pillow
into a more comfortable lump, then sank back into
the comfy warmth.

Tick . . .

Winking open an eye, she did a quick scan of
her room, deemed it looked quite as it always had,
then returned to her blissful slumber.

She had to be imagining the noise; there was no
other explanation.

After sneaking into the house by way of the
kitchen entrance, Charlotte had crept past a
dozing Nelly, who slept in a chair before the

kitchen hearth with a wooden club in her arms as she often did ever since the incident several months ago with the intruder.

Then Charlotte had tiptoed upstairs, careful not to step on the second stair from the top as it creaked miserably and would most likely awaken her parents, especially her father.

She had then padded into the sanctuary of her room. After her maid helped her unbutton the back, she had dismissed her. Back in the carriage, Charlotte had spied a bit of blood on the hem of her chemise and didn't want the maid babbling to all in creation what she had seen.

She washed, changed into her nightdress, brushed out her hair, and then crawled into bed to relive making love to Rothbury over and over while she stared at the ceiling.

However, the events and news of the day left her mind muddled and her muscles heavy and tired. And as she crawled into her bed and slid under the coverlet, her languorous body quickly succumbed to a deep, restful slumber. She had never felt so relaxed in her life.

Tick . . . tick. . .

With an annoyed groan, she flipped over to her back.

Tick . . . tick . . . tick-tack . . .

Sighing loudly, she tossed back the covers and swung her legs to the side of the bed. Lifting heavy arms, she pulled on her robe.

The ticking sound came from the balcony doors.

Lighting a candle, she padded toward the sound, approaching the French doors cautiously. Maybe she should call for Nelly?

She jumped with a start as a tiny crumb of a pebble nicked the windowpane.

"What in the world?"

Someone outside and below her balcony whistled low.

Setting the candle down behind her, Charlotte pushed open the curtain, unlocked the handle, and pushed open the doors.

Pulling her night rail more snuggly under her chin, she stepped onto the small balcony and looked down into the kitchen garden below.

A tall, achingly handsome, tawny-haired scoundrel stood grinning up at her, one hand behind his back.

Rothbury.

It was in that very moment that she realized she loved him. With all her heart. He was her friend, recently her lover, and now and forever, her husband. It was all quite remarkable. She could only hope someday he might come to love her half as much. Physical love, he was an expert at, but real love? How could a man raised by a band of rapscallions know anything about love?

"What are you doing here?" she whispered.

"Looking for a way up."

A sneaking suspicion nagged at her. "Have you been friendly with the whiskey bottle again?"

His laugh was low, sultry. "No. I've only had a splash of brandy."

"What? No Shakespeare for me?"

His grin turned wry. "No. No Shakespeare. But I do have these." From behind his back, he brought out a fist full of pink tulips, their blooms closed against the night.

She smiled, almost laughed even. It was difficult, but she forced a note of disapproval into her tone. "Those aren't from my mother's garden, are they? She'll throttle you."

"No," he said, making a grand show of looking insulted. "I would never."

"Sorry," she said with a cringe.

"They're from your neighbor's garden, actually."

She did laugh then, smothering it with the sleeve of her nightrail. "Come up before someone sees you."

Putting the small bouquet in the band of his breeches, Rothbury began to scale the maple tree, which was actually a clump of four smaller maples sharing the same main trunk, next to her balcony.

The upper branches shuddered and the leaves shook as he climbed up. And then silence.

Dear Lord, had he fallen? She hadn't heard anything.

A second later, Rothbury's hands grasped the banister. Charlotte offered him a hand, but he declined, swinging his long legs over in one quick move.

As he stood before her, she just couldn't fathom that this was now her husband. But what *was* he doing here?

"What are you doing here?" she asked, taking the flowers from him. Some of their petals had fallen off from the bumpy climb. "I mean, I'm happy to see you, but why aren't you home?"

"Wherever my wife sleeps is my home."

"You can't sleep here," she said gently, stepping back into her room. She yawned. "Do you know what time it is? It must be near dawn, I imagine."

Yawning himself, he followed her in. "It's half past four."

Taking long, leisurely strides, he slowly walked

the perimeter of her room, stopping every so often to pick up some bauble or knickknack and examine it.

Closing the curtains, she shut the French doors and locked the handle.

"I will not stay," he said, picking up a small container on her dressing table. He unscrewed the lid and waved it under his nose. "Lemons." He smiled. "Is this why you always smell like lemons?"

"I-I suppose." She sat on a blue-striped bench at the foot of her bed. "It's a concoction my mother and I made. It keeps freckles at bay. I didn't know you noticed how I smelled."

He turned, his steady gaze on her. "I wager there are a lot of things you didn't know I noticed about you."

A shiver shot through her. Gazing down to her lap, she realized she had forgotten about the tulips.

She rose. "Excuse me." Walking to a row of bookshelves in the corner, she took her time in choosing the perfect vase from a selection of four. Finally, she decided upon a white vase with pink stripes, which would match pink tulips to perfection. Then she poured water into it from the pitcher on her washstand, and placed the flowers in their vase upon her writing desk near a window.

After admiring it for a spell, she turned . . . and found Rothbury sound asleep on her bed.

Maybe he was faking?

She crept closer.

His chest rose and fell evenly, his head turned into the softness of her pillow that, up until his arrival, she had been enjoying as well.

He looked . . . younger. All traces of his cynical smile had vanished. He also looked . . . comfortable and warm. She yawned.

She supposed it wouldn't hurt if she were to curl up beside him for just a little while.

Feigning sleep, Rothbury barely moved when he felt Charlotte climb into bed with him.

He kept his breathing slow and steady, which was a remarkable feat considering his senses came alive whenever she walked into a room, let alone rested her fair head on his chest, yawned into his shirt, and snuggled against his side.

Her body heat radiated alongside him. She smelled simply wonderful. Lightly like lemons and . . . he inhaled deeply . . . jasmine.

A soft moan came from her, not unlike the sounds she had made in his carriage not more than two hours ago. She had been exquisite. He felt so undeserving of her and yet yearned to hear the words tumble from her lips. How absurdly happy he'd be even if for the whole of one day she could look at him the way she looked at Tristan.

For so damn long he had taken the role of a seducer, a manipulator. A role he fell easily into under the old earl's guidance—though "guidance" didn't quite fit his less-than-noble father.

But the lifestyle that was so much a part of his father's and his father's brothers' lives had no place in Rothbury's heart.

When he was a boy, he would rather have hunted, ridden, been of help on the horse farm, gone fishing, or even played card games with his grandmother (unsurprisingly, she was a horrid cheat) than be anywhere near his bawdy, drunk, and sometimes violent father.

In fact, should Rothbury have shown, either with his words or with his facial expressions, that he was unhappy spending time with his father, that's when the old earl would become especially violent. Perhaps that's why Adam had become so accustomed to hiding his true feelings.

And the older he got, the more his mother pushed him away—assuming that it was inevitable that he'd join right in with the Faramond males' manner of living. It was in his blood, so therefore he would be like them and all the Faramond men before him. Carousers, gamblers, debauchers; lazy, heartless spendthrifts.

Adam couldn't fathom what had lured Josephine Aubry into the arms of a man like his father. Considerable charm, perhaps? Maybe it was an arranged marriage? He didn't know, but then he'd never had the opportunity to ask.

Charlotte stirred beside him.

Opening one eye a slit, he peeked at her slumbering form. She looked exactly like he had imagined she would, down to the white cotton night rail.

No. He was wrong. She was even more beautiful than he could have ever imagined.

He smiled, sure she was sleeping deeply now. Part of him wanted to kiss her, part of him couldn't wait until he could make love to her again, and still part of him was content to simply rest here with his wife.

His wife.

There were so many things he wanted to tell her. And he would, eventually, in his own time, but right now as she cuddled so trustingly up to his side, he allowed himself to admit everything.

In low tones so as not to wake her, he spoke,

in his mother's language, of all the things he wouldn't say if she understood. He wasn't ready to bare his heart, not when he wasn't sure if her affections still resided with his friend.

So he told her all about his mother, all about the things they did together, all the things he missed about her. And then he told her about that day, the day she left him, just packed up her bags and left him. He was only eight and had no idea at that time how much worse it was going to get once she was gone. But she wouldn't listen to his pleas—she just shoved him away.

He told her that if it weren't for his grandmother, he'd probably be dead. 'Twas the reason he liked to make her happy whenever it was within his power to do so.

And then, when he was done, he told his sleeping wife, in French of course, how he had loved her all along. He told her everything he knew.

But what he could not know was that Charlotte was very much awake.

Chapter 20

A Gentleman takes care not to upset a
Lady's nerves.

Hyacinth always sang in the mornings.

Not songs one would find in a book, or
even at church, for that matter. Just little songs she
made up as she moved about the house to begin
her day. Truly, she hummed more than sang, for
they rarely had words.

But it was a sound Charlotte had been accustomed to hearing every single morning of her
life.

Sprawling on her back in her bed, her cat's
warm, heavy body curled on her stomach, Charlotte couldn't help but smile.

Hyacinth was a woman of routine. She ate all
her meals at the exact same time every day; she

always worked on her needlepoint in the evenings, and never in any other room but the salon; and she even had the maids adhere to a tight schedule. And she always, without fail, brought Charlotte a cup of chocolate in the morning.

Taking a deep breath, Charlotte could almost smell the delicious aroma now.

She stretched, disturbing the cat at her belly.

Her eyes flew open.

"I don't have a cat!" she yelped, jolting up in bed.

With sleepy eyes, Rothbury looked at her with such a grumpy expression on his usual austerely handsome features, she rather thought if she weren't so frantic, she would have laughed.

"What are you still doing in here?"

"Not sleeping anymore, that's for sure."

"You need to get out," she started to yell, then lowered her voice. "My mother will be in here any minute."

"Is it time to eat? Your stomach is growling furiously. Can I get you something?"

She whacked him in the head with her pillow. "Rothbury, do you even know where you are? Do you even know who I am?"

He ran a hand through his hair, eyeing her dubiously. "Susie? Joan? Margaret? Lola?"

"Stop it," she said, laughing. "Just get out. Get out." She shooed him off the bed.

And then the door handle clicked. Her mother was coming into the room.

"Come-back-come-back-come-back," she whispered, holding the blankets open so he could dive under them quicker.

"I fail to see the point," came his deep, muffled tones from under the pink coverlet. "Not only am I your husband, but your mother also still believes that I'm like your Uncle Herbert."

"I still do not want her to find out this way."

"Worried she'll swoon?"

"My mother doesn't swoon."

The door creaked open, having been pushed by Hyacinth's backside as she backed into the room, one hand carrying Charlotte's chocolate, the other holding a plate of toast.

"Good morning, my dear!" Hyacinth beamed as she strode across the room. She passed Charlotte's bed in order to retrieve the wooden bed tray that sat on a chair near the dressing table.

"I've got your chocolate, of course," she said, now carrying the tray. She gave Charlotte's room a quick perusal as she returned to the bed.

On a normal day, Charlotte would have assisted her mother with the tray. On a normal day, Charlotte wouldn't have a handsome man under her covers currently blowing hot air on her thigh.

"I'll take the tray," she said, holding out her arms. She couldn't very well let her mother place it on Rothbury's head.

Normally, this would be the point where Hyacinth would leave. But her mother just stood there, staring at Charlotte, her hands on her hips.

Charlotte took an innocent bite of her toast. Not that bites of toast were notoriously guilty-looking.

Hyacinth smiled tightly.

Charlotte chewed.

"Well," her mother said, finally. "I guess I'll go see if your father needs me."

Charlotte took another bite.

Turning, Hyacinth strode out of the room, hands still on hips.

When the door closed, Charlotte breathed a sigh of relief.

But it was short-lived, for the door sprung open.

Strangely, Hyacinth closed the door behind her this time. And stranger still, now her mother's arms were crossed tightly over her chest.

"What is it, Mother?" Charlotte asked through a mouthful of toast. She hoped to distract her mother further by spurring a stern lecture about the pure savagery of speaking with one's mouth full.

It didn't work.

"The Martins," Hyacinth said sternly.

Charlotte blinked. "The Martins?"

"Yes, the Martins."

"Mother, are you all right? Why are you saying the neighbors' names?"

Hyacinth took a deep breath. "Because, my dear, the Martins came to call this morning."

"This early?"

"Yes, it seems they had a thief in their garden last night."

Charlotte's head started to pound.

"And do you know what the funny thing is?"

Charlotte shook her head.

"This thief stole, of all things . . . tulips. Not unlike the ones you have on your dressing table, my dear."

"Are you accusing me of stealing the Martins' flowers?"

"No. I am not. For the Martins caught sight of just who stole their flowers before the thief dashed away. And they said that they couldn't be sure, but they thought it was a man. The Earl of Rothbury, to be precise."

"How odd," Charlotte squeaked.

"Do you know what else is odd?"

Charlotte shook her head.

"That lump under your covers."

In the end, Hyacinth swooned. But not because Rothbury was in her daughter's room, and not because he was now her daughter's husband. No, she swooned once it became clear that Rothbury was not like dear Uncle Herbert in the least.

Chapter 21

*Every Gentleman knows the most elegant
way to get married is by special license.*

Three hours later, the new Countess of Rothbury was being handed up into the Faramond carriage, which would, naturally, bring her
straight to her awaiting husband in a handful of
minutes.

Charlotte could hardly wait.

After her mother's initial shock crumbled away,
they had all sat down together, including the pious
Mr. Greene.

Charlotte's father was a bit of a homebody who
busied himself with the reading and interpreting
of numerous religious tracts, much to her and her
mother's dismay. He stayed with them in the town

house for the Season, but never joined them at any social gatherings.

It was her father's reaction to the current situation that worried Charlotte the most.

However, with Hyacinth's calming presence, Charlotte and Rothbury explained just how their marriage had come about, adding the fact that they were both rather blissfully happy with the outcome.

Hyacinth's shoulders visibly relaxed, but William Greene's countenance changed from disbelief to astonishment, and then, finally, a squinty-eyed glare aimed directly at Rothbury.

Charlotte nearly groaned aloud, for she knew what was coming.

William's posture changed. He stood rigid, his chin held high.

"We must assemble in the morning room," he said pointedly to her new husband.

Her father rose and after a brief hesitation, Rothbury unfolded himself from his chair as well and followed Mr. Greene from the room. He turned for a moment, glancing at Charlotte and raising his brow, but she merely shrugged innocently and waved him on.

Poor, poor Rothbury.

There was nothing like a stern lecture about upholding the holy vows of matrimony from a pious old man to scare away one's new husband. It was all too bad; she rather liked being a married woman.

For the next half hour, her father droned on and on. All the while, Rothbury patiently listened.

And Charlotte knew it was patiently, for she spied on them by peeking through the crack in the door that opened to her father's study.

Sitting in a wing-back chair, his long legs stretched out before him, Rothbury nodded slowly at all the appropriate times, elbows on the arms of the chair, long fingers steepled.

And then, possibly because he hadn't had his tea yet, her father's lecture veered wildly off course, delving into the sins of the flesh.

Charlotte nearly groaned. But then she stopped. Quite suddenly, she realized Rothbury had found her gaze in the crack in the door. He knew she was there, listening. He winked.

And for all her past misinterpretations of that particular gesture, she knew without a doubt just what that wink promised.

So, it was with much anticipation that she now stepped down from the carriage and stared up at his stylish town house.

The front door opened and Rothbury was there, looking as wickedly handsome as ever. Those hooded eyes of his burned into her with such a stark intensity, she wondered how she never noticed it before—perhaps because he was so good at hiding his feelings. He took her hands in his.

"Welcome home, Countess," he said warmly, bringing her hands up to his tantalizing mouth for a kiss.

He escorted her inside the elegantly appointed foyer, his hand hot on her back the entire time.

Lined up in the hall were all his servants waiting to meet their new mistress. Charlotte greeted them all with a warm smile. When they were finished, Rothbury dismissed them back to their duties.

"Come," he said, grabbing hold of her hand. "I'll show you our rooms. Though I think you might remember the way."

She smiled, thinking of the last time she was in his house, sneaking in like a thief.

First, he showed her the countess's room, spacious and feminine, the walls covered in silk wallpaper, a pattern of tiny, lilac-colored flowers and light green vines.

As their marriage was indeed a surprise, the

room hadn't been readied yet, and crisp white sheets yet covered all of the furniture.

"The room will be ready for you by the end of the day, I promise. You can redecorate it if you'd like, it's entirely your decision. But you will always, *always*, sleep with me in there." He lifted his head in the direction of a connecting door on the right.

"Even if I'm angry with you?" she quipped.

"Yes, especially if you're angry with me."

He walked her around the room, hand still held in his, leading her to the connecting door.

Opening it, he gave her hand a tug, swinging her arm a touch, meaning her to enter first.

Unlike the last time she was here, his bedchamber was now awash in light. The colors were masculine, deep brown and tan, offset by a splash of dark burgundy here and there.

His huge bed crouched directly in front of where she stood. A sudden profound urge to run and jump atop it like a child came over her, but she resisted.

"Well, it is a beautiful . . ."

Her words trailed off when she felt his fingers quickly, expertly, undoing the row of buttons running down the back of her berry-colored day dress.

She swallowed hard, a profound desire welled

up within her instantly, making her feel over-heated and shaky.

Roughly, he tugged her dress down. She helped by pulling her arms through the sleeves. He slid her chemise off next, untying her corset, while she yanked off her gloves and kicked off her shoes. Soon she stood naked before him, wearing nothing but her spectacles, stockings, and . . . her bonnet.

She giggled, reaching up to untie the ribbon.

"No, wait," he said, darkly, turning her around to face him. "Always in my imagination . . . I've waited for this sight."

She watched as his throat convulsed. His chest rising powerfully, his eyes hooded and focused as he stared at her body. He raised his hand, brushing the backs of his fingers against her breast.

Charlotte was a little surprised to see that his hand shook a little.

He stepped closer to her, his chest brushing her hardened nipples. It felt so deliciously wicked being practically naked and he still so properly dressed.

He tipped her chin up and pressed a soft kiss on her lips. Pulling back, he looked into her eyes, "Charlotte, I never thought for a second that this moment would come. Had I, I would have chased you relentlessly from the start. I never thought I'd win you. I've loved you for so long."

Her heart soared. He sank his mouth atop hers, his lips slowly moving over her mouth with such tenderness, it made her heart ache.

She reached up, threading her fingers in his tawny hair and moaning into his mouth when his tongue dipped languorously inside. Their bodies pressed tightly together, his hands holding her backside to the hard knot of his arousal, grinding her into him.

Moaning, she pulled impatiently at his clothes, wanting to see him naked, wanting to feel skin upon skin, but he denied her. His fingers now roamed over her back, at the nape of her neck, knocking her bonnet askew.

The kiss seemed to go on forever, so slowly escalating into an almost ferocious onslaught. She felt as if she were on fire. Boldly she rubbed her breasts against his shirt, a silent plea for him to touch her.

His hand now came to a stop at her shoulders. He broke the kiss as he set her away from him, his eyes glistening with passion as his gaze raked over her entire body.

Both of them breathing heavily, he smoothed

his warm hands over her breasts, squeezing them, running his thumbs over the pebbled tips.

She grabbed the top of his head and pushed him down.

Gladly, Rothbury licked at them, suckled them, savoring the feel of her in his mouth. She shuddered and he moaned.

He couldn't wait any longer. He had to taste her. All of her.

Dropping to his knees before her, he loved her, worshiped her with his mouth, kissing her stomach, her hips, her thighs, and finally reaching her moist, intimate center.

She cried out his name and he knew she was shocked at his behavior, but he didn't care.

He devoured her, holding her tightly against his mouth as he drank of her.

Alternating between swirls of his tongue and long, languid licks, he let her moans and sighs be his guide to pleasuring her. Her body shook and he knew she was close. He quickened his movements.

He slid his hands from her bottom around to her waist, and to her rib cage. Reaching her breasts, he plucked at her nipples while he suckled the tiny nubbin of flesh hidden in her folds.

She screamed. And he continued his sweet torture until her knees buckled.

He caught her to him. Holding her close he carried her to his bed, his cock so fiendishly hard he thought he'd go mad if he didn't take her at that moment.

In a stunningly short amount of time, he rid himself of his clothes and joined her on the bed. Her legs spread for him and he sank himself between her thighs.

Her limbs shaking, Charlotte wrapped her legs around his waist and eagerly met her husband's lips for a kiss.

His body was simply magnificent, she thought, running her hands down his muscled back, over the hard muscles of his arms and chest.

Reaching between their bodies, she shyly touched his arousal. Hot and hard, but smooth at the same time. She squeezed the tip.

He broke their kiss to take a big gulp of air.

"Did I hurt you?" she asked appalled that she should have done such a thing at a time like this.

His eyes shut tight, he shook his head quickly, pressing his lips together.

"Rothbury," she whispered. "I need to feel you inside of me again."

His eyes fluttered open, then met her gaze.

Staring into her eyes, he positioned himself at her opening, then with one hand at her hip, he entered her slowly at first, thinking she must be tender from the day before.

She arched against him, silently giving him leave to enter more fully.

And he did, then, nearly losing himself in that second.

Together they began to move, their rhythm steady and firm. Soon her moans grew more desperate and her heels pressed into his buttocks.

He increased the pace, pumping into her wildly now, determined to bring them both to utter bliss.

And when they did, he groaned her name over and over. "Charlotte . . . my Charlotte . . ."

They clung together for long minutes, until their breathing slowed, until their hearts steadied, until they both fell into a deep satisfied sleep.

When Charlotte awoke, moonlight was pouring in through the tall windows across the room. Rothbury lay next to her on his stomach, his arms folded under his pillow.

Her stomach growled painfully. For a second she thought of waking Rothbury and asking him where the kitchens were located, but instead decided to find them for herself.

She kissed his back. He muttered something incoherent.

Sliding from the bed, she tiptoed to the connecting door and stepped inside the adjoined room. Surprisingly, the room was shrouded in shadows, but she was able to locate her bags.

Looking through them, she quickly found a nightdress and robe and dressed.

Quietly, she slipped into the hall. Her stomach growled so loudly just then, she feared she might have awoken everyone in the house.

Terribly hungry, she made her way down the stairs, hoping she could find the kitchens in the dark.

At the bottom of the stairs, the pungent scent of roses filled the air.

Charlotte crinkled her nose as she turned down a hallway toward the back of the house. There must be a vase of them nearby, she pondered. And by the smell of them, they had long since bloomed and needed to be thrown out.

But the further she walked, the stronger the smell became.

Up ahead, a patch of white sat on the floor. On closer inspection, Charlotte realized it was a sheet of paper. There was writing on it. She bent to pick it up.

> Rothbury,
>   *I cannot do this any longer. My affection resides elsewhere and I must go to him now. Please do not try to contact me.*
>
>   *Charlotte*

"What in the world? I didn't write this."

And then a slice of pain bloomed on the top of her head and all went black.

A loud thump woke Rothbury.

He sat up in bed with a start, his eyes alighting on the empty space next to him in bed.

"Charlotte."

Rothbury knew instantly something was dreadfully wrong. Throwing off the covers, he leaped from the bed.

He dressed with haste, dashing down the hall, taking the stairs three at a time.

He didn't know where she went to, or what that noise was, but a knot of dread tightened in his chest.

At the bottom of the stairs the nearly overwhelming aroma of roses assaulted his nostrils. He knew that smell.

Grabbing a brass candle holder as he passed the side table in the front hall, Rothbury took care that his footfalls went unheard.

He saw the sheet of paper as soon as he turned the corner. Sliding it closer to himself to take a look, he bent to retrieve it without taking his eyes from the dark hall before him.

He held it up, letting his gaze skim the words briefly.

Only for a second he felt as if his heart stopped. And then, he pushed the thought away.

The back door slammed shut. He raced toward the sound, catching a glimpse of two figures, one holding the other by the hair, her muffled cry seeping into his soul.

Charlotte.

He knew who had his wife in their cruel grip. He knew without a doubt.

Other than their collision in the hallway at the Hawthornes' masquerade ball, Charlotte couldn't think of a single occasion involving Lady Gilton that would warrant such violence.

But then, when one was being dragged by her hair down a dark alley, a letter opener at her throat, it was entirely possible that some imagined slight had slipped her mind.

"Little mousy bitch," Lady Gilton said through her teeth. "Thought I would give him up so easily, did you?"

Abruptly, she paused, panting from the strain of pulling a resisting Charlotte along.

Charlotte stumbled, and as a result, the letter opener punctured her skin. She inhaled sharply at the pain.

"Damn it to hell! Got yourself nicked, did you? He'll be disappointed. Wants you perfect and unsullied."

"Who?"

"Witherby. Your new lover," she said with a sickly sweet smile in her tone. "I'm to take you to him. Of course, he'll be quite disappointed to know you've probably given yourself to my Rothbury before he could get to you."

A sudden and powerful anger rose up in Charlotte. She twisted in her captor's hold, freeing herself and kicking Lady Gilton in the stomach in the process.

Falling back against a brick wall, Lady Gilton snarled, holding the letter opener menacingly above her head. But just before she would have lunged at Charlotte, a pistol cocked from some place behind her.

Lady Gilton froze.

Charlotte spun around.

"Rothbury," Lady Gilton whispered.

He shook his head. "What in the hell are you doing, Cordelia?"

"I'm . . . I'm helping her," she rushed out, looking like a wild animal that had been cornered. "I'm taking her away. She doesn't want to be with you . . ."

"And you do, I suppose."

"Of course I do."

"Well, if you're trying to endear yourself to me, you're failing."

Cordelia gulped.

"You see, my dear," he said, his eyes taking on a wicked gleam. "I don't like my wife being manhandled."

"Your *wife*?"

"Indeed."

She looked at Charlotte then, her eyes large and hurt. "I love him," Lady Gilton said suddenly. "So much, that I . . . I think I could kill you for him." She looked down at her hands as if she had never seen them before. "What's wrong with me?"

As she spoke, Rothbury moved closer and closer to Lady Gilton.

When he grabbed her arm, she didn't even fight him.

"We're going back to the house now," he said, "I'm sending for your husband."

"Oh, no. No, you mustn't." She shook her head. "I'll go. I'll go," she said, her voice sounding hollow.

But in the end, he did discreetly send for her husband. And they discussed privately the possibly unstable state of Lady Gilton's mind. Lord Gilton, having many affairs outside of marriage himself, knew his wife did the same, but was surprised to find his wife at Rothbury's town house.

The pair left an hour later, Lady Gilton muttering to herself.

As soon as they left, Charlotte ran to Rothbury, hugging him tightly.

He held her close, pressing kisses in her hair.

She looked up at him. "You didn't think it was I who wrote the letter, did you? You knew it wasn't I?"

He gave her an unsteady nod. "Well, I . . . I hoped."

"I love you," she said. "I do. And I'm never going to leave you."

He smiled, his own love shining in his eyes. "You're not lying?"

"No, of course not." And she suddenly remembered something. "I have lied to you, though."

"I suppose we're even. I have as well."

"Well, not really. You misled me. But I have . . . well, I guess I have misled you as well."

He raised a questioning brow.

"That night, when you came to my house and ended up in my bed. I heard you talking softly. It woke me. So I pretended to sleep."

"Pretending to sleep? That's how you misled me? Charlotte, that's hardly worth bringing up."

"Perhaps. Well, then, you might not be so surprised to know another little secret. I can understand French fluently.

Late the next day, Charlotte stretched like a lazy cat on her husband's bed.

They had recently made love, for the third time that day, and her limbs felt gloriously heavy.

Could anyone die of happiness? she wondered, grinning.

News of their secret wedding had now reached London and the salver in the front hall held an avalanche of invitations. No doubt from all the biggest gossipmongers.

Rothbury had just stepped out into the hall, his solicitor needing him to look over some sort of letter.

The door swung open slowly. Charlotte, naked,

sat up, clutching the sheet to her chest, a sudden alarm quickening the pace of her heart as she saw the look of shock on her husband's face.

"What is it?"

He held up the letter. "It's a note, Charlotte."

"And . . ."

"From Father Armstrong. It seems, upon further investigation, the bridge we crossed was still on English soil. The Scottish village of Dirleton is about two miles down the lane."

"Which means . . ."

"That I am truly a despoiler of innocents, and you, my dear, lovely woman, are not my wife. We are not married."

A moment of silence filled the air as they both stared at each other.

And then they both laughed, great big soul-cleansing laughs.

Joining her on their bed, he continued to chuckle. Then the chuckling turned into kissing, soon changing into sighs of pleasure, then admissions of love, then plans of obtaining a secret license later in the day . . .

Epilogue

Aubry Park
August 1814

"In the presence of God and in front of all these witnesses, I, Adam Bastien Aubry Faramond, give myself to you, Charlotte Faye Greene, to be your husband and take you now to be my wife. I promise to love you, to be faithful and loyal to you, for as long as we live . . ."

"And in the beyond," Charlotte mouthed for Rothbury's eyes only.

"And in the beyond," Rothbury softly repeated, to the delight of the wedding guests assembled on the south lawn.

Standing before the ironwork arbor, now heavy with ivy and honeysuckle blooms, he held up the ring his grandmother purchased from the blacksmith along with the one he purchased himself in Town—a sparkling sapphire between diamonds.

"I give you this ring in God's name, as a symbol of my promise, and all that we share," he said, letting the power of the love he felt for his wife sparkle in his eyes just as brightly and as precious as the stones of the ring dazzling in the sunlight.

"In the presence of God and all these witnesses, I . . ."

In a chair off to the side of the couple sat a very smug-looking Louisette, who turned to her companion, Miss Drake, and muttered, in perfect English, "See. I told you I would get that boy to the altar eventually. All I had to do was pretend I was a loon."

Next month, don't miss these exciting new love stories only from Avon Books

When Seducing a Duke by Kathryn Smith
Rose Danvers charms her way into the glittering masked ball with only one man on her mind. She would risk certain scandal for a kiss from Greyden Kane, Duke of Ryeton—though she lusts for much, much more . . .

Captured by Beverly Jenkins
On a dangerous mission against the Crown, the notorious privateer Dominic LeVeq has just captured a British frigate. Dominic is utterly entranced by the stunning slave on board, and offers to grant her freedom in exchange for a forbidden night in his bed.

Out of the Darkness by Jaime Rush
Rand Brandenburg can see the future, but his power has made him a target and could get him killed. Now he must hide out with others like him, including a mysterious redhead who has his heart soaring.

Taken by the Laird by Margo Maguire
A young lady escapes to Scotland in the dead of night, desperate to avoid the horrid marriage her guardian had arranged. She finds shelter at Castle Glenloch and intends to stay for just one night . . . until she encounters Laird Glenloch, and all her plans vanish into the Highland air.

Visit www.AuthorTracker.com for exclusive information on your favorite HarperCollins authors.

REL 0909

Available wherever books are sold or please call 1-800-331-3761 to order.

At Avon Books, we know your passion for romance—once you finish one of our novels, you find yourself wanting more.

May we tempt you with . . .

- **Excerpts** from our upcoming releases.

- Entertaining **extras**, including authors' personal photo albums and book lists.

- Behind-the-scenes **scoop** on your favorite characters and series.

- **Sweepstakes** for the chance to win free books, romantic getaways, and other fun prizes.

- Writing **tips** from our authors and editors.

- **Blog** with our authors and find out why they love to write romance.

- **Exclusive content** that's not contained within the pages of our novels.

Join us at
www.avonbooks.com

AVON

An Imprint of HarperCollins*Publishers*
www.avonromance.com

Available wherever books are sold or please call 1-800-331-3761 to order.

FTH 0708